My Life Being A Sensitive

*Spirits exist around us every moment of the day -
we are never truly alone.*

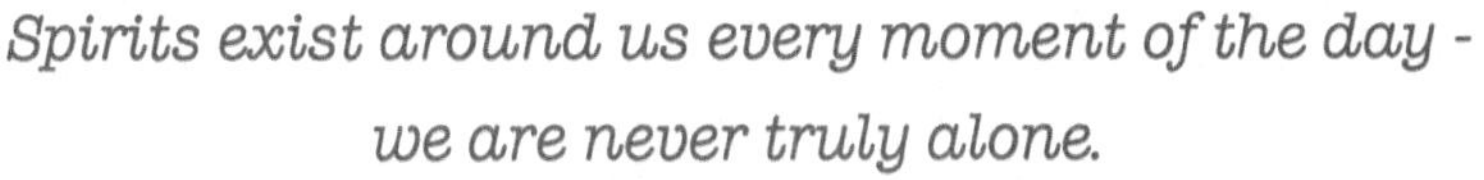

*Just like our living counterparts - some are evil, and
some are here to help us.*

You must be sensitive to the difference.

Chapter 1

Be Aware

A simple white clapboard house with black trim and dark shingles, bought from a Sears Catalogue circa 1940, sat on Marsalis Street in Fort Worth, Texas, a quiet suburb on the East side of downtown made up of working-class families. One unfortunate residence survived mishaps that impacted its inhabitants for years. The unassuming residence maintained its secrets between the living and the dead until a boy with a gift arrived. He would ultimately reveal and bring to an end the horror held within.

The second owner of the white clapboard house was a woman in her mid-thirties. She moved into the residence with her husband and five children in 1966. She was intent the structure would become a home, a place for her family, and a domain she could control. It was appropriate to assume the new residents had no knowledge of the house's sordid history. With its series of past events, this new address might have been considered malum-in-se, pure evil in action. It stood to reason the new family was not warned about the previous tenants or the horror that had taken place on this property. Had they been made aware, one would surmise they would have never agreed to call it home.

An occasional light left on in the night, a random toilet flush after everyone was in bed, a faucet left dripping; these were commonplace occurrences. Events which were easily explained in a house with seven people living in it. The parents, who worked different shifts in order to avoid each other and their gaggle of five children, did their best to survive. It was a place where someone was always coming and going. So much movement made the unusual appear normal at the white clapboard house, even when something strange occurred within its four walls. The oddities were ignored, unnoticed, by the family members living in the white clapboard house.

No one bothered with the comings and goings of the dead until the year I turned five. I was the fifth child to be born into this family; my arrival would be a nuisance to my four older siblings, who were all busy with their own lives. My oldest sister was ten years my senior, the ages of the others counted down to a brother who was barely five years old the day I arrived. He had the pleasure of being the baby in the family until I came along.

It is important to note my parents never intended to have another child; their focus was on things other than another mouth to feed. Proof I had not been planned for was in my nickname, Boo Boo.

According to the Websters unabridged dictionary:

boo-boo/'bōōbōō
noun, slang, informal
1. a mistake, an error, a stupid or foolish action, a blunder.

My early years consisted of being passed from one sibling to another as far back as I can recall. Each of them managed my existence with as little effort as possible. They were simply following my parents' leadership style: stay busy leading one's own life. Time left over for attention to me was nil. Looking back, I have concluded my sisters and brothers did the best they could with the information they had, and for that matter, I guess my parents did as well.

It was the Jones era: all focus and effort were put into keeping up with them. House, car, clothes, and outward appearances were all that mattered. How others perceived us carried high value in our minds.

As they attended school and worked, I was left to my own devices most of the time. I was never in danger as someone was always at home, regardless of their limited engagement. Maybe all this alone time was why I began to notice others around me. The ones that my family couldn't see or perhaps wouldn't.

The first recollection I have of those on the other side was when I was five. The house we resided in had a smaller abode located behind it; it was aptly dubbed the "little house." Initially built by the property's first owner, it was intended to serve as a small guest house. Running water and plumbing were non-existent; it was merely a place to lodge and, perhaps, utilize the bottle of water next to the hot plate to prepare a cup of coffee prior to joining the family being visited.

It was a summer evening, July, as best I recall. My birthday had recently passed, and my siblings had not yet returned to school. In the usual upheaval of comings and goings, the family was in a constant state of chaos. The illuminating street lamps signaled to the neighborhood children it was time to return home. Seeing the bulbs begin their arc toward brightness, my two older brothers peddled their bikes home after a day of shenanigans with the neighboring youth. In their plight to ensure they were indoors before dark, they left their transportation in front of the house.

Barreling through the front screen door and into the room shared by the three of us, they kicked the toys I was playing with to various corners of the room. It certainly was not my fault my toys were strewn across the hardwood floor between our beds and considered to be in their way. I believe it was on purpose that my oldest brother, storming in with reckless abandon, kicked one of my favorite playthings under his bed.

The bedroom we shared consisted of a bunk bed directly across from a twin bed where my oldest brother slept; my toy was now located underneath it. The walls, initially painted white, had become a dingy yellow over time. The color faded from a mixture of age and three messy boys. Two large side-by-side windows flanked the ten-foot area between the beds in the middle of the off-white walls. Their floor-to-ceiling span offered a view of the backyard, the little house, and the garden just beyond. The large uncarpeted floor in front of the large windows was my favorite place to sit and play while enjoying my trinkets.

My toy soldier lying on his side under my brother's bed begged me for retrieval. I began my journey to rescue the little green man from under the mattress and boxed springs just as I heard my mother calling for my brothers.

Wooden sandal in hand, the matriarch of the white clapboard house blew into the room, where she began scolding my brothers for leaving their bicycles in the driveway. From where the bikes landed, they blocked her pursuit of parking her car in the garage. This had been noted many times before as a no-no. Chasing them out of the bedroom with her punishment tool ready to strike, she looked back into the room for me. But alas, I had disappeared under the bed and was being comforted by my little green army man. My miniature friend and I avoided involvement in the ensuing tribunal about to begin, all in response to her being inconvenienced.

I remained quietly under the bed for a few minutes while the shouting and gnashing of teeth were in process. I heard my oldest brother arrive in the backyard; this allowed me to hope I was in the clear. I crawled from my hiding space; I arrived at the double-hung window just in time to observe the judgment being passed. My oldest brother was always eager to please my mom; my other brother appeared to gain sadistic pleasure from seeing just how far he could push things. The first bike arrived in its storage place without issue, neatly propped in front of the little house, held upright by its kickstand. Enter bike number two, quickly rolling down the sidewalk without a rider. A perfect aim resulted in a direct hit into the other; a bicycle derby instigated by brother number two had begun.

My mother lacked a sense of humor that day; the banging of the bicycles into one another triggered the release of her built-up tension. My brothers, in their short pants, would be the recipients of my mother's favorite punishment device, her wooden sandal. The sound of the shoe's hardened sole smacking against uncovered flesh did not catch my attention. I was intrigued by the four red eyes looking out from the little house just above the mangled bicycles. The glare of the glass from the window they stood behind blocked most of their details. I managed to decipher a simple flowered house dress with a white collar and one-half of a dark-colored bow tie on the companion.

The red eyes above the half-bow tie turned to look at me; the set belonging to the collared frock followed. As soon as all our eyes met, they were gone. I don't remember running out the back door of the house into the backyard. I don't recall telling my mother what I saw, but I do remember getting drawn into the shoe attack and told I was to never speak of it again.

From that day forward, I hated going into that little house. Each time I did, I felt their presence in the place. I knew they were watching me. Beyond sensing them around me, the eyes belonging to the bow tie or frock remained unseen. I was never quite sure whether I should fear them or fear talking about them. Not understanding their presence or motive, I was diligent in my efficiency when visiting the little house.

Years passed, my parents divorced, and my siblings either married or joined the military; the end result was most of them moved away. Even as the number of residents in the house dwindled, the odd incidents of lights being turned on and the toilet flushing at odd hours continued to occur. It had become the norm, and I thought little of it at the time.

Christmas Day, the year I turned nine, my oldest brother bought my mother a clothes dryer as a gift. This was a wonderful gift as we continued utilizing clotheslines to dry our garments year-round. The new appliance needed a home; it was decided the little house would become a laundry room. With the last sister in the house getting married the following summer, the open-ended task of laundry was assigned to me. This required I spend additional time in the little house, way more than I wanted.

Each and every time I entered the little house, I could sense they were there. They never revealed themselves to me when I was in their proximity, and eventually, I came to realize they meant me no harm.

My mother, now a divorced white female (her declaration - not mine), worked most of the time to make ends meet. This left one older brother at home with me to manage the house and take care of the chores; he did not see duties as necessary and welcomed the rapture from our mother for ignoring her assignments to him. In some sad, sick twisted way, it was his way of getting attention from her. It would be their feuding that would summon the floating red eyes to the little house once again.

Mom and my brother began arguing over his not washing something she had asked him to. Intent on avoiding the imminent maternal explosion, I walked out the back door of the house while they fought. I moved down the curved sidewalk towards the laundry room in hopes of resolving the core issue before it escalated.

It was late fall, and the early evening air was crisp with a bit of moisture hanging aloft. Moving into the cold on my way to the little house, I quickly realized my thin t-shirt was inadequate for keeping me warm. I opened the little house's front door and immediately felt a significant difference in temperature between inside and out. The rooms were sweltering; full of moist air, an oppressive damp heat hovered in the atmosphere. My immediate assessment was the clothes dryer vent had clogged, creating a high moisture level in the room. As I flipped on the light switch, heading for the laundry devices, I noticed the dryer door was open, and the washing machine lid up. Neither device housed any garments.

Looking at the empty appliances, I began to sense the red-eyed couple was present, although this time, the energy was very different. I heard my mother's verbal assault bombarding my brother as they marched toward the little house. The closer they got, the warmer the room became. I stood there, all my thirteen years of fear coming to the forefront; something terrible was about to happen. My brother reached the threshold of the little house just as my mother pushed him at full force through the opening, all the while screaming at him; she was entirely out of control. He fell through the doorway, his toe catching the lip of the door seal. Tumbling forward, he lost his balance. He attempted to steady himself on the round table in the middle of the room. Hitting the ugly green tile floor, the sound of bone snapping was deafening. It sounded to me as if I had broken my arm. In all her rage, Mother lifted her arm to strike him again with her favorite weapon of choice. As her hand began to swing downward, it stopped suddenly. Her arms were abruptly lifted upward, both now above her head, held by an invisible force. An unseen entity removed the shoe in her left hand from her grip. The wooden sandal traveled at great speed through the window on the far side of the room, landing somewhere in the garden just beyond. As the shoe exited the window, the red eyes and bow tie appeared. I looked into the red pupils as a soft pair of hands began to gently rub my shoulders, petting and soothing me. I continued to watch Mom's feet rise from the floor as she kicked and screamed, begging for freedom.

My mother continued her ascent until her hands were pushing against the ceiling. Her legs continued to flail around as she turned her head to look at me. Her eyes were drawn to something beyond me. Suddenly she was released from her captor, falling to the floor. Landing on her bare feet, she stumbled backward across the tile floor and out the door. Turning away from my brother and me, she quickly ran from the room, leaving us behind. The red eyes were now gone.

I crossed quickly to my brother, hoping to comfort him; he was out cold. It was either the pain of a broken limb or a head injury that took him to unconsciousness. Perhaps it was the fear of seeing Mother float upwards. I began calling his name, gently working on waking him. Once he regained awareness and could manage a sentence, I helped him stand. We began our journey to the white clapboard house. Walking through the back door, we found Mother standing in the middle of the family room, fully dressed to leave. Her hair was now combed, her lipstick perfectly applied, and her purse in hand.

"Get in the car; we need to take you to the hospital to have that looked at. I can't believe you tripped over the door ledge. You are such a clumsy boy."

As they backed down the driveway, the car making its way toward the local emergency room, I began to feel despondent. All of a sudden, I didn't want to be left alone. As I had done many times over the years, I sought refuge at a nearby neighbor's home. A wonderful couple in their sixties, a man and a woman whom I considered my grandparents, if not by blood, then by fate. Being after dark, Pa Day was concerned to find me knocking on their door. It was apparent to him something was seriously out of order. He ushered me through the door with a pat on my back, just like he did when I was three years old; when he found me wandering the neighborhood unattended. Being quick to know how to soothe me, Ma Day was in and out of the kitchen in a second, returning with a slice of chocolate pie for me to consume.

Finishing my pie, I placed the fork on the plate now residing on the couch's arm. Wiping my mouth with my shirt sleeve, I remained silent. Being the kind people they were, they allowed me to sit still, everyone in dutiful silence. Pa Day reached for his clicker and silenced the television, letting the room become free of noise or distraction. Remaining on the couch, quietly staring at the floor, I was summoned back to reality when Ma Day broke the silence by asking what had happened. I was hesitant to tell them Mom had pushed my brother, causing him to fall. It had been made clear to me from as far back as I can remember that what happened in that white clapboard house on Marsalis St. stayed in that white clapboard house. I paused for another minute while deciding if I should tell them about the red-eyed couple. Reasoning they would dismiss the story as me being a silly boy, and that would be the end of it, I began.

I regaled them with the tale of Mom being lifted off the floor by the red-eyed man and how the red-eyed woman was soothingly touching me. When I finished revealing my story, there was a long pause before a response was made. I was concerned I had Boo-

Boo'd! Maybe I shouldn't have told them. I raised my eyes to see Ma and Pa Day looking intensely at each other. Ma Day was the first to speak, "You should tell him. He obviously knows they are there."

"Son, I know you've heard me talk about being on the police force prior to my retiring. One of the reasons I quit was because of an incident that happened on this very street. In the house where you live. Have your parents ever talked about it?"

"No, sir," I stated inquisitively.

He slid to the front of his overstuffed chair and began his pipe-packing ritual until the device was full of fresh tobacco. He reached for his lighter before sliding back into the chair while lighting the pipe.

Taking a deep draw from it, he began: "A couple in their early forties lived there before your family moved in. The woman, as sweet as your Ma Day, and her husband, well, he was my good fishing buddy. He and I would sit on the train trestle by the creek most evenings enjoying beer and pretending to fish. Good folk, they were."

He paused talking, taking another deep draw on his pipe, seemingly contemplating how to finish his story. Ma Day exited her chair; retrieving the plate and fork from the couch's sidearm, she departed for the kitchen. Once the faucet began releasing its water, Pa Day continued.

"Those lovely people were killed in that storehouse your mom uses as a laundry room. I worked at the crime scene and decided to retire shortly after. I saw what true evil could do, and it shook me to my core."

"Can I ask you what they were wearing when they were killed?" I don't know what prompted me to ask such a question; it just popped into my head.

"That's an odd question. What does that matter?"

"Did she have a collared house dress on, and he a dark bow tie?"

Pa Day's eyes shot up over his pipe, looking directly into mine. "How did you know that? Did your mother tell you that?"

"That's what I saw them wearing," I responded.

We sat quietly until Ma Day retreated from the kitchen. Walking through the doorway, she placed her apron on its hook, drying her hands on it before crossing to her chair directly across from me. "They never caught who did it or found out why," she said while settling into her chair.

"Pa Day, why did you ask me if my mother told me what the people who died were wearing?"

He continued to puff on his pipe for a while before answering me. "One afternoon, sometime after your family moved in, your mom knocked on that very front door. She handed me a cigar box containing a part of the man's bow tie along with a button from a woman's dress. She claimed to have found them in the garden while preparing the soil for planting."

"The cigar box and clothing articles were from inside that little house; I saw them when I was there. The bow tie remnant alongside the pearl button were both on the floor in that little house. Both were lying in puddles of blood on the floor, right beside the table where the bodies had been placed. It didn't make sense. The murders were brutal attacks, but the killer took the time to lay the victims on the table with care. The murderer even made sure to close the dead couple's eyes and put their arms across their chest. Moreover, both articles in the box were clean when your mom gave them to me, free from blood or dirt."

Each of us was startled by an unexpected knock on the front door; Pa Day left his chair to open it. It was my mother.

"I assumed I would find him here. Hope he wasn't any trouble. His poor brother fell and broke his arm; I had to take him to the hospital, but I'm sure he told you all about it."

As only Ma Day could, she shifted the subject. "Oh no, sorry to hear he's hurt. Hope it's not too serious. Boo didn't mention it at all; he just said you had to run an errand. He was here earlier today when I was baking a chocolate pie; I just thought he came up with an excuse to get a slice. No worries on our part. Now you two should run along home. It's getting close to time for the nightly news."

Mother and I walked separately back to the white clapboard house, she under the street under the lamps and me through the neighbors' front yards. Between Ma and Pa Day and the red-eye couple, I felt protected. It would be twenty-seven years before I would learn the truth about what happened to the red-eyed couple.

Chapter 2

Don't Poke The Ghost

Odd things continued to occur over time at the white clapboard house. I am not sure why I had grown accustomed to the unexplained events; I just quit paying attention to them anymore. I knew someone, something, continued to watch over me.

Looking back, I realize there were numerous times I could have been seriously hurt due to someone's stupidity. The overseers kept me safe, making sure I always survived.

When I was around seven or eight, long before the broken arm incident, my brothers and I were playing in the garden area on Marsalis St. just before Easter. I remember the time of year because the garden had not been planted yet, allowing us lots of room to roam in the dirt. Mom insisted on planting her crops on Good Friday; she believed planting on that day kept the evil spirits at bay. The boys (how I refer to my older brothers) had a new bow and arrow set they received as a Christmas gift from an uncle. One of them came up with the bright idea to test how high they could shoot an arrow into the sky. This was a literal test of gravities' nature. The theory that every action has an equal reaction was proven that day; the arrows launched upwards, soon returning downward toward us. One strong pull on the bow, an arrow, complete with its deer tip, was on its sky-bound trip. As the projectile made its return trip, people started screaming at me to watch out. I panicked and immediately went into duck and cover. Isn't that what they teach you in school? When things are falling, bend over and cover your head! The arrow was headed straight for me, and had it struck me; I would have most likely been paralyzed if not killed. My brothers panicked, seeing the arrow's downward trajectory; each of them standing by, watching. What they observed was the arrow slicing between my butt cheeks ahead of piercing the earth. Ripping my shorts wide open while not rendering a scratch on me. There was no logic to be applied here; merely a matter of powers from beyond protecting me. I could share numerous other incidents to drive the point home. I don't believe I truly appreciated the fact I had guardians until years later when my protectors would prove their existence and value to me.

My mother remarried my freshman year of high school and immediately began birthing more children. The oddities in the white clapboard house had continued on, less frequent than before but still existing. The man my mother chose for a second go-round of matrimonial bliss carried a controlling air about him; this kept my mom subdued. Her new mindset seemed to keep the spirits quiet as well. The connection between her energy and theirs was notable to me. When she was in a foul mood, the entities became very active. Nothing like what happened in the little house with my brother occurred again; still, I saw a pattern of unexplained incidents happen when mom was unhappy or expressed her displeasure outwardly.

During my first year at university, circumstances dictated I lived at home. Receipt of a full scholarship afforded me the opportunity to attend a private school, but the funds awarded did not cover the expense of living on campus. The financial gifts were insufficient to cover tuition and living expenses. As it was, my family lived hand to mouth, leaving the cost of a dorm room and food simply too much to bear.

Fall term began, and like most freshmen, I was figuring out the where and hows of education beyond high school's safety. I was really struggling with it all. I was fortunate to not have to work, but the responsibilities of school were wearing me down. Adding to the stress of these new surroundings and rituals, I fell in love for the first time. His name was Andy. Attempting to balance it all was new to me; someone showing love to me was odd to my psyche. I was incredibly cautious as this was all very scary to me.

The fifth week into my first college semester, my stepdad's mom suddenly became ill and was not expected to live. It was decided the family would drive to California to see her. Being a dutiful wife under my stepdad's hard hand, my mother quickly packed suitcases and ice chests for the road trip. My stepdad assumed I would take leave from school and go with them; the assumption was a massive misunderstanding on his part. I would not leave Andy or school behind because of his travel whim. I hardly knew his mom, so it was of no emotional consequence to me.

I woke up at 3:28 AM on Wednesday morning to a series of noises in the kitchen. My assumption was my mother was toiling away, preparing for their trip. I felt disturbed and couldn't shake it. Coming out of my deep sleep, I realized the sound was repetitive, a groaning of sorts. My immediate reaction was mom must have been sparring with my stepdad again. I was concerned the argument was most likely my fault. Earlier that evening, I had taken a stand against my stepdad, telling him to fuck off when he threatened to whip me with a belt.

I pulled a pair of shorts from the floor and slipped into them; standing up, I moved into the hallway from my bedroom. The house's one and only bathroom was between my and my parent's bedroom. It appeared to be occupied; the door was closed, and the light was on. I naturally assumed a member of the family was utilizing the toilet. I walked past the bathroom door and exited the hallway into the living room. Looking to my right, I visually checked the front door to confirm it was closed and its deadbolt in the locked position. Turning to my left, I headed for the kitchen. Turning the corner, my peripheral vision caught the bathroom light turn off. I paused, waiting to see who was up at this hour. After the bathroom went dark, the toilet flushed, but the door didn't open. Standing there, now fully awake, I held firm. I felt a negative energy flowing around me. From the opposite end of the bedroom hallway, I heard my parent's bedroom door open. My stepfather appeared in the dark hallway; he looked at me before he opened the bathroom door and went in, closing the door behind him. I returned to the hallway and peered into their bedroom to see my mother sound asleep.

I couldn't conceive who would have been in the bathroom, all the adults in the house were accounted for, and no one had exited the bathroom when my stepdad went in. Moving on to the kitchen, I heard the bathroom door open and close. After it closed, three swift bangs rapped on the bathroom door. I assumed it was my stepfather making a point of some kind.

I moved through the kitchen, passing on into the family room. No one was awake. There were no sounds, only the kitchen lights on. My younger brothers and sister were all asleep in the room they shared at the back of the house. I entered their room. Moving from bed to bed, I checked on each of them.

The nightlight glow confirmed their eyes were closed; each of them sound asleep. As best I could tell, all was normal in the house except for the negative pressure pushing against me.

Retreating to my room, I turned off the kitchen lights as I moved into the living room. I crossed to the front door to inspect the deadbolt one more time. Everything was as it should be. Walking towards the shared hallway between my parent's room and mine, I heard the toilet flush and the bathroom door open. There stood my stepfather. "What are you doing up?" he grumbled at me.

I was startled to see him as I had heard the bathroom door slam while I was in the other part of the house. "I was checking on the little ones. I thought I heard something."

He stared through me and asked, "Is that why you were banging on the bathroom door?"

"I was in the kitchen when I heard that."

We both turned to see if Mom was still asleep. "You need to stop fucking with me, kid. I don't have to let you live here. If I pushed it, your mother would put you out on the streets."

I am not sure where my nerve came from or who entered my body at that moment, but I stood very tall as I responded. "Good luck with that. You haven't persuaded her to give you title to the house, so don't think she is so in love with you that she would stop protecting herself or me. You may have her fooled for now, but just be mindful, so did my dad. And well, you know how well that worked out for him. Good night!"

I walked past him and into my room. Closing the door behind me, I collapsed onto my bed, where I quickly fell asleep. The moans and door banging were all forgotten.

When I awoke the next morning, I immediately realized I was late leaving for class again. Tardiness had become an all too common occurrence for me. Throwing on the nearest clothes I could reach, I bolted for the front door. Entering the living room, I noticed the luggage and travel gear were absent. It dawned on me the family had left on their trip, leaving me home alone.

I grabbed my car keys and tore out the door, heading for school. I took the first empty parking spot I found on campus. Pulling my seldom-used books from the back seat of my car, I ran for class. I arrived at Wesley Hall to find Andy sitting on the steps leading to the building. He spotted me coming up the walk and quickly trotted down the steps to me. Hugging and kissing me, he said, "I am so happy to see you! I was worried about you!"

"I overslept. Come on, I can't miss another of Dr. Lambert's classes, or he is going to drop me!"

"Dr. Lambert's class was yesterday! You didn't show up for it. Today is Thursday, Babe."

"It was Wednesday morning when I fell asleep. No way I slept for more than 24 hours."

"That's why I have been so freaked out; I called when you weren't in class. I drove by your house, your car was in the drive, but your parent's van was gone. I just assumed your parents forced you to go with them to California. Then I dreamt you died in an accident. I called your house again this morning; still no answer. I have been sitting here, not knowing what to do."

"My parents left for Cali without me. I don't remember anything; them saying goodbye, any noises from the babies, nothing. I assume they are mad at me. The old fart and I got into it before they left. Weird that I slept through your calling."

"Are you sure you are okay? This is really strange."

I took Andy's hand as we began walking to the quad; I was starving. Scarfing down a cold-cut sandwich, we made plans for the weekend. Since my family was out of town, Andy was coming to stay with me. Neither of us was out to our parents, even though most of our friends had figured it out. We still had to keep a low profile as we attended a Methodist school below the Mason-Dixon line. Even after the Stonewall riots, it was prudent to keep certain things low-key while living in the South. Besides, it was nobody's business what we did under the covers. In retrospect, holding his hand on campus was probably a dead giveaway.

The reality was we had not done anything under the covers or anywhere else. Andy was my first serious boyfriend; he was the one I wanted to build a life with. I had been on the make with guys since I was fourteen, but that was merely casual sex and generally nothing more than mutual masturbation. I was looking forward to Andy staying the weekend to explore our relationship's more intimate side.

Finished with our snack, we parted ways and headed to our afternoon classes. Saying goodbye, we confirmed our plan to see each other at my house after he got off work Friday night. Neither of us had classes that Friday, so we planned to talk on the phone before he went to work.

I cleaned all day Friday; I wanted to make that white clapboard house on Marsalis St. look as lovely as possible. With my mom's marriage to my stepfather, we had migrated from keeping up with the Joneses to being just plain white trash. My stepdad didn't care what others thought of him unless it was to consider him good-time Charlie. I didn't want Andy to judge me by the home I was living in; he came from the moneyed Westside of Fort Worth. His parents made him work to cover insurance and gas expenses for the Porsche 911 they bought him for high school graduation. I was deeply concerned I would never reach his standards and would undoubtedly struggle to convince his parents I was good enough for him.

The day quickly passed as I scrubbed the white clapboard house from top to bottom. Somehow we missed our call, making the evening so excruciatingly slow for me. Waiting for Andy to arrive at my house, I was ecstatic when I heard his Porsche pull into the driveway. Bounding out the front door, I jumped off the front porch moving towards him. I noticed him acting strangely; he had slowly exited his car and remained by its open door, not moving. I pulled him from behind the door and hugged him with all the might I could muster. His response was lackluster; my heart began to sink. "What's wrong?"

"You said you weren't out to your parents."

"That's true, but so what? You know they aren't here; they are in California."

"Then who was that I saw watching us through the curtains?"

"Which curtains?"

"The far ones on the left, the big double window."

Leaving Andy by his car, I flew back into the house, heading directly into my parent's bedroom. The curtains were askew when I entered the room, but no one was there. I looked around the room, and suddenly the air began to chill. I began to shake uncontrollably as the temperature continued dropping rapidly. I screamed out loud for help but only heard a groan sputter forth.

Along with the freezing chill surrounding me, I felt my body being pulled onto my parent's mattress. Every minute that passed, I was getting weaker. I felt hands reaching out for me as the room faded to black.

When I came to, I was in the passenger seat of Andy's car. He was feverishly slapping my face and calling out my name. I saw his arm raise before his hand swiped across my face; I didn't feel a thing.

"Baby, don't leave me!"

I gasped and began to cough. Suddenly the pain from him hitting me was real; the impact of his hand hitting me intensified. I looked into his eyes and wispily asked him to stop. He fell back into his seat and began to cry. Regaining some strength, I reached for his hand and began to look around. We were sitting in the Piggly Wiggly parking lot. "How did we get here?"

In between sobs, he began to tell me what had happened. "You took off into the house; I could see someone looking out at me as you leaped up the front steps. Then they were gone. You pulled back the drapes and smiled at me, so I assumed everything was fine. I crawled back into the car and waited for you to return."

"Ten minutes or so passed, and you still weren't back. I was getting anxious; I was afraid your parents or one of your siblings saw us hug. I was scared you were fighting, so I just sat there, prepared to take off if necessary. When I rechecked my watch, I caught a glimpse of something in the side view mirror. I quickly looked over and caught sight of someone standing by the passenger door. I rolled the window down to speak with a sweet little old lady who was standing there. She leaned her head into the car, looked at me, and calmly said I should go inside. 'He is in serious danger; it's up to you to save him.'"

As Andy continued to tell me about the events we participated in, I began to feel my strength returning.

"My adrenaline kicked in; I ran into the house to get you. I found you lying on the bed, unconscious, pale, and cold to the touch. Something tripped me when I walked into the room. From the floor, I reached for your feet and began pulling you towards me. It felt like someone was on the other side of the wall pulling you towards them. I forced my way up to your side and put your arms around my shoulders. I lifted you off the bed; it took all my strength to get you up. Free of the mattress, we turned to leave just as the wooden bookshelf against the wall began to creak. One of the front legs snapped in half; the entire case with all its contents fell to the bed where you had just been lying. As we got to the door, I turned to look back; the bed was entirely crushed."

"I carried you out the front door and down the steps; the little old lady was still beside the car holding the passenger door open. I dropped you in the seat; I turned to thank her while closing the door. She looked at me and said, 'Go quickly away, do not tell anybody what happened here. It will only bring pain for all who are involved.' I ran around the car, and as I slid into the driver's seat, I started the car before sliding the gearshift into reverse. I quickly looked around for the woman; I looked everywhere, but she had disappeared from sight!"

Looking at Andy, I could see how afraid he was. I didn't blame him, for this was way more intense than I had ever encountered. I took his hand and held it to my chest to feel my heartbeat.

"I slammed my car door shut and sped out of there. I didn't know what to do; I saw the parking lot and pulled in. You were still cold and out of it. The lady said not to tell anyone. I don't know what I would have told them if I had taken you to the hospital, so I pulled in here and started CPR on you. I have never been so scared in my life.”

I reassured him I was fine and all would all be okay before I asked him a question. “Andy, what was the old lady wearing?”

“She was in a flowered housedress with a white collar.”

“Did you notice if she was missing a button at the collar like it had been cut off?”

Andy began to cry uncontrollably. He was trying to tell me something, but I wasn’t understanding. We sat there in the parking lot for close to an hour. Just holding hands, trying to gain a grip on the recent events. Suddenly, Andy wiped the tears from his eyes and righted himself in his seat.

As he started the car, he said, “Put your seatbelt on. We are going to my house. My parents will be in bed; we can sleep in the pool house. I think it’s time I had that talk with them anyway. I care too much for you to risk losing you. I can’t let you go back to that house on Marsalis St.”

I obeyed. Not knowing what state the house was left in, doors unlocked, windows opened, etc., I was concerned about what would happen if we just left it as it was. I was tired, and I was scared; I resigned control to Andy.

Arriving at his house, I was a bit overwhelmed by it all. We approached the neighborhood's entrance gate, where Andy briefly conversed with the guard explaining a friend in need. I didn't understand why he needed to explain to the guard until I deciphered it wasn't the neighborhood entrance; it was Andy's, or should I clarify, it was the gate to his parent's home.

We crept through the sideyard to the pool house. Entering the French doors, we kicked off our shoes and fell down on the sofa. Andy reclined in such a manner that I could lay repose between his legs, my head against his chest. Finally, settling down from the evening's wild ride, sleep began finding its way to us.

"Do you remember yesterday when I said I dreamed you died?"

"I do."

"The way I found out you died in the dream was from a little old lady standing by my car; she told me you had been crushed by a falling bookcase. It was, well, the same old lady at your house tonight. Why did you ask me if the collar was torn and missing a button?"

I looked up at him and gently kissed his lips before saying, "This isn't the first time she has saved me."

Andy lifted my head so he could see into my eyes. "There is more."

"Oh fuck, I can't take anymore tonight."

"That woman, I know who she was."

Chapter 3

Revelations

Waking up the following day with coffee urns and orange juice on the sofa table in front of me was a pleasant surprise. The coffee's aroma brought me slowly out of my slumber. Beyond the brewed bean smell in the air, there were lingering notes of sandalwood and tea rose. I stretched my legs and toes; my face wore a smile from having spent the night in Andy's arms. My senses began to sharpen as I realized he wasn't there next to me. Opening my eyes, my focus adjusted towards the far end of the sofa; alas, there he was. As my pupils began to cooperate, I took note of the delicate features on his sweet face. I was quickly taken aback, realizing how much Andy favored his mother; it was she at the other end of the couch.

Her smile was sweet but a bit distant. I couldn't blame her; I doubted she had a clue who I was or why I was in her pool house. Or did she? Maybe Andy arose early to have "the talk" with his parents after all.

"Good morning, Henry. I hope the sofa was suitable for sleeping on. I believe it to be quite comfortable for lounging, though I am not quite sure how it performs for slumbering."

Her accent was a lovely soft British timbre. From my love of linguistics, I garnered a touch of a Surrey accent. It made sense, Andy was actually called Andrew, and his last name was Dench.

"Good morning, Mrs. Dench. I hope my being here isn't terribly inconvenient, and I go by Hank."

"Only if you consider having my son coming out of the closet inconvenient, Henry."

I couldn't read the tone; it wasn't sarcastic or demeaning; it was merely proper English directness. I quickly assessed her; there were no tear stains, no puffy eyes, and her mascara was perfectly placed. Status; there had been no drama when Andy told them I was there.

But where was he? My question was quickly answered as Mrs. Dench was a brilliant mind reader. "Andrew has gone to his room to shower and change clothes. He should be back shortly. He said there was unpleasantness at your home last night, which is why he brought you here. Am I to assume you don't have toiletries or a change of clothes?"

"Yes, ma'am."

"There is a bathroom right there you may use to clean up. I requested Carlton bring a razor, toothbrush, shampoo, etc., for you. Please prepare your-self for the day; Andrew will fetch you in a bit."

"Thank you so very much. I am truly appreciative."

"May I ask if your parents are aware of your being homosexual? Excuse me - Gay?"

"That is not a conversation we have had, and if I may be direct, never will. My family is very basic; they are people who only believe in what they can control. I expect my father and stepmother will understand and maintain a relationship with me. I suspect my mother and stepdad will not. My mother is incredibly religious; this will not settle well with her."

"If she is a woman of faith, a Christian, then why do you not believe she will work through this with you?"

"I said she was religious; being Christ-like and reli-gious rarely coincide."

"Well said, Henry. May I ask why you continue to live there knowing your sexuality is an issue?"

After the night I had just gone through, I wasn't pre-pared to be a guest on a daytime talk show. I re-sponded out of courtesy and respect. "I am doing my best to get through college and start a career. My life has been a series of events beyond my control, and I am pushing forward with the lessons I've learned.

The goal is to achieve a better life than what I was raised in."

While clarifying my position with and around my family with Mrs. Dench, a man I didn't know entered the room and nodded to me. Dressed in a waistcoat, white tie, shirt with vest, and pinstriped pants, I assumed he to be Carlton, the manservant. Andy had spoken of him on occasion, telling of his long tenure with their family; he had been around all of Andy's life. Crossing to a disguised mirrored door, he pulled on the virtually invisible handle; he entered the pool bathroom, leaving a bag of toiletries on the vanity. He quietly returned to the sofa table, leaving the bathroom door ajar. I assumed the door was left open so I would know where the facilities were. He removed the coffee service and once more nodded to us as he took his leave. He never spoke a word.

After Carlton left the pool house, Andy's mom rose from her perch. Making her exit, she said, "Please go about your morning ritual. I have made lunch reservations at the club for the four of us. There is much to discuss."

Watching her through the glass doors as she elegantly crossed by the pool and up towards their home, I made my way into the small pool bathroom to pull myself together. This weekend was not working out exactly as I had planned. And, by the way, when I say small pool bathroom, that is sarcasm. It was the size of my bedroom at home. I began preparing for a welcomed shower; removing my shirt up and over my head, I noticed bruises on my wrists. The dark purple marks in the shape of fingers. I recalled Andy saying he felt as if someone was pulling me away from him. I continued undressing, looking down my front for other unexplained markings. There were minor scratches on my face; this was to be expected from Andy trying to revive me. Removing my pants, I found my ankles were slightly bruised as well. That fit the story; Andy claimed he was trying to pull me from the bed.

I continued checking for anomalies in the reflective surface. Nothing else was visible to me; I was somewhat relieved. I didn't know what to think of the finger marks on my wrist. I didn't remember a thing after going into my parents' bedroom until I woke to him slapping me.

I moved into the glass and tile shower, adjusting the temperature until I found the setting I liked best; a toasty warm shower was in order. I lowered myself to the tile floor to sit, my knees gently tucked under my chin, the water streaming over me. As the glass walls and doors fogged over, I began to relax. I must have stayed there for a long while. When Andy entered the bathroom calling to me, he startled me. He had never seen me without clothes, so I was grateful I was huddled on the floor where not everything was visible.

Opening the shower door, he said we would depart for lunch soon; he wanted to know if I needed anything. I smiled at him and committed to being right out. He returned the smile before closing the shower door, retreating to the other room to wait for me. I rose from the floor, used the razor to clear my stubble away, and began to feel somewhat refreshed. This was the best my energy had been in some time.

I vigorously dried off, wrapping the towel around my waist as I looked into the mirror. I sought to control my wavy locks; my hair had always looked unkempt, and today was no different. My dad always said my out-of-control hair was just part of my charm.

Leaving the bathroom, I found Andy sitting on the sofa waiting for me. I reached for my jeans on the floor and turned away from him to put them on. Purposefully, I dropped my towel as I slid my jeans up over my ass. I looked over my shoulder, expecting to see him smirk as I attempted to tease him. He was staring at me with concern.

"Did I cross a line? Did you not like what you saw?"

"Umm, I don't like seeing that at all."

"I am sorry. I thought we were headed to that level of intimacy."

He rose and walked towards me. Taking me by the hand, he guided me to the middle of the room. He didn't say a word, just turned me to face him. "It's not your ass. Look over your shoulder into the mirror."

I turned my head as far as possible while Andy held my shoulders straight, the mirror revealing what he observed. My eyes opened wide when I spotted the bruises on my back, each one deep purple and black. Eight handprints were embedded in my skin. Four on each side, each angled perfectly to suggest I was being pulled downward. I turned back to him and looked into his eyes. "I'm scared. What else happened in that room last night?"

"When I was trying to pull you off the bed, you were stuck to it."

I pushed back from him and raised my wrist into the air. "Look at these." The visible handprints around my wrists startled him. Staring into each other's eyes, we were caught off guard when Carlton cleared his throat, announcing his presence.

"Your mother sent these for Mr. Notenburg. She deems them appropriate for lunch."

Andy reached for the hanger, taking the clothes from Carlton. Releasing the articles to Andy, he nodded and once again was gone.

"My mother was a fashion designer in her younger days; she has a good eye for size. I am sure they will fit you wonderfully. I think your tennis shoes will set off the outfit perfectly. Get dressed for lunch; my father is already at the club and is not an indulgent man. Lots of great things about him; patience is not one of them."

"Andy."

"Yes, Babe."

"I am afraid."

"We will be fine. It's all very odd, but we will figure it out together. I got you."

Andy exited through the glass doors, gliding across the coping. I proceeded to dress in the clothes deemed appropriate for the club. I looked in the mirror and quite liked the white cotton shirt combined with the khaki pants. Andy was right; his mother did have an eye for fit. I was surprised at how well the clothes embraced my body. The sleeves on the unstructured blue cotton jacket should have been pushed up, but I wanted to hide the bruises on my wrists. I grabbed the tan belt from my jeans, tucked the shirt into the khakis, and slipped on my tennis shoes. Checking myself in the mirror one more time, I decided I needed to add one little thing to the ensemble. I tightly rolled the cuffs of the khakis upwards to my ankles, revealing my bare skin. The bruises were faint around my ankles; I was confident no one would notice them.

"Hank Notenburg - you look good!" I muttered while looking in the mirror. The real purpose of my mirror review was to check for any signs of apparent wounds. It was nice to have found an upside to all of the craziness.

I left the pool house and walked up the path of the beautifully landscaped yard. The sunlight seeping through the large oak trees revealed a beautiful retreat, perfectly appointed with flowers and shrubs. The yard was worthy of a formal English garden. I imagined Andy's parents had their home in the UK transplanted to Fort Worth, providing a sense of the place where they were raised. I didn't know much about Andy's family and was curious to learn. Walking up the cobblestone steps, I spotted Andy at the top, looking down at me, beaming. This all suited him; it was apparent he belonged here. I did not have that same confidence in myself.

Lunch with his parents was uneventful; his father asked lots of questions about my future plans and how I had managed a scholarship to a private school. I was very upfront with him; it was quite simple, hard work, and good people put me there. Andy and his mother remained relatively quiet during the interview; I sensed this was a make-or-break for me.

His father acknowledged he suspected Andrew was gay from an early age. Andy's mom interjected that, having worked in fashion; she was quite comfortable around gay men. Mr. Dench revealed he had an older sister who identified as a lesbian. Seeing all the challenges she had in life, he vowed should he have a homosexual child, that child would be treated fairly and equally. His exactness and profound love of his son touched me, and if I am honest, it made me jealous.

Being the inquisitive boy I have always been, I asked Andy's father how he had made his fortune. Andy and his mother were aghast I would ask such a question. Mr. Dench laughed, "The old-fashioned way, my boy. I inherited it!"

Everyone at the table shared a giggle over the response. Then he said something that shifted my perspective significantly. "Hank, you need to understand and be able to discern the difference between Riche and Nouveau-riche. People who have had money all their lives don't think about it; they enjoy it. They enjoy the people it allows into their life. Those who have recently acquired significant amounts of money spend their life proving their value to everyone they meet. It's important to them people know how much they have acquired and what it means to them. They don't have joy; they just have things."

His theory made me smile as it was logical to me. The history of keeping up with the Joneses' never made anyone happy in my family; we just had to have more.

"I had an older sister who gave it all up to find a life of happiness, a life of love. She married a man my father completely disapproved of, pushing the two of them to leave Cambridge and start a life together here. They lived in a simple home with an acre of land here in Fort Worth. She was twenty years my senior, so I don't really remember much about her growing up, except she always looked on the bright side. She always wanted to help others. Her husband, always in his silly, out-of-fashion bow ties, made her happy. I visited them once in the fifties. It is one of the reasons we decided to live here after we got married in '64."

The waiter interrupted our conversation, inquiring if we wanted desserts or required anything more. After the bill had been resolved with the stroke of a pen, we left the table. Walking to the car, I asked Mr. Dench what had happened to his sister, who had lived here. "You spoke of your sister in the past tense. Am I to assume she is deceased?"

"She and her husband were murdered in their home; when discovered in their garden house, each of their throats had been slashed. It was never determined who the killer was; there was no significant evidence to follow up on. The poor man who investigated the case told me strange things had occurred during the investigation. He said he had never seen such evil before as he did in that garden house."

What Pa Day said to me about the couple killed in the little house was immediately in my head. Was this coincidence? It was all very queer. "And your other sister?"

As he was about to answer, the valet delivered his car keys; Andy's dad took the interruption as an opportunity to change the subject.

I said my goodbyes to Andy's parents before walking towards his car. I left Andy behind, thinking he might need a moment alone with his family. Kissing both his parents goodbye, he returned to my side and opened my car door for me. The valet observed him opening my door and quickly opened his. The young man delivering cars clearly winked at both of us as he closed the driver's door. The world around us was changing. Good or bad, I didn't know.

"My mom said you are welcome to stay with us until your parents get back."

"What exactly did you tell your parents?"

"I told them someone broke into your house and was attacking you when I showed up. I said they took off hearing me enter the house."

"Andy, I have a question for you."

"Yes, it was my aunt I saw outside your house and who came to me in my dream."

"How'd you know I was going to ask that?"

"Educated guess, my dad told you about his sister and what happened to her. You are a smart man, babe. I figured you would ask sooner or later."

"We need to go back to my house."

"I assumed you would say that as well. I am not keen on that idea. We can drive by, but I am not making any promises I will stop."

"Fair enough."

Driving across town, my mind was racing at speeds equal to the tires of Andy's nine-eleven.

Turning onto Marsalis St, the hair on my arms began to rise. The creek running alongside the street and disappearing into the woods by the railroad tracks appeared agitated. Andy slowed the car to a crawl as we approached the double driveway to the house. Everything in view was completely normal. The front door was closed, and the drapes opened just like any other day. My car was parked in the driveway exactly as I had left it. Nothing was out of sync. Fence gates were closed, their visible locks in place.

Suddenly Andy swerved the car into the driveway and parked. "This is not how it was when we left here last night. Does anyone else have keys?"

We crawled slowly from the car, anxious some wild event might occur. Standing in the driveway, the hair on my arms began to settle; the eery feeling I previously had suddenly calmed. I closed the car door and headed to the steps of the white clapboard house. I pulled on the screen door to enter; the handle was locked. I reached for my keys only to realize I didn't have them; they were in my jeans at the pool house. I looked through the living room windows; everything was in its place. I turned to see Andy standing in the front yard, staring into my parent's bedroom window. I leaped from the front porch into the flower bed, landing on the ground beside him. Looking in the window revealed everything was perfect in the room. The bookcase against the wall, no broken leg, all the books in their place.

I looked at Andy. "This isn't how you described the room when we left."

"I swear what I told you was true. The books were everywhere. The bed was smashed halfway through the floor. The shelf's left leg was at a ninety-degree angle sticking out from the base from being broken."

"I believe you. This is not the first weird incident to happen in this house."

We closed in on the window slowly, one inch at a time. I wanted a complete view of the room. Everything was just like my parents had left it. Turning to go, my eye fixated on something out of place. A book lay on the bed where my mother slept; this book was off-limits to everyone in the house. No one in the family beyond my mom was allowed to look in this book. And yet, there it was, laying on her pillow, open. I pointed it out to Andy.

A wedding photo was lying prone on the book's edge, facing the window allowing complete visibility. Andy gasped. "That's a wedding photo of my dad's sister and the bow-tied brother-in-law! Why would that be in your house? Dad keeps that exact photo on the mantle in his study."

"I have no idea."

Bringing us out of our trance, we heard a distant call.

"Boo Boo. Hey, Boo Boo" It was Ma Day calling for me from down the street.

I turned and waved to her, "Be right there."

Andy continued to observe the wedding photo through the window. The hair on my arms was be-ginning to rise again; I felt someone watching us from the crawlspace underneath the white clapboard house. "Andy, honey, let's go. I need to stop by and check on Ma Day. I would also like for you to meet her. She is one of the most important people in my life."

Backing away from the window, he simply said, "Okay." Andy drove up the road to Ma Day's house, parking his car in the street. I walked my usual path through the neighbors' yards; I didn't want her to know anything was off.

"I tried to call you several times, and there wasn't any answer. Is everything all right?"

"Yes, ma'am, I spent the night at my friend's house last night." I motioned Andy out of the car and introduced him to Ma Day. "This is Andy. I am staying with him and his parents until the folks get back."

"Nice to meet you, Andrew. Everything okay at the house? The Piersons said they heard quite a ruckus at your house last night, then saw you boys take off in the car."

"Yea, Andy was coming to get me, and someone had gotten into the house. He scared them off. All is good."

"Boo, don't lie to me. I feared your parents leaving you alone would stir up the past."

Andy and I looking at each other, turned our eyes back to Ma Day after her comment. "What do you mean?" I asked.

"Why don't you boys come inside? Let's have a soda and visit."

We followed Ma Day into her house. She motioned for us to have a seat on the couch while she disappeared into the kitchen. The sound of ice clinking into thick-walled glasses came from the kitchen; soon after, a familiar sound of fizz signaled a fresh carbonated beverage was being opened. A few moments later, she appeared with a tray carrying three full glasses and a plate of cookies, freshly made, no doubt.

Ma Day settled into her floral patterned rocker, which now sat where Pa Days' chair had been when he was alive. Gently rocking in her chair, she took a sip of soda before clinking her glass down on the side table. "I knew your aunt and uncle pretty well. I don't imagine you were born when they passed."

"His aunt and uncle?" I asked.

"They lived in the same house you do now. They were the couple Pa Day told you about being killed in the little house." She had all the details correct, but how did she know who Andy was? Andy responded to her question about knowing them.

"No, ma'am, I never met them. Only have seen a couple of pictures of them. May I ask how you knew I was related to them?"

Taking another sip of her soda, she smiled. "Because you look exactly like your father when he was your age. Same haircut and everything. You do have your mom's nose and lips, though. How are your parents?"

I cocked my head sideways. "How do you know his parents? I am very confused."

"When your dad was around fifteen or sixteen, he spent one summer here with his aunt and uncle. Such a delightful young man he was; he had such a good time. Your dad's brother-in-law would take him down to the creek with Pa and spend the night fishing. I think it did him good to see something beyond Cambridge and to learn there could be life beyond Oxford. Becoming an only child after your grandparents disowned your aunts, he became concerned that money would always rule his life. I am guessing he figured out how to manage happiness and money. I met your mom when they first moved here, just before you were born, I think."

Andy looked at me; I could sense he wanted to know more. "You can ask her anything. We are an open book; if she doesn't think you need to know, she'll tell you so."

Andy paused before speaking, carefully gathering his words. "My father never talked about his other sister, the sister who was —— different. Did you know anything about her?"

"I wasn't sure if he would ever mention her. Her being homosexual is what caused the family upheaval and why your aunts moved from England."

We were offered more homemade cookies and refills of drinks as we visited for a while. I could tell Ma Day liked Andy; I sensed she knew we were an item but would allow me to tell her when I felt I was ready.

"Oh, it was quite a stir when the news came out that the family's oldest girl was homosexual. Conservative English family with royal ties; she was immediately sent off to a sanitarium. Your dad told me how hard it was on him to lose both his sisters. He said her being homosexual wasn't a choice; it was just part of her being. Don't think he ever forgave your grandparents for that. How much do you know about how they died?"

Andy shook his head from side to side. "Very little. Dad has only mentioned the incident twice. Once today and one other time."

"Both your aunts were here in Fort Worth when the murders happened. The eldest had been in the mental hospital in Big Springs and had been released for a family visit. She was with a friend at the house the day they were killed. I saw them leaving, but of course, I didn't have a clue what had occurred at the time. She was not seen again after that awful day until her death; she never checked back into the hospital."

"Do you know if my dad knew she was here in Texas?"

Ma Day thought about it for a minute. "Oh yes, her sister would have most likely taken him to visit the mental hospital the summer he was here. Someone was paying the bills for the hospital; I suppose there could have been a trust fund taking care of it. I just always assumed your dad knew about it."

"Ma Day," I said, "Do you believe in life after death? The spirit world?"

"I don't really know. It seems like your soul ought to go somewhere; I have always thought about it as heaven, but perhaps heaven is just around us. I will say your Pa Day believed others lived amongst us. He said he saw things that could only have happened with help from the other side. What he saw in that little house shook his very being. I never thought he would leave the police force, but whatever happened that night scared him. Did you ever wonder why he would never go to your house?"

"I sure do miss him," I said reverently.

With a tear in her eye, she said, "I do too."

Taking that as a cue, it was time to go; I picked up the dishes and returned them to the kitchen. I didn't wash them as that was a no-no in Ma Day's house; guests did not clean up after themselves.

I hugged her goodbye, just hard enough of a grip to not break any of her seventy-plus-year-old bones. Moving aside, I gave room for Andy to hug her too. He thanked her for the time and for providing some insight into his family's past.

We walked to the car from her house quietly. Looking to the West, we both commented the sun had set. It had been a long visit, well worth every minute spent.

Seated in the car, Andy turned the ignition to start it. Releasing the clutch, Andy checked his rearview mirror prior to pulling away from the curb. "The front porch light is on at your house."

"That's nice; it can just stay that way."

Chapter 4

Saying Goodbye

For the two weeks my parents were traveling, I spent my days and nights in Andy's pool house. By the time the parental units returned, the physical bruises had healed, but new emotional ones were forming.

After discovering his aunt had been sent away to live in a sanitarium, something changed in Andy. He became obsessed with what his father knew and why the family wouldn't discuss it. As more information about his aunt was garnered, Andy methodically started pushing me away. Less and less time was spent with me; luckily for me, I had friends to fall back on.

Things on Marsalis St. returned to their norm. Since their return from California, my stepdad had become very subdued. It was obvious to everyone in the family, and all my mother would say is the trip was not as productive as he had hoped. My older siblings and I agreed it must have had something to do with his mother's estate; apparently, he wouldn't receive any family money. I never really knew for sure if that was the case as we barely spoke any longer; we avoided each other at all costs. This worked out well for me as I was drowning in schoolwork and doing all I could to keep up. High School had not adequately prepared me for college, and it was evident. Even graduating number four in my class with an A average did not set me up for success; college classes were all-consuming.

Midterms arrived and were finally over; the big reveal of grades made it clear I was barely passing. This news only heightened my desire for Thanksgiving break to arrive, time to let my mind take a breather. I suggested to Andy we get away for a few days before Thanksgiving and take a break from the world around us. I hoped we could rekindle what had been so lovely at the beginning of the semester.

Andy declined my invitation; his excuse was he had some family business to attend to in West Texas. I suspected he was going to snoop around the mental hospital where his aunt resided. The numerous times he engaged his dad in conversation about his sister were not fruitful. His dad was curious why Andy suddenly was so keen to know about his aunt; he repeatedly asked Andy to leave it be. Mr. Dench was not a man to be easily riled. Still, when Andy continued to bring the subject up, the anger in his father was reminiscent of the red-eyed couple on Marsalis St.

Classes completed, the break began with only one commitment for me; Thanksgiving day at the country club with the Dench family. Andy's mom invited me to join them for lunch; she and I hoped the four of us together would bring Andy out of his funk.

Giving my mother the news I would not be home for turkey day led to a tirade of biblical proportions. All her children would be at her house this year; this required me to stay as well. She forbade me from hanging out with my, as she put it, rich-snooty-friends.

I did my best to keep my mother from meeting Andy. My inner voice said it was best to keep the two of them apart and never tell her his name. Freshly dressed and ready to leave for the country club against my mother's wishes, the telephone rang on Marsalis St. My little sister answered the phone before calling out that the call was for me.

"Hello, Henry. So glad I caught you before you left. There's been a bit of a row at our house, and Andy has requested I retract my lunch invitation to you. I am terribly sorry about this. I truly enjoy our time together, but I am sure you understand we need to work this out."

"I get it."

"Thank you for not making me choose family over friends."

"Before you go. May I ask a favor?"

"Certainly."

"Andy is angry with me, and I don't know why. I am not asking you to get in the middle of it; I just wanted to ask if you would remain my friend. You know what I mean? Should things not work out with him, could we still lunch and shop together?"

"Let's cross that path should we come to it. Andrew has had bouts of unhappiness previously; this, too, shall pass. Enjoy your holiday with your family." And with that said, the next thing I heard was a dial tone.

I remained at home with my family and pretended all was well. They would not have understood the challenges I was encountering, educationally or emotionally, and likely would not have cared. The weekend passed, and once again, Monday arrived. Classes were back in session, and I returned to my studies, intent on focusing on school and little else. Unsure of what the future held for Andy and me, a preoccupation was needed. The threat of losing my scholarship was the perfect distraction.

Sitting in my usual seat in Psyche 101, Andy walked into the class we shared. I wasn't sure what to expect from him when he saw me. He settled into his usual seat next to me. Reaching across the aisle, he took my hand, and without looking at me, he apologized for how he acted over break.

Life with him continued to go up and down over the next four weeks. One day Andy was like his old self, and then the next, he would be standoffish. Thank god I had Donna and Todd to hold me up and keep me focused on school.

Todd, Donna, and I were a threesome of sorts. This three-way started during Fish Camp right after Donna, and I met Todd. He and I quickly became best friends. Even though the two of them were romantically involved, they often made sure to include me in their adventures. Donna and I had been friends since junior high. Classmates assumed we were in love, and we were, just not romantically. People thought it odd the three of us were together most of the time. We went so far as to buy matching silver bracelets with our names engraved equal distances apart on them, symbolizing our triangle.

The last week of the semester was full of emotional stress when dealing with Andy. Final exams were done, and I was exhausted from school and the turmoil with him. During our up weeks, I spent time with his parents, enjoying the holiday traditions they observed. The more time I spent at his home, the more a sense of belonging overcame me. His dad taught me the ins and outs of wine and cigars, all the old-world protocols lost on modern society. How important a good set of legs were on wine, the proper way to assess a bottle recently opened, advising one does not lick the cork of the bottle to determine its moisture content. Skill sets I would have never known otherwise. The time spent with his parents created hope in the three of us that whatever was bothering Andy would pass.

On the last day of the fall semester, Mrs. Dench planned a celebration for him and me. She was very proud of Andy for managing through the first term. A term which was, for many, the most challenging semester of higher learning. I arrived at their home around 5:00 PM; shortly thereafter, Mr. Dench and I partook in a cocktail and cigar while dinner was finalized. Just as Mr. Dench and I finished our Manhattan, Andy's mom entered the study and announced Andy wasn't home and dinner was ready. She suggested we not wait for him. I assumed another argument had occurred; I was beginning to believe it had something to do with me. I could tell Mrs. Dench was hurt by Andy skipping her planned event.

Andy's father and I were discussing holiday plans; they had committed to taking us to their cabin in Colorado to ski the day after Christmas. I had never been skiing and was very excited to try it. I also hoped the getaway, spending time with Andy, would help him and me reconnect. Unaware Andy had entered the living room, he interrupted my and Mr. Dench's conversation with an announcement. "I am not fucking going skiing if Hank will be there." His statement was a complete surprise to everyone in the room. It was apparent that something was amiss, but the language took the announcement to an entirely different level.

Andy's dad, being a very astute man, pardoned him and his wife from the room. "You two boys need to talk this out tonight." Closing the door behind them, Andy turned to me and stared. He leaned back into the door and said, "I can't do this anymore. I can't be with you; I need you to go."

"You have been acting out at me since Thanksgiving break. I know some weird shit happened at my parent's house early on, but we seemed so happy until you went away at Thanksgiving. Please tell me what is going on."

"I don't know how to tell you," he said softly.

"Are you in love with someone else? Did I do something to irritate you?"

"Babe, it isn't you directly, but it has to do with you. Ma Day talking about my aunt started me thinking about things my dad had said, none of it added up. She was right; my dad knew about the sanitarium and the trust fund in place to manage her expenses. He has kept it a secret to keep loose ends from unraveling."

Doing my best to hold back my tears, I said, "I love you, and what you are saying doesn't have anything to do with me. Why are you tossing me aside?"

"It has to do with your family."

"Is it because we are poor? Really? Is that it?"

"No, it's not that." Andy reached into his coat pocket and retrieved a picture. He slowly turned the black-and-white photo around before handing it to me. The date imprinted on the photo's edge was 1953. I intently studied the two people within, trying to understand why this would push him away.

"I don't know who these individuals are."

"Yes, you do. Well, you know one of them."

I continued to dissect the picture, and soon the recognition came. "Oh my god, that's my mother!"

"She was the last person my aunt was seen with in 1960. Your mom was the person who checked my aunt out of the hospital; she was the woman who delivered death to that house on Marsalis St. The In/Out ledger from the hospital records confirms it."

Andy presented me with a photocopy of the document; there, it was in black and white. "Released to Norma De Lyon per the Dench Executive Trust."

"I couldn't find out anything else, only that my aunt never returned. I remembered the picture of my aunt and uncle in the book on your mom's bed. I went to your house one day last week and met your mother. I needed to confirm her maiden name. She corrected my pronunciation of the name, 'It's Duh - Lee - on,' thus confirming it was her birth name."

"I asked her if she ever had a friend named Gert Dench. She admitted she had known Gert before getting married. She asked me to have a seat as she left the living room; she returned with the album we saw on her bed. She was carrying the book containing the picture of my aunt and uncle. She sat down next to me and questioned why I was asking about Gert. I told her I was researching family genealogy."

"Your mom said she had not seen Gert in years, not since the terrible accident. Sitting there, staring at me, your mom became very quiet. The living room began to chill, the exact same cold we felt when I pulled you from the house. The fact that your family wound up living in the same place my family was killed and your mom having checked Gert out of the mental ward is too much. I don't know what's happening, but I can't subject my family to turmoil. You must go and never return or have anything to do with my family." Tears streamed down his face; the agony in his eyes was all it took for me to stand up and leave. I loved him too much to be the cause of any pain he felt. I left their house without saying goodbye to his parents.

Starting my car, I began to cry. Once again, my family had created unnecessary angst for me. I dreaded going home, back to that house on Marsalis St., the little white clapboard house where demons were lying just below the foundation.

The photo of my young mother with the crazy woman, still fresh in my mind, meant Andy was right. Why was my family living in that house? What spirits were circling around us? A portal of damnation? It was all overwhelming me.

I turned my car right at University instead of left that night. I couldn't return to Marsalis St. A cocktail was in order. I crossed through downtown towards Jennings Street, the land of gay bars; three of them, to be exact.

Walking into The Lumber Company, I was greeted by Big Mama. "Child, where have you been? You finally turn legal to drink and stop coming to the bar. There has to be a man in your life!"

"You're wise, mama."

"Well, it's the holidays, and he ain't with you. I know what that means; he is either gone home to his wife and kids or ain't willin' to take you home to meet the parents."

I just smiled and handed him my cover charge. I didn't really want to talk about it.

"Uh-huh. Come on in, child. Have a drink, and find comfort in the arms of another man. You know the quickest way to forget about that one is to crawl under another! Heh, heh." Big Mama was right; drinks leading to a man at his place meant I wouldn't have to go home.

I am not sure how much alcohol I consumed that night, but it was enough for me to not know where I was waking up or who the sexy Latino boy wrapped around me was.

Trying to recall if I drove or if I needed to walk back to the bar for my car, I scanned the room. In pressing need of water and aspirin, I looked around to plan my escape. Stretching my arm towards my watch on the table, I heard him speak.

"There is water in the fridge and aspirin in the bathroom, Papi."

"Oh, thanks; I didn't mean to wake you."

"You think we slept? Aye, no baby, and if you don't remember, I am losing my magic." That said, he jumped up from where we were on the floor and walked away. Looking at his ass and other assets, I was disappointed I didn't remember anything. He returned shortly with water and aspirin, especially for me.

"Don't worry, Papi, we didn't do anything. You were seriously fucked up last night, though. Talking about ghosts trying to kill you and your mother cracking some woman out of an insane asylum. You were telling some wacky shit! It was good, though; you should write a book!"

"Thank you for the water and meds." Taking a sip of liquid, I sat up. The apartment had little furniture, and the pallet on the hard floor was most uncomfortable. But mission accomplished, I hadn't had to go home. "What's your name?"

"Jaime Laverde Castillo. I know, very typical Latino. But don't stereotype me!"

"How did I get here?"

"I drove you in your car. Big Mama asked me to take care of you. He must really like you 'cause he doesn't normally take care of the drunks."

"I don't usually drink like that; crazy things going on in my life."

"Big Mama said you just got dumped. Pobrecito."

"Why are we in bed together naked if we didn't do anything?"

"You asked me to hold you. Then you took off all your clothes and pulled me up to you. I don't sleep in clothes. Once you were asleep, I undressed and cuddled up next to you. It was nice. But I need to be honest with you; you aren't my type."

"Well, I don't think I was offering anything, but good to know. Can I buy you some breakfast for taking care of me?"

"Thank you, and I appreciate it, but I have to get to work. So put on your clothes and let's vamanos. You know what you could do is drop me off at work so I don't have to take the bus; that would be a great payment in kind."

All dressed and in the car, Jaime and I headed for his job. The winter morning had turned somewhat cold. It was brisk but pleasant; the weather was waking me up from a night of drinking.

"Who is Todd? Is he the one who broke your heart, and why you drank so much?"

"Todd? Huh? Not sure what you are talking about."

"You kept asking Todd to not leave you in your sleep last night. Very passionately, you were begging him not to go. It was obviously someone you love."

The memory was faint, but it didn't make any sense to me. Arriving at the corner of Main and 28th Street, Jaime spoke. "Jus' pull around the side here. Thanks for dropping me. Saved me from being late."

"Least I could do - thanks for keeping me safe and out of jail. Hope to cross paths again."

Jaime exited the car and walked around the front of it. He stopped and smiled at me; then, he approached the driver's side window. Motioning for me to roll it down, he leaned into the car and gave me a soft kiss on the lips. Standing back up, he smiled and turned to walk away. Without looking back at me, he said, "I lied to you; you are my type. I think you are totally fucking hot!" Off into the side door of the market he went.

I decided to head back to Marsalis St. I didn't want to go home but was reasonably sure my mom would be in a snit because I didn't come home last night. She had threatened to kick me out if I didn't start being more respectful of her house rules.

Driving down Marsalis St, I approached the curb in front of the white clapboard house. The driveway full of parked cars meant I would have to leave mine in the street. Family members in town for Christmas were taking over the house.

The effects of the long night of drinking were lingering; my brain remained in a fog as I stumbled out of my car. Walking through the front door, I was greeted with distant relatives making their once-a-year visit to Fort Worth. "The Pretend Tour" is what I called it. A group of people who always talk bad about each other behind their backs yet pretend to be in love for the sake of a holiday. I was certain we weren't the only family in the world who participated in such craziness.

Excusing myself, I moved to the only bathroom in the house and relieved my bladder. Exiting the bathroom, I found my friend Donna standing in the hallway with tear-stained swollen eyes. "We have to talk right now," she blurted out.

One of the obnoxious family members nearby overheard and immediately announced there would soon be another baby in the house. Was my family really that clueless?

"Let's go to my room."

I walked Donna down the hallway to my bedroom. Looking around the room, I realized Mom was glad I didn't come home last night. My not being there left a bed available for a guest to inhabit. Pushing a cousin's luggage from atop the bed, we sat. Finally settled on the bed, I looked at Donna and asked, "What's wrong? Is something wrong with Andy?"

"You don't know? You haven't heard?"

Panic began to take control over me, "No, what?"

"It's not Andy. It's Todd."

"Todd? What's going on?"

"Todd died last night. The Christmas tree in his living room caught fire. His parents got everyone else out. He wasn't in his bed, so they thought he wasn't home. He had fallen asleep on the couch upstairs." Donna was full-on in tears.

She was distraught, as any girlfriend would have been at the loss of someone she loved. Holding her, I let her cry without saying a word. It wasn't long before my mom blew into the room and began her assault on me; she assumed I had done something to cause the tears to stream down Donna's face. As twisted as it was, correcting Mom and explaining that Donna's boyfriend had died in a fire gave me great pleasure. My mother did not like being corrected; she turned heel and returned to her guests.

Coming out of my hangover funk, it started coming back to me; what Jaime said about me asking Todd not to leave me. I recalled seeing Todd lying on the couch, smelling the smoke. I could hear him calling out my name, asking me for help.

"It's my fault. We stayed out past his curfew. I am sure he went up the back stairs to not wake his parents," Donna spurted out between tears.

Continuing to hold her, I didn't know how to tell her he had come to me. Why would his spirit find me to say goodbye? I held Donna's head up and looked at her. "I know you are going to think I am crazy, but remember me telling you about the spirits I have encountered. I doubt you have ever believed me, but now you must. Todd came to me last night to say goodbye. I repeatedly asked him not to go, but he said he had to."

Donna stared at me with a desire to believe what I was saying. "How do I know what you're saying is true? That you aren't just trying to make me feel better."

"Todd said to tell you he loves you and will be with you always."

"Hank, stop!"

"Donna, he said to tell you he wants you to keep the baby. To raise him with help from his parents and, most of all, to name him Morgan after his father."

She immediately stopped crying and looked at me. "I only told him I was pregnant last night. That's why we were out so late. We discussed my having an abortion. He said he needed to think about it and would let me know what he wanted. There is no way you could have known.”

“Well, it appears he found a way to give you his answer.”

The noises of Christmas coming from my family grew rowdier as we sat there silently holding hands. I was grateful for the time with her; it took the thoughts of Andy from my mind.

“Hank? Have you really been visited by the other side before?” Donna sheepishly asked.

“Yes, many times. Some were not so good, and some very special. Moments like Todd coming to give me information. Often times they seem like dreams. Where’s the ring Todd gave you?”

As she answered, she finally believed it was true. The ring was in her glove box. She wasn’t ready to let anyone know he had proposed.

“My Pa Day came to me when he left his body as well. I was at summer camp, fishing by myself on the pier. He sat next to me and reminded me to cast softly so I didn’t scare the fish. He told me I was special and one day would need to be prepared to use my gifts for good to help the people I love. I didn’t know what that meant until now.”

The memory of Pa Day telling me about the box containing the tie and the pearl button, the one my mother delivered to him free of blood or dirt, was fresh in my mind's eye, just as was Todd lying on the couch talking to me. "Donna? When he left you last night, was Todd wearing a red polo and 'our' bracelet?"

"He was; why?"

"Just confirming to myself it was him."

Donna stood from the bed and announced she needed to use the toilet. Leaving my bedroom, Donna turned right into the bathroom as I proceeded into the living room, looking for my mom. Sitting on the sofa, she was talking with one of her sisters.

"Hate to interrupt but will anyhow. I am going to Donna's house and get her settled in. I will be back after-while."

Just as my mom began to share her displeasure with my leaving while company was visiting, the front door blew open. Through the door came two delivery men alongside my older sister. They were delivering Mom's Christmas present, a new cookstove. She and her husband lived in Hawaii, home early for the holidays; they were dropping off gifts before they returned.

My sister gave me a big hug, followed by a hardy handshake from my brother-in-law. Donna exited the bathroom into the whirlwind of delivery men and family in the living room. My sister gave Donna a hug before stepping back and assessing her from head to toe. Hearing my sister advising how having a baby would be her greatest journey, Donna cast me the evil eye.

"I didn't say anything, I swear." I crossed to Donna and took her hand, and out the front door we went. Walking to her car, I told her I was going home with her to get her settled. She declined the offer saying she needed to be alone. Now that Todd was gone and a child was on the way, she needed to decide what her future looked like. I escorted her to her car, honored her request, and let her be alone. Waving goodbye as she drove off, I hollered, "Call me later! Say goodnight to me!"

I settled on the bumper of my car, taking a moment to observe the neighbors' holiday decorations, trying to absorb recent events. The last twenty-four hours had brought a breakup, death, and life. Good lord, what was next? Sitting there in the cold, I was soon joined by my Aunt Linda Fae. Dropping onto the cold bumper with a cocktail in one hand and a cigarette hanging from her lip, she spoke, "What's up, Boo?"

"Give me a drink of that!" I said. Smelling the liquor rising from the glass, I took a sip of the vodka tonic; I felt a little better. The hair of the dog, I guess.

My aunt and I had been allies all my life. She didn't mind my eccentricities, and I didn't mind her being a lush. She lived just far enough away from us to be close but not always around. My stepdad didn't like her because she had no issue telling him to piss off or whatever clever new phrase she may have picked up at the local watering hole.

"Linda, you and Mom have always been close. Did you two always hang out together when you were young?"

"Up until your mom ran off in high school, we were always together."

"What do you mean ran off? I have never heard about that." The night was in my favor; she was loaded just enough to still stand but drunk enough to talk about things she shouldn't.

"Hell yeah, she took off the year before she got pregnant with your oldest sister. When she came back home, she told all kinds of wild stories about parties, going to seances, and hanging out in graveyards. Weird shit."

"That doesn't sound like my mom. Are you sure it wasn't Gracie doing that crazy stuff?"

"I'm sure because Gracie and I had to pick up all the slack at home. Your mom met some girl from England at a party here in Fort Worth; they were inseparable."

"England?"

"She was really butch. The time I met her, I thought she was a man. Deep British voice with a sexy accent. I was kind of in love until I figured out she didn't have a cock."

"Do you remember her name?" I was intrigued.

"Good god, that's been a long time ago. I don't remember its name. Ha-ha." She was proud of herself for making a joke about a woman who identified as a man. So much for me thinking the world was moving forward. Linda stood, raised her glass, and declared it was time for another cocktail. I stayed on my perch, observing her fall up the driveway towards the house.

On her approach to the front steps, the front door opened. It was my mother shouting out into the night. "Boo, phone!"

Leaving the hard bumper that had imprinted its curve into my ass cheeks, I headed to the house to answer the phone. I assumed it was Donna letting me know she was all settled in.

"Hello."

"Is this Hank? Or Boo Boo, as they call you?"

"Yes. Who is this?"

"You need to wind your neck in and not ask questions about me. Best to leave sleeping hounds where they bloody lie."

"Who is this? What are you talking about?" I felt the receiver getting cold, the same cold I felt that night in Mom's room. I stood very still, and when I exhaled, my breath produced a fog around the phone's mouthpiece.

"If Andy hadn't intervened, you wouldn't be standing there right now!"

I looked around again, people were laughing, carrying on, and having a good time, but it was all in slow motion. The environment around me had decelerated, and time was being altered.

"You know who this is. Andy showed you my picture recently."

I recalled the woman in the picture with Mom; the lady Andy had said was his aunt. It was Gert. The woman who had been removed from the sanitarium by my mother.

"Next time I visit Marsalis St., it will be unpleasant for everyone. Stop digging into the past, into your mom's life, or I will come."

Two fingers snapped in front of my face. "Boo, are you ok?"

The phone was no longer in my hand, time returned to normal, no cold chill any longer. It was my mother.

"Mom, who answered the phone?"

"I did; why?"

"Did you recognize who it was? Who was on the other end?" Looking at her square in the eye, I said, "Why would you put me on the phone with Gert?"

Her eyes grew wide. "Where did you hear that name?"

"I know things I probably shouldn't?"

"Is that why that snooty young man was asking me questions about his family?"

"It has something to do with the fact that you have a picture of the people who used to live in this very house, the ones who were murdered. Why is their photo hidden in your secret book?"

Mom pulled back while staring at me. "Why were you in my book?"

"I wasn't. It was lying open on your bed when you were in California. I saw them."

By now, the jovial demeanor in the house had screeched to a halt. All ears were intent on hearing what Mother and I were arguing about. Everyone visiting the white clapboard house knew about the book and its forbidden access. They were in dire need of knowing what I had done to learn the information I spewed.

Not waiting on a response, I pushed past her and headed to my room. I grabbed the first warm thing to wear I could find. I had no intentions of coming back that night, or perhaps ever. Mom didn't follow, and I am not quite sure why. Through the front door, I went, headed towards my car. I didn't speak to anyone. I didn't want any questions, and my mind was made up. I was getting out of there.

Pulling the front door closed behind me; I saw Mother still standing in the same place I had left her, probably in shock. I was intent on leaving the spirits who belonged to that white clapboard house there, along with Gert and the memories of her.

Starting my car, I could tell I was being watched. I didn't know by whom, and I didn't want to know.

Chapter 5

They Always Come Back

Looking at the car's clock, I realized it was getting late; I had better make a plan for a place to stay. Since exiting the white clapboard house, I occupied the last several hours driving around the city. Diverting my attention from life by looking at Christmas decorations on display. Neighborhood by neighborhood, I toured the city.

I was sure if I didn't return home and face my mom, it would mark the end of me ever returning to Marsalis St. Based on my phone call with Gert, I decided it was best not to return. Knowing I had little choice, I did what I had to do.

My stepmom had been suggesting for years that I move in with them; it was time to take her up on the offer. My dad and I developed a decent relationship after my parents parted ways, and I truly adored my stepmother. I recently came out to her, and she did her best to support me in any way possible.

My father's intense self-focus pushed him to only participate in activities where he appeared as the hero in the storyline. There had never been a moment when he didn't take the standing ovation for something if the opportunity presented itself. Somehow he always managed to make it about him. My being threatened and his allowing me to live in his home would be the perfect story for him to play protector. So, I played my card.

Knocking on their front door, I stood on the porch without my coat on, shivering for effect. Observing my dad over the years, I knew how to put on a production that would garner sympathy on a grand scale. Dad opened the door, and seeing me without a coat on and shivering, he pulled me inside. He wrapped his arms around me to warm me. It was a genuine gesture, and I certainly appreciated the warmth of his touch. He did his best to be a loving father even though he was clueless about how he set people aside.

"I need to stay here tonight if it's okay. Things are not good with Mom and me at the moment." My statement lacking emotion, prompted him to announce my presence to my stepmom, who happened to already be in bed.

"Of course, it is. Is everything okay? Why don't you have your coat on?" His voice revealing concern. "Don't say another word. You know where the guest room is; go rest, and we will talk tomorrow."

I walked through their kitchen towards the guest room located at the back of the house. I grabbed a soda from the refrigerator and found my way to the bed. Laying down on top of the covers, I was asleep in seconds. Life had caught up with me.

The next morning my stepmom woke me offering a fresh cup of coffee; my feelings of melancholy were evident to her. She smiled and asked, "Do you want to talk about what happened?"

"Good morning," I mumbled.

"I am cooking breakfast; come to the kitchen."

I motioned an okay and looked over at the clock to see the time was 10:54 AM. I had been asleep for nearly twelve hours. Sipping my coffee, I began collecting my thoughts. What a psychotic couple of days it had been.

Walking to the kitchen, I could smell the ham hocks on the griddle. For all her craziness, one thing my stepmom could do was cook. "Dang, that smells good," I muttered, sitting down at the kitchen table.

"'Bout ten more minutes till it's done. So what did you and your mom fight about? Did she find out about Andy?"

"Yes, but not in the way you are implying. Turns out Mom has a past with Andy's aunt." Sharing the new-found information with my stepmom, my dad walked into the room. "Who does your mother have a past with?"

My dad was always up for dirt on my mom. He wanted all the seedy details. "I didn't even connect the dots until now. Of course, you would know. Andy's aunt was Gert Dench."

"That's a name I haven't heard in a long time. She and your mom were quite a troublesome pair. I brought your mom to Fort Worth to a party; that's where they met. Your mom was around 15, and boy, did she have some wild times."

"Apparently so," my stepmother shared her opinion before filling the plates with food. Placing breakfast on the table, she settled in next to me to hear the tale I never knew.

"We headed this way from Big Springs on a Friday afternoon, right after school. Didn't tell anyone, just took off. I had friends that had moved up here, and we decided to see what they were up to. We ended up at a party and had a wild evening. Your mom disappeared on me, and when I finally found her, she was with Gert. At first, I thought it was a man she was sitting with. I didn't like the implications, so I told her we needed to go. She had to be in her bed before your grandmother left for work, or there would be all kinds of hell to be paid."

Hearing this story of my prudish, religious, self-appreciating mother left me stunned. These were not the same two women.

"Your mom refused to leave with me. Said she had found where she wanted to be and that I could just go back without her."

Before my dad could continue, my stepmom chimed in, "And with your nasty temper, you turned tail and hoofed it back west."

My dad gave her a disapproving look, which was returned equally by my stepmom. Finally, releasing the unhappy glare between them, Dad turned his attention back to me.

"Turns out, she stayed in Fort Worth for four days until something happened that forced Gert put her on the bus back to West Texas. She called me and told me to pick her up at the station before taking her home. I didn't do it. I told her I wasn't going to take the rap for her staying gone and scaring the hell out of everyone. Your mother said if I didn't, she would tell everyone she had been with me. I caught her off guard when I informed her your granny had been at my house Saturday morning looking for her. They knew I was in town and that she wasn't with me."

Sitting there, taking this all in, I began to put the pieces together. The picture would have been from the party, or at least from that weekend. But why would Mom have checked her out of the hospital all those years later?

"I hadn't heard the Dench's name again until you started dating Andy. I had pretty much forgotten about them. You do know that's why the house on Marsalis St. is in your mom's name, right?"

Questioning my dad, "I had always assumed it was awarded to her in the divorce."

"My name was never on that deed. That house was gifted to your mom by Gert Dench."

"But I was told the house belonged to Gert's sister and brother-in-law."

"From what I heard, they lived in Gert's house while she was in the institution. A few years after they were killed, it was deeded to your mom. I fought your mom about moving into that house; when I finally gave in, it was the end of our relationship. Everything deteriorated once we got settled. In all fairness, we were already fighting most of the time, but the battles became physical after moving in."

"Dad, what happened to Gert?"

"I guess she died in the sanitarium in Big Springs. Why?"

Pushing my plate toward the center of the table, I leaned in and looked directly at my father. "Were you aware Mom checked Gert out of the hospital just prior to the murders?"

His usually pale skin went pink, "I did not know that."

We sat there wrestling with the implications of my mother's involvement with the murders. I didn't tell them about the red-eyed couple in the little house or the information garnered from Pa Day regarding the cigar box and its contents. I thought it best to leave certain things a secret.

Each of us quietly drawing our own conclusions, the telephone rang, interrupting the silence. My step-mom rose to answer it; after an abrupt response, she told the person on the phone to hold the line. She looked at my dad and suggested he take the call in the living room. Placing the receiver back on the hook when Dad arrived at the extension, she began to clear the dishes without speaking. I walked over to the sink, standing next to her; I began to help. We stood there, washing and drying dishes while my father was on the phone. Neither of us said a word. When Dad returned to the kitchen, he placed his hands on my shoulders.

"I am going to your mom's house to collect your things. You are going to stay here with us for the rest of the school year. After that, we will see what we can do about getting you on campus. For your safety, you are not to go back to that house ever again."

The holidays came and went; my stepmother did her best to make them memorable for me. Even with the unruly behavior of my family, I had never missed a Christmas Eve with them.

Donna and I attended Todd's funeral and moved on with our lives. She decided to keep the baby, for which I was thrilled. It made me happy to know a little piece of Todd would still exist in the world. Telling me she was moving to live with her dad in Los Angeles, the pile of loss I felt grew exponentially. I knew she needed to go; living with her dad would provide her a path to attend school and work while her family helped raise the baby. I understood but was sad to lose them too. Before she left, she confided in me she had picked a name for the baby; she was going to name it Morgan Daniel. Morgan, after Todd's father, and Daniel, after my middle name. I was truly honored; it confirmed she believed what I told her about Todd saying goodbye to me.

Starting the spring semester was a challenge for me; no Andy, no Todd, no Donna. Three key components of my campus life were all gone in the blink of an eye. I often caught a glimpse of Andy on campus, even though he had changed his class schedule. My assumption was he altered his classes to avoid us being in the same room at the same time.

I later learned he had changed his major, which ensured we would have little interaction. Andy did his best to guarantee all interaction between us ceased. When I did see him, I knew he was unhappy, but I was miserable as well. He made this choice, and I felt like I still didn't have the whole story. I didn't reach out to his mother as I knew that would be miscon- strued as me trying to hang on. Somewhere deep in- side me, I knew we both needed to move on.

I pushed through the second term; improving my grades, I managed to retain my scholarship for the second year. I also snagged a work-study job for the following year; it paid just enough money to cover dorm expenses if I lived in the jock's dorm. Residing in OC Hall was going to be interesting as I was now totally out on campus. Fate was kind as I was as- signed to share a room with the baseball team's gay pitcher. He was not out of the closet, and people thought he was cool for being willing to share a room with me.

Summer passed quickly while I worked waiting ta- bles to save money for the upcoming school year. I kept busy, spending most of my time by myself. I read some excellent books, listened to some good music, and allowed my soul to heal. Stepping away from the white clapboard house had proven a good thing. There were no more spirits visited, no more cold rooms, and no more unexplained bruises. The closest I would get to the white clapboard house was to stop and visit Ma Day at least once a month to help with whatever she needed doing. She was aging, and time was taking its toll on her. I was so grateful her kids let her live in her own home with the aid of a daily nurse.

In late August, just before the term was to begin, I was at my dad's doing yard work. I loved working the flowerbeds and being out in the dirt. I had garnered this skillset from Ma Day; I utilized her green thumb expertise to make Dad's little yard shine.

Nearing the end of planting six flats of pansies in the front flowerbed, my stepmom came out of the house and placed a fresh glass of soda on the stoop for me. It was a little early to plant, but I knew I wouldn't have time when school started the following week. With a bit of extra watering, I felt the flowers would survive until cooler weather arrived.

I got up off my knees and moved to the porch; sitting down, I lifted the thick glass container full of coke and ice and thought of Ma Day; how many times we had shared a glass after a hot day working in the yard. Feeling the refreshing carbonation go across my palate, I felt a slight breeze waft across my skin, and with it was the smell of tuberose. It was then she put her hand on my arm and reminded me how the purple pansies were her favorite too. I took the last sip of my drink and heard her say, "I love you. Fix things with your mom."

I smiled and returned to my planting, shedding a tear for her with each flower placed into the ground. Picking up the trash, the phone inside the house rang. I heard my dad say he would let me know, and he hung up the phone. I migrated towards the door just as he came outside. He saw the tears in my eyes. "I guess you already know."

He hugged me once more while I cried. My tears were not from sadness but gratitude for an amazing woman who had been in my life. I refused to admit some of the tears were for knowing I had to face my mother just as Ma Day had told me to.

Ma Day had compiled her burial wishes a few years before she passed; one of her requests was that I sing and play piano at her service. I was honored to do it; she was the one who gave me my love of music and allowed me my creativity.

Channeling her spirit on the day of the funeral, I sat at the piano in front of the church. I played her favorite song, Sweet Georgia Brown. Her other request was for "Peace in the Valley" to be sung as a reminder to attendees where she was. After the service, I was standing by Ma Day's casket when my mother approached me and complimented me on my performance. "That wasn't me; that was Ma Day one last time."

"I understand," was her response.

"Son, I think we need to talk about some things. You know I don't approve of your choices or lifestyle, but your little brothers and sister constantly ask about you. Would you please come to see them?"

In her subtle controlling way, she managed to speak with disdain towards the world. It wasn't just me that she talked to with the authoritative tone of Marie Antoinette; it was everyone. By the time she finally stopped lecturing, and only after we had been asked to move away from the coffin, she managed to offend me on every possible level.

Controlling my response very carefully, I said, "I do miss the kids terribly. I would love to see them but not at that house. Get someone to bring them to the duck pond or the community center."

"All right. When are you back in school?"

"Day after tomorrow. You can leave me a message at the dorm. The number is listed; OC Hall."

"I am sorry I am not who you want me to be," she said.

"That's about you, Mom. I am the one who isn't who you want me to be. All I have ever wanted from you is for you to be real with me. I know about your past. I know you aren't the supreme mistress of the church, the grand dame you envision yourself to be, and quite frankly, I don't care. But I won't tolerate you judging me for being true to myself when you don't have the balls to do that for yourself."

For the first time I could recall, she did not speak or retaliate. She must have heard some truth in what I said. At that juncture, I found hope we might reconcile and have some type of relationship. Perhaps we might exorcise the demons from the past. No one will ever understand how much courage it took for me to draw that line in the sand.

I felt a hand on my shoulder, a recognizable touch I had missed. Mom nodded to the person behind me and excused herself, turning to go. Walking away, I heard her say, "I will call you for next Saturday about the duck pond."

I knew it was Andy standing behind me. I could smell his familiar scent and feel his intimate touch. I was afraid to turn around, scared all my feelings would surface, and I wouldn't know how to control them.

Pulling on my shoulder to turn, I began to pivot only to realize it wasn't Andy; it was Mr. Dench. "Wonderful job in there; she loved those songs. I can still remember her playing and singing them from my youth."

"Oh my goodness, I thought,"

"You thought it was Andy, and that's okay. I didn't want to leave without saying hello to you."

"Thank you for the compliment; that's very kind. Are you here alone? Where's that beautiful wife of yours?"

"She and Andy went to the car. I told them I had to go use the restroom. I need you to know things have been rough on us as well. We thought you would be a part of our lives for a long time. Andy will not tell us what happened, and we respect that. But he is so sad; he misses you so."

"I miss him more than any of you can imagine. But this is on him; he is choosing for us to not be together. I can't fight with or alter his choices, but I would welcome all of you back with open arms in an instant."

Mr. Dench reached out for me, pulling me close. I could smell Andy on his skin. It stirred emotions in me that I hoped were gone. Releasing me, he turned and walked away without saying a word. It had never crossed my mind they would be at the funeral; I didn't have any clue he remembered Ma Day.

My sophomore year flew past; I spent almost every Saturday I wasn't working doing something with my younger siblings. Mom would drop them off wherever we agreed to meet and retrieve them when our play date was over. Time had begun to soften Mother; it started with simple hellos and goodbyes, eventually leading to small conversations after each visit. Eventually, we managed to meet for dinner with the kids and enjoy the time together. We found a relationship based on friendship without the ugly parent/child past as a part of it.

The babies soon weren't babies anymore. My younger sister was blossoming and causing my mother all kinds of hell. I believed it to be payback for Mom's younger years. The boys were involved in various activities, keeping them busy and mostly out of trouble; my stepfather was absent most of the time. Time was passing very quickly.

Two weeks after graduation, I began the arduous task of finding a job. My degree was in Vocal Performance with a minor in Business Admin. This made it difficult to land an office job. Even so, I kept pursuing opportunities, my resume circling the globe. At one point, I thought about contacting Mr. Dench for networking but decided it best not to.

My dad and stepmom had built a new home in the countryside a few hours from town. This meant their little house on the Northside of Fort Worth was vacant. They allowed me to take up permanent residence in their previous home while I got on my feet. Once I was working, I would pay rent and keep the place up for them. It was a win-win for everyone.

Come mid-July; I was desperate to find a job. My dad needed the rent money, and I was tired of ramen noodles for dinner every night. After an unsuccessful interview one Wednesday afternoon, I stopped by the Lumber Company to enjoy a refreshing beverage. Big Mama greeted me with a hearty hello and a toothless grin. Teasing me about the fancy shirt and tie I had on, I was prompted to share my job challenges with him. Big Mama, who always had a kind heart towards me, told me his nephew ran housekeeping for a hotel downtown and was hiring people to work in the laundry. He needed muscular guys to move the wet laundry baskets from station to station.

Initially, I was too proud to think about doing it. I had a degree, after all, and that was a laborer's job. Sipping on my drink, realizing my pocketbook was lacking inhabitants, I put my ego aside. "What's his name?" I asked.

Big Mama smiled a big toothless grin. "Go to the Hyatt on 5th downtown and ask to speak to the housekeeping manager. He will take care of you."

Finishing my cocktail, I made my goodbyes and headed to the hotel. It was on my way home, and I knew if I didn't do it right then, my ego would talk me out of it. I parked on a side street without meters and headed inside by way of the hotel's revolving door. I knew exactly where the laundry rooms were; one of my older sisters had worked there while she was in high school.

Walking down the small spiraling stairwell, barely big enough for one person, I reminded myself I needed money. The ugly brown paint on the walls and metal rails had been freshly painted, and the concrete steps had recently been washed. Whoever maintained this hotel was picky; I liked that. I reached the bottom step and spotted the manager's door across the vast open space. I made my way towards it, passing the large washing machines working hard to clean the soiled sheets and towels, the noise deafening.

Approaching the door to the manager's office, I saw the light click off; my surprise attack on the manager had been thwarted. Suddenly someone stood up and waved their hands around madly inside the small room; the light reappeared. "God damn sensors!"

My immediate response was to run, but I needed a job, and I was indeed not above hard work. I stepped up to the door and knocked.

"Entrar." Spoken in a Castilian dialect.

I mumbled, "Oh shit, I don't speak Spanish!" I misjudged the level of my vocal output due to the noisy machines surrounding me.

"Not a problem. If you speak English, we are okay! Come in."

Embarrassed, I pushed on the door, stood up straight, and crossed the threshold. The man behind the desk was busy shuffling papers, obviously unconcerned with the gringo that had just entered his office. "What can I help you with?"

"Big Mama sent me. Said you were hiring, and I need a job."

The man looked up from behind the desk. "Big Mama, huh?"

When our eyes met, I remembered that kiss in the parking lot. It was Jaime.

"That man has a death wish. O Dios Mio! How the hell are you? So many times, I have thought of you."

"Jaime! Wow! What a surprise! Oh wait, are you really hiring, or is Big Mama up to something?"

With a chuckle, he replied, "Both."

It was unfortunate that I didn't get the job. Due to our past engagement, Jaime refused to hire me. Jaime said it was against company policy to sleep with his employees, and he had waited too long for me to find my way back to him.

Within a month, Jaime moved into the cozy house I was pseudo-renting from my dad. His taking on rent allowed me time to continue searching for a job. Eventually, I found a position in a manufacturing company located close by. It was a new world for me; I knew nothing about pharmaceuticals but was willing to learn. They were open to young college graduates finding their way. They believed it promoted loyalty.

Jaime had no family in the States beyond Big Mama; this made my limited engagements with my family an issue for him. He pushed me to become more involved with them, and they came to accept us as a couple over time. Wounds were healing, and I decidedly chose to leave the past alone.

Visit's to the white clapboard house was reasonably often and without incident. Jaime and I eventually moved from my dad's house and bought a place of our own. The timing on this was predestined; when I told my dad we were moving, he confided in me he and my stepmom were divorcing. He planned to return to his home and be content living in it companionless.

Before we knew it, Jaime and I were celebrating six years together. My little sister was getting married, one brother had moved on without a word to the family about his plans, and the other had joined the military. One more time, everyone around me seemed to be settling into their own lives.

It became a tradition for Jaime and Mom to cook a meal together every Saturday. For some reason I can't explain. The two of them had bonded, a pairing I would have never expected. During our recent visits to Marsalis St., I noticed the only child still living at home was spending all his time in his room. He had been born with a mental deficiency and would always live at home with his mom. It was a choice she made when he was young, and I respected her for that.

Mom and Jaime were in the kitchen making pasta during our weekly dinner visit; they were acting silly. For some reason, I didn't want to participate. I left the kitchen and walked into my brother's room. He was having the conversation of his life with someone I couldn't see. His communication skills were, how should I say, mushy. He had difficulty enunciating hard consonants, and I struggled to understand him; I always had. If I pushed him to repeat anything, he became irritated and would then clearly state, "Fuck off."

I didn't interrupt his conversation as it was quite intense. I retreated from his room and back to the kitchen; sitting down at the kitchen table, I asked Mom who my brother was talking to. Her response was, "He's praying and talking to Jesus. Does it all the time."

Jaime's eyes met mine from across the room. Without either of us saying a word, we shared our thoughts by making crazy eyes for the pair of them.

My stepdad had made it a point to not be around when we came over; he didn't like Jaime. It probably had something to do with the fact my stepdad liked to hang out at the gay bar just a few blocks from Marsalis St. Jaime ran into him a couple of times at the bar during happy hour. When Jaime told me about it, I laughed and confirmed my stepdad would drink with anyone as long as the beer was cheap. In my opinion, a one-dollar draft beer was right up his alley.

The duo completed preparing dinner. The three of us sat at the table to consume the pasta with meat sauce. My younger brother refused to leave the conversation he was having in his room. Sitting at the kitchen table, we heard something strike the front of the house with great force. Jaime and I jumped from the table and exited the front door to investigate. Clearing the front porch, we found nothing.

Looking around for evidence of what we heard, I saw my brother standing at the window looking at us. That familiar sense appeared; someone, something, was observing us from under the house. It had been years since I had felt that feeling, but it was there, very faint but very real to me.

Jaime and I proceeded up the steps to where my mom was standing on the porch holding the screen door open. "Mom, has that been happening lately?"

"I haven't heard that before. That was weird."

My brother entered the living room; he walked past Jaime and straight to me. Putting his finger on my chest, he began poking me. Accusingly assaulting my chest bone repeatedly, he spoke as clearly as a college professor; every word perfectly sounded out. "She's mad at you."

Jaime and I looked at each other, then I asked, "Who's mad at me?"

"Why don't you go back to your room?" my mother suggested to my brother while she deflected his hand from my chest.

"She says she warned you before."

"Mom? What is he talking about?"

"He doesn't know."

"Jaime, let's do the dishes quickly and head home." He could hear the concern in my voice and said, "Yeah, I think that is a good idea." I had never shared with Jaime the incidents on Marsalis St., the murders, or the freaky incident with Andy. I didn't think it was essential to bring up the past. I thought I would just mind my neck in, just as Gert had told me to.

As Jaime passed the door to the hallway on his way to the kitchen, an enormous bang hit the wall closest to my mom and brother. I pushed passed Mother, moving into the hallway with Jaime following quickly behind me.

On the floor beside the wall was Mom's secret book. An indentation in the sheetrock wall to our left remained from where it had been struck. The dent mirrored the book's outline, the leather-bound spine leaving an exact three-d replica in the wall. Jaime reached for the book.

"Leave it; I don't want the energy in the book polluting you."

Backing up from the room, we heard the back door of the house slam open against the wall and then quickly shut. It had not been unlocked the last time I was in the family room.

"Why don't you boys head on home? I will do the dishes," my mother softly said.

Her hand pointing towards the front door, I averted it. Moving through the house towards the back door, I encountered my stepfather standing in the kitchen. He had come home through the alleyway, leaving his car beside the garden. Obviously drunk, he pushed past me, calling for Mother. As he moved through the room, I could smell the cheap beer on him. Jaime motioned for me to look at my stepdad's face. He was bleeding, and it appeared his nose was broken.

"Norma, where the hell are you? I need some bandages."

"What the hell happened to you?" My mother said, looking him up and down.

"I wrecked the damn car. Didn't you hear it? Took out the whole damn tree. How could you not have heard it?"

Mom ran off to the storage closet to find a medicine kit. Opening the back door, I flipped the backyard spotlight on as I headed out of the house. I wanted to see the car for myself. The car was sitting there, not a scratch on it. I realized Jaime was over my shoulder looking as well. "Do you see any damage to the car?"

He giggled, "Nope. Looks like it always did."

Jaime returned to the house and began gathering our belongings; he sensed it was, indeed, time to go. Turning off the yard light, I began to close the back door. Ensuring the screen door was latched and the deadbolt turned, I left the doorway. Moving on to close the drapes on the large plate glass window overlooking the garden and little house, I saw them.

The red-eyed couple was looking at me once more.

Chapter 6

Spirits Creating Issues

The following Saturday, Jaime called my mom and canceled our scheduled cooking event. In all honesty, it didn't have anything to do with the strange events the week before; other matters occurred since that time which was the cause.

Jaime and I had another weekly ritual; we met for cocktails at Big Mama's bar on Friday nights after work. Jaime loved spending time with his uncle. Oddly enough, Big Mama was not homosexual; he just loved "the gays" and felt it a privilege to provide a place for the boys to drink without fear of being beaten up.

Big Mama witnessed terrible acts of hate against his best friend in high school, all because the boy was in love with another boy. The tragedies he witnessed prompted him to leave South America upon graduating from high school. Shortly after, he opened his first gay bar in Fort Worth. The reason he is called Big Mama is due to his size and gentle nature. He carries the weight of a sumo wrestler and the heart of an Abuela. He also has the meanness of a grandmother, the point being no one messes with him.

Jaime's mother threw him out of her home when she caught him getting a blowjob from another boy. Big Mama heard about the incident between Jaime and his mother from a family member; he immediately wired money to Jaime for his journey to the United States. We lived together for a year before I knew they were actually related.

I parked my car in my usual spot in front of the bar. It was just after 5:00 PM, and the happy hour crowd had not yet poured in. I was sure I would beat Jaime there; as expected, I didn't see his car. I walked into the bar, and to my surprise, there he was. Standing at the bar with Big Mama, his arms around another man. My initial response was not good; jealousy ran through my veins like never before.

The bright light behind me in the door prevented him from realizing it was me, at least for a moment. When the light waned, Jaime saw me and raised his glass in the air, yelling, "Salute!"

I realized happy hour had started without me much earlier that day; I was not amused. I reached for my cell phone to see if I had missed the voicemail invitation to join them earlier; there were no missed calls. I walked through the doorway and made my way across the bar towards the red patent leather and chrome bar stools. Big Mama met me halfway across the room and grabbed me, lifting me off the floor. "I am so excited for you both! This is such an amazing opportunity!"

My feet eventually returned to the floor; I was confused. Jaime rushed over to where I stood; grabbing my hand, he pulled me towards the man sitting with him. He then introduced me as his husband. The stranger stretched out his hand, offering a handshake. "I am thrilled to meet you. Jaime has talked about you for weeks now. Finally, I meet the man that makes him so happy."

"Nice to meet you, Mr...?"

Jaime realized I had no clue what was going on and quickly told me the gentleman's name. "We are celebrating, and at last, my sweet man is here to join in the festivities!"

Having several friends of Latin descent, I recognized fiesta mode; I had walked into the middle of a party. Throwing my jealousy to the curb, I grabbed a shot of brown liquor from the bar and screamed, "Salute!" I didn't know what we were celebrating, but if it made Jaime this happy, we would celebrate!

Saturday morning arrived with the need for a Brome-seltzer and lots of water. Laying in our cozy king-sized bed, I took his hand and asked him to stop the world from spinning. Jaime bounded up from the bed, "White people just don't know how to party!"

"I am going to take offense at that as soon as I feel better."

"Come downstairs when you feel like it; I am going to make Arepas and eggs. That will help your hangover!" And he was gone.

Soon the smell of cilantro, onion, and chorizo began wafting up the stairs; what a fantastic aroma for my aching head. As always, food had been a significant reason for me to do something; once more, it prompted me up off the bed and towards the kitchen.

Jaime was dancing in the kitchen while he cooked; this was a part of his ritual. A lovely samba was blaring from the CD player, and his sexy round ass and hips moved in sync with his feet as they formed figure eights. Watching him sway to and fro made me smile.

Sliding onto a barstool at the kitchen island, I reduced the volume of the music. This was his first inclination I entered the room. He leaned across the countertop and kissed me. I could taste the fresh herbs on his lips. Rotating back to the arepas on the stove so they didn't burn, he said, "I hope you are up for an adventure!"

"Jaime, my love, I enjoyed the partying last night, and you know I am bonkers in love with you, but I sense something is going on that you are not telling me."

He filled my plate with food and gingerly set it down in front of me. Placing both hands on the counter and looking across at me, he said, "I have been offered the head of housekeeping for Para Rios Hotels, global!"

"Baby, I am so happy for you. But what are you not telling me?"

After you live with someone long enough, you learn subtle clues to their behavior. For example, when I arrived at the bar, he introduced me to the man with him, giving no indication of who the stranger was; this implied he didn't want to talk right then.

His family's past and the pain they inflicted on him left him terribly guarded. I totally appreciated and understood the emotional impact. What this translated to was he had to come to a conclusion about what he wanted prior to talking to me about it. I surmised he had been in the process of deciding what he desired before telling me. He crawled onto the stool next to me at the counter. "The job requires relocation to Palm Springs."

The critical piece of information he left out of that statement was a pronoun, such as he or we. I wasn't able to discern if he was requesting I go with him or if he wanted to go on his own.

Diving into my comfort food, I kept my mouth full, so I wouldn't speak. Anything I might say would most likely come out wrong. I also knew if I didn't talk, he would be driven to.

"I know this is a big ask. But it's a great opportunity for me. It's what I have been working for since I came to the US. You are so important to me, and I don't want this to split us up, but I have to do it."

What I was hearing was the job was more important to him than I was. In reality, his ego was more important to him than anything. I continued to eat. When I finished, I leaned forward over the counter and dropped my dishes in the sink. "Please call my mother and tell her we won't be coming for dinner tonight."

En route to the backyard, I left the room without saying another word. I needed to get into the dirt, generate some sweat, and do something to clear my head. He was right; this was an excellent opportunity for him. However, I also had a job that I liked, a place that provided a future for me. I didn't want to give up my chance for success either.

After a couple of hours of toiling in the backyard, I called into the house, requesting Jaime bring me a drink. When I was processing, he knew it was best to just leave me to what I was focused on and let me come to him when it was time to talk. My asking for a drink was the signal for the next step.

I sat down on a lounger and waited for him to arrive with my beverage. Before taking the chair directly across from me, he handed me my drink. "You need to know I want you to go with me and will understand if you choose not to. Your career is just as important as mine."

After taking a sip from my glass, I replied. "You accepted the job without discussing it with me first. By doing that, you are forcing me to choose between my work and you. That said, I will not put a career over family. I choose you over the job."

Yes, it was a guilt play, but it was honest. "When do you have to report to work?"

"I will give the hotel two weeks' notice and then head straight out there."

"Ok, I will stay here to sell the house and come out there as soon as possible."

"Since this is such an upheaval for you, I will make sure there is a home waiting for you when you get there. Let's ship the furniture out, and when you get there, everything will be in place."

Guilt card play?: Successful.

I went to work on Monday and discussed this life event with my boss; my intent was to give notice that once the house was sold, I would be leaving. My boss graciously accepted my resignation. Three days later, she surprised me with the suggestion I work remotely. "With the technology available, there isn't any reason you can't manage the day-to-day tasks in Palm Springs and then report to the office one week a month for meetings and client visits."

I took this as a compliment; it indicated she viewed me as an asset to the company and believed I did a good job. The house was put up for sale, Jaime moved, furniture shipped, and before you knew it, I was in the car on my way to California.

The stress of the job quickly took its toll on Jaime. When he wasn't at work, his time was spent drinking with colleagues or friends. His alcohol consumption had increased exponentially. On numerous occasions, specifically when I was back in Fort Worth at the factory, he would not appear at home for days. He would leave work and spend his free time out and about consuming beverages and making new friends.

Nine months into the job, Jaime was released from his commitment to the company. This was a massive blow to his ego. With no reason to stay, we agreed to cancel our lease, pay the fines, and move back to Texas. As events unfolded, it came to light that while

I was back in Fort Worth working, Jaime had spent every dime he acquired partying.

Reviewing our finances confirmed there wasn't enough money between us to pay the lease off, hire movers to return the furniture to Fort Worth, and find us a place to reside. The small amount of money earned from the sale of the house in Texas would quickly be consumed by the move back. I was very thankful my company had allowed me to keep my job. I am not sure what we would have done otherwise.

I managed to rent a large moving van and covered the initial expenses with a credit card. Paying the rent-house lease off with what cash we had, we were broke. I had no clue where we would live once we arrived. With the equity from the previous house in Texas now consumed, buying another piece of property was out of the question at this point in time.

As much as I hated the thought, I called my mother and asked if we could stay at the white clapboard house on Marsalis St. Much to my surprise, she didn't lecture me about the position I was in. Without my having to ask, she wired me money to cover expenses for the road trip back to Texas.

The white clapboard house had been sitting empty for over a year. After my stepdad passed, my mom decided to relocate to Florida. Her dead husband's government pension, along with her social security, provided her with enough income to move and live a comfortable life. My younger brother, who lived with her, had passed on as well, leaving her with no responsibilities in Texas. Now settled in Florida, she had a part-time job working with special needs children. This fed her soul and kept her active. It gave her purpose and was part of her softening over time.

Mom and I had reached an amicable place in our lives; however, she and Jaime had stopped talking. I wasn't sure why exactly, but something was said at my stepdad's funeral that caused the two of them to stop interacting. That was between them, and I didn't want to get involved. I had my own issues with Jaime that he and I needed to resolve.

Mom and I came to an agreement, Jaime and I would live in the house and do some renovation work for her. The intent was to fix the property to a sellable condition; she commented that she would never sell it but liked the idea of me renovating it.

We arrived in Fort Worth on a Friday morning. I had insisted we drive all night from Albuquerque so that we had the entire weekend to unload the truck. Walking through that front door would be a significant challenge for me; I remembered all too well Gert threatening me to never return.

I unlocked the deadbolt on the front door and walked in. All was calm and almost serene. I moved through every room in the house and didn't sense a thing. Moving out the back door through the yard, I followed the cement path leading to the little house. I put the key in the door, turned the lock, and pushed the door open. The room was covered in cobwebs, odd bits of furniture, and pieces of junk my mother refused to throw away. I moved through the little house's front room, where the red-eyed couple seemed to stay, and into the dilapidated kitchen. I felt nothing.

Returning to the main house, I was met by Big Mama and a group of young men. He brought his employees to help us unload the truck, and I was so appreciative of the effort.

I left the truck unloading to Jaime and the crew; it was up to him to direct everyone as to where he wanted the furniture placed. I required sustenance; leaving them busy at work, I proceeded on a mission to find food to feed everyone. Grabbing the keys to the car mom kept at her Texas home, I walked out the back door, down the steps, and around the side of the house. The tall gate separating the front and back yards allowed me access to the car, thereby avoiding the work crew.

The gate appeared as if it hadn't been moved in many years; it was stuck and wouldn't budge. I was determined to get it open. I pulled and tugged on the metal handle until the gate finally gave way, swinging open towards me. Opening the gate, I was face to face with a white-haired woman I didn't recognize. We both let out a yelp from being startled; after a minute, I realized it was my oldest sister, whom I had not seen in over 20 years.

The most senior member of the family who still resided in Fort Worth had been coerced to keep a watchful eye on the white clapboard house. Her home was less than a mile away, making it convenient for her to drive by regularly. Passing by today, she saw the moving van in the front yard and concluded we had arrived.

"I was just heading out to get some food for the worker bees. Want to join me and catch up a bit?"

My sister agreed and offered to drive. Considering how tired I was, I took her up on her proposal. We chatted niceties and top-level family business while making our way to a local fast-food joint. Completing my purchase, she returned me to Marsalis St., Dropping me back at the house; she asked me to visit her sometime.

I reached for the door handle and responded, "Feel free to stop by here anytime for a visit as well."

"I won't set foot in that house. The last time I was in there was when 'your' stepfather died. Something was terribly off about all of it. I am not one to be easily frightened, but the way he died didn't make sense."

"What are you saying? Mom said he had a heart attack while taking a shower."

"Mom was out of town; she had gone to Big Springs to visit someone."

"She never told me that."

"I only know because I was the one who found him."

"Why was that? Did you just happen to stop by?" I was surprised none of this had been shared with me before.

"I got a call from the neighbor saying the grill in the backyard was on fire. She claimed she rang the doorbell and knocked several times, but no one answered. With the eight-foot privacy fence between the yards, she couldn't determine exactly what was going on. When she didn't get a response at the house, she called me, assuming I had keys to get in. She said she knew mom was gone; they had spoken that morning."

While telling me the story, it quickly became evident that my sister had been rattled. "I didn't have keys to the house but got in my car and came down to check. Mom's car was gone, confirming what the neighbor had said. I knocked on the door and looked through the windows. I saw the back door was open and assumed he was out there. I tried the doorknob, and it wasn't locked. I let myself in and walked through to the backyard. The grill was open; the briquettes were loaded but not lit. Two steaks were on the cooking grates, uncooked, not even seared. There had been no fire in the grill that day."

While my sister spelled out how the steaks were uncooked on the grill, Jaime tapped on the car's window, scaring the bejesus out of us. Standing next to the car, he pointed to the food. I rolled down the window and handed the paper bag to him without speaking; I rolled the window back up and asked my sister to continue.

"Walking back into the house, I heard the bathroom door shut. I went and knocked on it; there was no response. The tub faucet turned on, and the shower began to run. I could only assume he was in there. I knocked again. The light turned off, but the water was still running. I reached for the doorknob and began to open the door. It was stuck. It felt as if someone was pushing from the other side. I hollered at him, 'That's really funny - now what's going on?' Suddenly the door freed. When it slid partially open, I saw his hand on the floor. I ran to the kitchen and called 911. I didn't go into the bathroom at all. I stayed in the kitchen right by the phone. When the paramedics arrived, the shower was off. He was fully dressed, his apron on, you know, the one he liked to grill in."

"Oh, my god. I had no idea all this happened."

"I told Mom what had happened, and she dismissed it as me being confused."

"Why would she do that?"

"I don't know. But the other weird part is they said he had been dead for well over four hours when I found him."

Standing back in the front yard, I watched my sister drive away. I felt terrible for her having to deal with my stepdad's death. I pondered if his death had released the house from its demons; I didn't feel anything for a change. I purposefully looked inside the grates into the crawlspace under the house; nothing was looking back. Perhaps his dying had appeased the conflict between Gert and Mom. I didn't know what to think, but I trusted my senses that everything was ok, finally.

Big Mama exited the front door of the house. "Now that's how Big Mama gets things done. The truck is all unloaded, baby. Now you get some rest."

I hugged Big Mama and thanked him for his assistance.

"Anything for my boys. Now I have to get to the bar. I hear glasses begging for ice cubes and liquor! You boys, come see me this weekend." And in a whoosh of hairpins, Big Mama and the entourage took their leave with food in hand.

As they exited the front door, I said my goodbyes to the young men. I entered the house to find Jaime sitting on the couch in the living room, falling asleep. I wasn't going to be far behind him. Gently shaking him, I offered, "I will make up the bed real quick so we can crash. We can worry about putting everything together later."

"The crew put our bed together; I was digging in the box for the sheets, and I guess I fell asleep."

I grabbed the sheets Jaime had retrieved from the moving boxes. "Why don't you go out and lock up the truck, and I will make up the bed."

To my surprise, Big Mama's crew had put our bed in the room I played in when I was a toddler. The headboard was placed directly in front of the windows where I first saw the red-eyed couple. Looking out the window for the red-eyed couple one more time, I laughed to myself and quickly made our bed. Tossing a blanket across the bed, I heard the front door close. Soon Jaime was dropping his clothes to the floor.

"Going to take a quick shower before crawling in." Passing by me, he kissed me and patted me on the butt. I remembered what my sister had just told me.

"Leave the door open for me."

Giggling, he called out, "You pervert!"

Sleep was restless that first night, primarily due to being tired from the journey. I didn't have odd dreams or hear weird noises; it was simply exhaustion overwhelming me. The weekend was quickly over, and I was back at the office. Jaime had decided to lay low and start working on the house renovations. He confided in me he wasn't ready to go back to work and needed some time to detox. He wanted to figure out who he wanted to be. Seeing how deflated his ego was, I agreed to let him do some soul-searching.

Before we knew it, fall had arrived, and the nights were beginning to get cold. Projects around the house had been haphazard at best. Jaime wasn't really focused on anything but reading entrepreneur magazines. I hoped he would find his passion soon.

My need to not live in constant discord made it easy to persuade myself to hire a contractor to install central heat and air into the house. Growing up in the white clapboard house, we got by on gas heaters and swamp coolers. I needed and insisted on some controlled air. I also needed someone who could push the projects forward.

Jaime advocated an office be set up for him in the little house while the renovations were ongoing. I had hoped he would be more involved in overseeing the renovations, but this was not within his mindset. After a few arguments on the subject, I relinquished my hopes he would be interactive in the remodeling process. He was free to develop his homemade office, but not without his understanding I wouldn't spend time in the little house.

The contractor went to work installing AC while Jaime created his office in the little house. There was an old desk in storage my mother said he could use. I am not sure how he managed it, but the burl wood desk was out of the storage building and in his pseudo office. Cleaned and oiled, it looked pretty good. He was finally finding a purpose, and I was glad.

By the time we had forced air in the main house, Jaime had his personal space decorated. I didn't know where many of the things came from, and I thought it best not to ask. All the cobwebs were gone from within the little house; the round table in the front room was polished and had five chairs surrounding it. He had created a nice space away from the white clapboard house all for himself.

Jaime began spending more and more time in his tiny office. We managed a WIFI signal strong enough for his laptop to be functional in his new space. The intent was he could do job searches on the internet in peace and quiet away from the construction; at least, that was the plan. It was becoming the norm that I had to retrieve him from his cave every day when I got home. He had stopped cooking dinner, and the number of liquor bottles in the recycle bin was increasing quickly. His focus on liquid spirits and trying to grow up forced me to hire a full-time general contractor to manage the house renovations. I worked it out with my mom that she would pay for materials, and I would cover labor and management fees. This was the only way the house was ever going to get finished.

I was growing frustrated with fronting all the expenses and Jaime's spiral into himself. I decided it was time to have an uncomfortable conversation with him.

Arriving home from work one evening, I parked my truck in the drive. I sat for a few minutes, developing my approach to the conversation. I didn't like going into an argument blindly; a plan was necessary.

I was confident he was in his man cave as the house was completely dark; the GC and workers had gone for the day. I walked through the side gate and head-ed towards his office. On my way, I retrieved the re-cycling bin full of empty rum bottles; my plan was in action. I would request him to open the container, which had been emptied three days before, and ask why it was already full of empty liquor containers. Before even passing the front gate, I could hear the music from the little house blaring out Edith Piaf. I was good with that; it would mask the sound of the cart rolling on the sidewalk behind me.

The door to the little house was ajar, the cool night air leaving a slight chill in the dark front room. After walking through the entrance, I turned into the new-ly decorated office. Remnants of its former life as a small kitchen were still visible.

"Hey, sweet man! Is it that time already?"

Jaime was not himself. I didn't know if it was the booze or if he was high or what, but I knew I didn't like it. I had never seen him like this before.

"Yes, it's that time. A reminder your husband is home, and your fun must come to an end." The sar-casm struck him hard. We were not legally married, and I only used the term "husband" when I wanted to remind him he was neglecting his commitments.

Crossing in front of his desk, I took a seat in the chair across from him. It was an old kitchen chair I had grown up with; he must have retrieved it from the attic or storage along with the other furnishings. Looking across at him, I realized the bookcase behind him was the bookcase that had resided in my mom's bedroom while I was growing up. Seeing the wooden unit there unnerved me a little. Searching the shelves and their contents, I saw it. There it was, the book that had imprinted its spine into the wall of my mom's bedroom, the book containing the picture of the red-eyed couple.

"I can tell by your face, you see it." Jaime's eyes were dark and glassy.

"Why do you have that book? Where did you find it?"

He gave an odd grin and said, "It was on the bookcase in storage. It belongs there; they belong there."

"Are you fucking with me on this? You saw what it did to the wall in Mom's bedroom. I told you not to touch it as it is poison to the soul."

He lifted his glass and took another drink. "You think I drink too much, don't you?"

"Yes, as a matter of fact, I do, but that is not the point at the moment. There are things you don't know, events which I spared telling you about to avoid your being freaked out."

"I know about them."

I wasn't sure what he meant by the "them" reference: the events or the people. He reached down and slid open a desk drawer; from within the compartment, he produced a cigar box. A very old one, still in perfect condition. Laying the box on the desk before me, he requested I open it to see its contents.

"I know what's inside," I said cautiously.

He smiled before speaking, "How could you possibly know what is in there? They only arrived today."

I looked around the room for the red-eyed couple. They weren't there; I couldn't sense them. Why weren't they nearby to protect me?

He slid his chair up to the desk and pushed the box towards me. "Open it, please."

I couldn't control myself; I had to know if bow tie remnants and a button were inside. I reached for the edge of the lid and paused. Looking at him, I saw his smile had grown incredibly wide; I was being coerced into opening it. I threw the lid open. Its contents were not what I expected.

There was no clothing from the dead man and woman, only two cigars, each with a wedding band strategically placed on them.

"Will you marry me? Actually, marry me? I know I have been in a terrible funk lately, but I want you to know I am here no matter what. I want this to prove it to you."

"I am a bit surprised, to say the least. I don't know what to say."

"Please say yes. I was in your mom's book, the one you are asking about. When I saw the picture of the happy couple in there, it came to me that I had to ask you. It is time."

Chapter 7

After saying yes to participating in a civil union, Jaime and I discussed possible dates. Same-sex marriage was not legal in the United States, so I proposed we wait and see what the upcoming administration would do on the subject. The reality was I needed time to see if Jaime would move beyond his day-to-day funk. Waiting until after the elections that year to see who won the white house was the best path; it also allowed us time to save for the expense of a nuptial celebration. After some in-depth deliberation, Jaime confirmed he was agreeable to the plan.

Finishing the discussion, Jaime turned his chair ninety degrees while extending an arm towards the bookcase. His hand reached for the book containing the red-eyed couple's wedding picture. Retrieving the image from the book, he inquired if I knew who they were. I offered a brief overview of their history in relationship to the house, nothing more.

"I also found this love letter inside the book. I guess it was written by one of them; the only clue was the initials on it: To N, Love G."

In our brief conversations regarding his family, Mr. Dench never revealed the names of his sister and her husband, who died there on Marsalis St. It crossed my mind that Andy would know their identities. Still, I decided doing some research would be an ideal activity to keep Jaime busy.

I personally never found much pleasure in doing research, the thought of spending hours culling through old newspapers and such was not appealing to me. I reasonably assumed that in his downtime, which was plentiful, doing the search would be right up Jaime's alley. He appeared curious enough about them to do it, so I made a suggestion. He should check the obituary column for their names. "I know rough dates based on when the family moved into this house."

He was intrigued by the idea and committed to starting the research the next day. I began to recommend he check the police records as there would definitely be information about them available; thinking before I spoke, I chose to skip it.

The picture safely tucked away in the book, Jaime returned it to the case behind his desk. The love letter from G to N found its way into his jacket pocket, all set for his adventure the next day.

I was unsure who N and G were but was confident it wasn't the red-eyed couple. I left Jaime sitting there as I started my journey back to the white clapboard house. Walking up the steps to the back porch, I turned back to the little house. I was unsure what drove me to do so until I realized the red-eyed couple was watching me. I called out to Jaime, asking if he was coming. Hearing me call out to him, the red-eyed couple went dark.

Meeting in the kitchen, we began to prepare dinner. For a change, the energy flowing between us was soft and light. It was reminiscent of when we first moved in together.

My sleep was restless that night; I kept waking up to look around the room and peer out the window; there was nothing to see. All I could remember the next day was having a vision of Andy, dressed all in white, handsome as ever.

Sitting in one more useless planning meeting at work, I found myself mentally returning to the vision of Andy. I had not really thought of him in a long time. Knowing my ability to connect with those who had passed, and visioning him all in white, brought concern to the forefront of my mind. Finally, released from two hours of inane bickering, I returned to my office and closed the door. I knew it was risky, but I had to do it.

I dialed the phone number in my book for the Dench home. Landlines were rarely answered anymore; I didn't know if it would still be in service or not, but I proceeded with pushing the numbers on the keypad anyway. The phone rang four times before I decided to hang up. I didn't want to leave a message in case Andy was there. Returning the headset to its base, I heard, "Hello-o-o."

Hearing a voice on the other end, I quickly returned the receiver to my ear. "Good afternoon. Is this Mrs. Dench?"

"Yes."

"I don't know if you will remember me, but this is..."

"Hello, Henry. Of course, I remember you. It's lovely to hear from you."

"I know I am not supposed to connect with you guys, but I had to reach out."

"So nice to hear your voice."

"How are things with you and Mr. Dench? How's Andy, pardon me, Andrew?"

"We are well, for the most part. My dear husband continues to work beyond retirement, but it keeps him active. We are traveling extensively and enjoying life when he has downtime. Andrew finished his residency last year and has taken a job at the county hospital."

Hearing her talk about the family eased my mind. Now I understood why I saw him all in white; he was in his doctor's coat at the hospital. The conversation with her was a bit rigid, but I didn't give it too much thought; it had been a decade since I had spoken with her.

"And you, my dear? How are things with you? Rumor has it that you are doing very well in your career."

"I am well. Working and focused on the day-to-day. I enjoy what I do. Moving up the ladder, as they say. Who says I am doing well?" I was curious to know how she knew what was happening with me.

"You recall my husband was very fond of you. He is friends with one of your board of directors, so he indirectly keeps up with what's going on. But I don't think you are supposed to know that."

Now I understood the reason behind management's offer for me to work remotely and not leave the company. It had been Mr. Dench's doing. But why?

"It's our little secret. Glad to hear all is well with you guys. Is Andy happy?"

"He manages to get by as best he can. He has been focused on work and, hopefully, soon be focused solely on patients with HIV and their recovery."

"That is wonderful to hear. When did he move from finance to pre-med?" I heard her hand rubbing against the phone's mouthpiece as she covered it to call out that she would be right there.

"He graduated from Wesleyan in Pre-Med. Shortly after he started his residency, his boyfriend died from AIDS-related pneumonia. As with everything, he has become obsessed with saving others from that horrible tragedy."

"I am so happy for him, for all of you. If you think it appropriate, please tell him I called and that I think of him, of all of you, regularly."

"I will; I think that will make him happy. I must go, it was so nice to hear your voice. Lunch at the club sometime?"

With my agreement to have lunch with her at some future juncture in time, I hung up the phone. I didn't believe the invitation would be acted upon, but having the ask was heartwarming.

The rest of the day at the office was routine; follow-ups with clients and staff, all very uneventful until I arrived home. Jaime was not home when I pulled into the driveway; the house was completely dark. It was rare he was not around. Before getting out of my car, I grabbed my cell phone and pushed the memory dial for his cell phone. There was no answer. I pondered whether to go to The Lumber Company to see if he was there with Big Mama or just go inside and start dinner. I was tired and not in the frame of mind for a confrontation; staying home and cooking dinner was the better option. I entered the white clapboard house and began to cry. I don't know what, but something came over me; the waterworks began.

I didn't hear Jaime pull into the driveway or enter the house. He found me sitting on the living room couch, my eyes puffy and red. A light above the kitchen sink was the only illumination in the house. Knowing something was up, he sat next to me and questioned what was wrong. I confessed to him I didn't know, but a terrible wave of sadness hit me when I got home from work. In hindsight, I believe it was the wounds opened from talking to Mrs. Dench.

Moving from the couch to the kitchen, we began to prepare dinner. Jaime was a fantastic cook, but there was no such thing as a simple meal, and being from South America, dinner time was never before 8:00 P.M. Chopping, slicing, sautéing; all were in progress as he told me what he found out about the couple in the photo.

"It took some backtracking to figure out who the couple in the picture was, but I managed it. Their names were Edgar and Lily Beauchamp. They were married here after leaving their families in the UK. I found their wedding announcement in the archives.

The only family mentioned was a sister, Gert Dench. They married on June 19th, 1948."

As he spoke, I listened to the information as if I had never heard of the couple before. "After I found their names, I looked for their obits and found Gert Dench mentioned again."

Just hearing her name being spoken gave me chills. I prayed he wasn't summoning the past by speaking her name out loud.

"The obituaries didn't say much about the husband and wife except that they died side by side in 1960. There is something missing in all of this; I just haven't figured out what it is. I am going to search warranty deeds tomorrow to see what else I can find out."

The main course for dinner was placed in the oven, and vegetable preparation began. We sat down at the small kitchen counter made of temporary plywood to eat dinner that night while I struggled with whether or not to tell him what I knew. I thought about it for a while before querying if he was enjoying the search; he committed that he was. With that information, I decided to leave my knowledge tucked away and see what he came up with. "How did you backtrack to find their names?"

"Lily Dench was embossed in the lower front corner of the book holding their photo. I started with that. Once I saw their picture in the wedding announcement, it was fairly easy from there."

That night brought terrible dreams for me. I tossed and turned the entire night. Every time I would begin to sleep, my breath would disappear, and I would wake up gasping for air.

I asked Jaime the next morning if I had kept him awake from my restlessness; he said he hadn't heard a thing. I wondered how he could have missed it; perhaps it was just a dream.

Another day at the office passed by, and once again, over meal prep at home that evening, Jaime divulged the information he had uncovered that day. "Turns out Gert died a couple of years after her sister. Apparent suicide. The obit listed a Norma De Lyon as a survivor."

Hearing Jaime speak my mother's maiden name, I choked on my drink of wine.

"That name sounds very familiar to me. Do you know that name? And I think I have determined the love letter between N and G was between this Norma and Gert. Imagine two lesbians in 1950s Fort Worth, Texas!"

Finishing my glass of wine in one quick gulp, I replied, "Only one of them was a lesbian."

Jaime laid down the knife he was cutting an onion with and leaned into the makeshift countertop. "What do you know?"

"Norma De Lyon is my mother's maiden name."

"That's where I heard the name. Why did your mother have a love letter from Gert? Did your mother tell you all of this? Spill!"

"I never heard of my mother having a fling with Gert. My dad told me about Gert and my mom running around when my mom was in her teens. They met here in Fort Worth at a party. With the letter from Gert and the other information I have, this all points to something more sinister. I think we need to leave this alone."

"I am intrigued; tell me about it!" Jaime was over the moon to hear what I knew.

"I was hesitant to return to this house to live, but everything seemed settled and calm. Gert threatened to kill me if I didn't stop digging into the past."

"According to the death records, Gert died before you were born. How could she have threatened you?"

"The couple you found the picture of, the happy couple that prompted you to ask me to marry you. The woman in the photo was Gert's sister. That couple was murdered in the little house outback. It was never known who did it, although I think my mother knows."

"How would your mother know?"

"This house, which included the lots on both sides, belonged to Gert. The couple lived here in Gert's house. Gert, at some point, deeded the property to my mom. According to my dad, my family moved in not long after Gert died."

"Wish you would have told me dead people were roaming around here."

"I probably should have, but with all the stress of coming back, it was a demon I had to face, and why bring it up to you if you are not affected by it." I reached for the bottle of wine and poured the last of its contents into my glass. Jaime reached for another bottle and opened it. "Is there anything else I need to know about?"

Over dinner, I told him about the situation with the bruised hands and back, about the red-eyed couple, and how my boyfriend at the time rescued me. I shared with him the phone call from the other side and my confronting my mother about her former life.

I spoke it all, with the exception of me dating Gert's nephew.

Bottle number three of wine was consumed, dishes were done, and it was time for bed. Both of our minds reeling from the implications of where we lived and what we were in the middle of.

Sleep came quickly for me, and once again, terrible dreams were present. I was awakened at 3:57 A.M. by the phone. It was my mother, "Are you all right?"

"I think so; what's going on?"

"I had a dream that you died. I had to check on you."

"No, but I had a terrifying dream. I dreamt several hands were reaching up from the side of the bed, attempting to pull me off the bed and into the floor." Complete silence on the other end of the phone.

Waiting for my mother to respond, I heard Jaime, "Oh Dios mío, mi amore! What the hell happened to you?"

"What? What are you talking about?"

"Your back is covered in bruises, shapes of hands. Eight of them?"

Through the phone receiver, I heard Mother say, "Oh shit, they have returned!"

"Mom, what is going on? I think something is happening to me, and if you know what is going on, you need to tell me what it is."

"I'm on my way to Texas. Do not sleep in that house until I can get there." The phone disconnected.

Jaime stood beside his side of the bed, looking at my back.

"Jaime, look out the back window to the windows in the little house."

Acting on my request, Jaime pushed the blind slats open and looked out. "There are two sets of red eyes by the garden looking at the house. They look sad."

"Get some clothes on; we need to leave the house now." The last bit of direction left my mouth as the door to the bedroom slammed shut, the doorknob rattling before falling to the floor. Grabbing any clothing we could get our hands on, we crawled out the side window into the yard. I didn't have my car keys or know where we would go, but we had to leave.

Dressing in the garments in hand, we made our exit. Attempting to walk quickly from the house, we felt the ground beneath us to be muck enveloping our feet. Finding it difficult to move, I screamed out for help. Hoping for a neighbor's light to turn on, someone to rescue us from the quicksand we were being held in against our will.

I felt someone begin to pull on my arms, pulling me away from the house. I looked at Jaime; his arms were stretched above him. We were being pulled towards the little house. The red-eyed couple appeared, pulling with all their might towards their home.

A loud clang erupted; the glass windows in our bedroom shattered. Shards of glass unexpectedly flew through the air as if there had been an explosion. Freed from the muck we were stuck in, we landed abruptly in the yard. Jaime and I rolled to a stop. Lifting ourselves off the ground, we looked back at the house. The windows were intact; there was no sign of any violence. The red-eyed couple was gone.

We started towards each other to embrace, both of us immediately stopping in our tracks. Broken glass surrounded us, cutting into our feet as we attempted to walk. Within Jaime's reach laid a deck chair; he carefully lifted one leg over the glass and climbed into the chair. With both feet on the seat of the chair, he leaped to where the ground was free of obstacles. Lifting the chair into the air, he hurled it towards me for my escape.

Half-dressed and with bloodied feet, we were lost as to what to do. I leaned back on the picnic table in despair; I heard a slight clink. My keys had been delivered to us, presumably by the red-eyed couple.

"I have chanklas in my office. Let me get them."

"Aren't you scared to go in there?"

"They are obviously here to help us. They would have let the demons collect us if we weren't meant to be here."

Within an instant, Jaime returned with sandals and jackets in hand. Dressed enough to stay warm and be seen in public, we hurried past the white clapboard house and through the side gate.

Leaving the white clapboard house in the rearview mirror, we sought out an all-night diner for comfort food and sanctuary.

Chapter 8

They've Returned

I phoned work the next morning, advising I wouldn't be in the office for a few days, making excuses regarding a family emergency and that my mom was on her way into town. I would need to be available for her when she arrived. Sympathies offered came alongside the request to keep up with emails.

Jaime contacted friends he worked with at his former hotel; he managed two rooms at a very reasonable rate. It would be two days before Mom would arrive in Fort Worth from Florida. I left her a voicemail on her mobile phone, telling her we had procured rooms at the hotel downtown. I requested she meet us there.

Upon Mom's arrival, we met her in the hotel lobby. I needed information, and I wasn't overly concerned about her getting to her room. I wanted more details about the white clapboard house I grew up in. Allowing her time to visit the ladies' room, Jaime ordered some refreshments to eliminate any other avoidances of the conversation.

Sitting in the lobby, Mother divulged her sordid past with Gert from the perspective of being the victim.

She told us how she delivered the release paperwork to the sanitarium. The executor of the trust overseas, Gert, requested the necessary documents for a weekend pass. Along with the paperwork presented, Mom admitted to using her charms on the young man at the admitting desk. "No one would ever give a second thought to a young woman with the proper paperwork signing a patient out of the institute. It implied she had the family's knowledge and consent."

Mom returned to the beginning of it all. She shared stories of the shenanigans she participated in with Gert before she married my father and how she would sneak off with Gert to various destinations in West Texas. Gert, being older than her, had a lot of influence on her. Often alcohol was involved in their adventures, which is what she blamed getting pregnant on before she was married. "When Gert learned about my pregnancy, she offered to care for the baby and me. She told me not to worry about money or propriety; she promised she would handle the challenges."

Mom told of the arguments occurring between my dad and Gert. How Gert threatened to kill him after he found out a baby was on the way. "Gert wrote me a letter; after reading it, I knew I had to marry your dad, for all of our sakes. If I was married, Gert would be forced to leave us be. I had no idea she would go mad. She showed up at the hotel for the wedding, drunk and wild, cursing at the preacher, threatening guests, screaming out loud that she was in love with me."

For the first time ever, I witnessed an emotion other than anger in my mother's voice. This release was long overdue for her.

"Her announcing her sexual desires was all it took for some of the De Lyon boys to get the better of her and drag her outside. The preacher began staring at me with disdain; your father intervened, confirming that I was pregnant and that Gert was obviously out of her mind and certainly not the father. It was within days the Dench family had Gert committed. Her sister and husband moved into the house on Marsalis St. permanently after she was sent back to England. It wasn't long before her parents sent her to West Texas to be institutionalized. They disowned her because of her sexual preferences. Her family gained power of attorney over Gert's property. Selling off the neighboring parcels purchased with the house originally, the money gained from the sale went into a trust to cover the costs of the sanitarium."

Mom continued telling the story while the day passed by. Revealing the letters regularly sent from the sanitarium; how she never read them. "Each time a new one would arrive, I would put it with the others; they were curiously numbered in sequential order on the back of the envelopes. I bound them together with a lavender ribbon before sequestering them in a safe place. Just before I got pregnant with your brother Donald, I received the last letter I would ever get from her. It had been some time since the previous correspondence. Life with your father was not going very well, which prompted me to open the letter from Gert. It was an odd letter that included symbols she had drawn. Her phrasing was vague, but I knew what she meant. She hinted at subjects, writing things like, leave, you don't belong here, retreat to your home. It began, To N, and ended with Love, G."

"About a week after that letter, I received papers from the trust managing her affairs. Included was a weekend pass. The reason for the release was to see her sister in Fort Worth. It also noted Gert had specifically requested I pick her up and accompany her on the visit. The papers explicitly stated I must deliver the contents within the envelope without exception. It made sense to me no one in the family would go get her; the family had made it clear they didn't want anything to do with her."

Mom reached for her soda. Taking a moment to refresh herself, she sat quietly. Before she completed her first sip, I asked, "Was that not an alarm for you?"

"May I continue?" she responded. Annoyed by my pushing for information, she stared at me for a response. I nodded and let her proceed.

"I felt sorry for her; I thought it was partially my fault she had been locked away. She lost her freedom and family; perhaps this was a way to begin a reconnection for them. I didn't see any harm in driving to pick her up and bring her to see Lily and Edgar. With the necessary documents and signatures in place, I headed to Big Springs. All I needed to do was present them to the guards."

"The drive from Big Springs back to Fort Worth was pleasant and uneventful. Gert obsessively talked about seeing her family and how she longed for them. The first thing she wanted to do was to visit the house on Marsalis St. and see her sister and brother-in-law. Pulling up to the house, I parked on the street and let her go up alone. I didn't see any reason to get further involved; that was until I heard the shouting. I recognized Gert's deep voice flowing across the airwaves."

"I ran from the car into the house; no one was there. I looked out the window to the backyard to find Gert kicking in the door to the little house. The door flew open; Lily stood in its opening, threatening Gert with a knife. It was only a matter of seconds before Gert had the knife in her own hands. Edgar charged her with a baseball bat firmly in his grip. Striking her hard on the chest with the wooden bat, she fell to the ground on her back. Rebounding to her feet, she stood tall before cursing them."

"I ran down the steps from the house in hopes of stopping her. Drawing near her, I could smell something rotten about her; the pheromones she emitted were foul and made of stench."

"I pulled her attention away long enough for Lily to run past her towards the garden. Pushing me to the ground, she turned to chase her sister. Edgar grabbed her arm as she passed him; wielding the knife at him, she wounded him across his chest, cutting into his shirt and tie. I reached for her feet, trying to slow her down; she was out of my grip and after Lily without pause."

"With precision, Gert threw the knife at her sister, nicking her in the calf before falling into the dirt. Lily fell forward onto the grass. Gert ran to where Lily lay; landing on top of her, she began punching her with all her might. It was then Edgar retrieved the knife from the soil and struck a blow into Gert's back."

"Gert stopped hitting Lily and rose to a standing position. I vividly recall watching Gert reach around like a contortionist to remove the knife from her own back. With it in her hand, she struck her sister hard. The first strike towards her throat was softened when it hit the pearl button on her dress, severing the thread holding it on. The second strike completed the initial intent by penetrating the décolletage. I ran towards her as quickly as I could. Tackling her, we fell to the ground. She grabbed me by my hair and tossed me aside like a rag doll. 'I am going to kill them for what they have done. They took my child away from me and put me away, never telling him the truth about me!'"

"In the commotion of it all, I began to understand her brother was actually her son. The boy in England at Dench Manor was not her parent's child. Climbing from the ground to stand, I stopped my intercession. I decided if this was what she needed to do to save her child, who was I to stand in between their re-union? Edgar and Lily managed all their efforts to retreat to safety to no avail. Gert succeeded in her quest. Her sister died just beyond the front window of the little house, Edgar lying across the threshold, looking at his wife."

"Observing the gruesome scene from where I stood in the garden, I didn't know what to do. I suppose I was in shock and somewhat in fear for my own life. A glimmer of sunlight bounced off something in the dirt; a pearl button and part of his bow tie were to-gether in the soil. Picking them both up, I kicked dirt over the blood splatter on the ground and returned to Gert. She gingerly carried Lily and Edgar into the little house, benevolently placing their bodies on the table within. She said she didn't want them exposed to the nighttime chill. I dropped the button and bowtie remnants to the floor, letting them fall into the puddles of blood congealing on the tile. Gert ushered me outside and pulled the door closed, and we left."

"I intended that to be the end of it. I told Gert I couldn't go with her to Dench Manor to find her son; I feared what she might do in retaliation for my withdrawal from the quest. She smiled and said she understood. She then requested I take her downtown to the bus station to drop her off. Initially, I declined. Walking to the car, I realized I was being watched. Fearing being the only person seen leaving that day, I called out to Gert to come along. I didn't want to be the most likely suspect for the murders."

"Ma Day was the person who saw the two of you leave that day, wasn't it?" I stated as a matter of fact. My statement caught her off guard.

"How did you know that?"

"That's irrelevant; I want to know what happened to Gert and how you wound up with the house?"

"How'd you know about the house being left to me? Oh, wait, never mind. Your dad must have told you."

"Yes," was my only response.

"I had terrible nightmares after the murders. I feared the police would come for me eventually. The neighbor had seen me at the house; my name was on the documents at the sanitarium, and it was only a matter of time before the police came to ask me questions. I was afraid of having a baby in jail and going crazy like Gert. Time passed, and nothing came of it. I did not hear from her after I left her at the bus station."

"Several stories about the Beauchamp murders were reported in the paper, but it remained an unsolved mystery for four years. Gert wasn't seen around the area again until the next-door neighbor reported smelling something rotten within the house. The police found her lying in the bathtub dead. She had quietly returned to the house unobserved; she died from self-inflicted stab wounds. The coroner told the papers the injuries inflicted were exactly the same depth and force as the wounds inflicted on Lily and Edgar. The newspapers described it as a satanic-style ritual."

"I didn't know anything about her death until I saw the article in the paper. The obituary had Norma De Lyon listed as a relative, but no one knew me by my maiden name except for your father; I can only guess he did not see the paper that day. So I moved on, waiting every day for something to happen. Another story in the paper told of the murders being solved; a policeman was quoted saying he was glad the case had been closed."

"A month after discovering I was pregnant with you, I received a letter from Gert's attorney. It contained a note from Gert apologizing for what she had put me through. She promised no one would ever know what had happened that gruesome day. Included with the letter was an attorney's contact information. The letter remained sealed, so I assumed no one else knew its contents. I called the number on the card and said I was a friend of Gert Dench's; a lawyer came on the line. He requested I come by his office to sign some paperwork. I had no idea what it possibly could have been."

"After curiosity got the best of me, I made the appointment to see him. Gert had signed the house over to me just before her death. She hoped I would leave your father and find happiness. The attorney read me a note from his files: 'After I am gone, please use the house as a place to provide for your family. I promised you I would always take care of you, and now you know I will. There are many reasons for my actions, but none of them are important now as I have gone too far into the darkness to turn back.'"

"The attorney placed the papers in front of me to sign. After executing all the forms, the lawyer handed me a receipt for the back taxes he had also paid per Gert. She also left a check for $2,800.00 to cover any additional expenses. I wanted to ask about her son but selfishly decided to remain silent."

Jaime and I were doing our best to take in all this information. It explained a lot about my mom's behavior towards me over the years; I had long ago forgiven her, but it didn't explain the supernatural phenomena.

"As you have always known, I was not thrilled about having another child. But it was not for the reason you probably think. My father had been able to reach out to the dead, as had his grandfather. I had always been concerned one of my children would inherit his ability. After my experience with Gert, I knew deep down inside it would be you. I was concerned for your safety before you were even born. When you were little, you talked about your play dates in the garden with the older couple. I didn't pay it much mind until the day you described in detail what the couple wore. I knew right then and there you were able to see the other side."

"My fears were confirmed after you mentioned them, and the odd things at the house began to occur. I never dreamed it had anything to do with Gert until she called you on the phone that Christmas. I knew then you had to leave the house."

"Shortly after we moved into the house, I found the pearl button and bow tie sitting on the back porch, neatly tucked together and clean. I put them in the cigar box I kept Gert's letters in and delivered the box to Pa Day. I didn't tell him why or how I had them; I just left them with him. He had been the investigator on the murders. I was never quite sure why he never pursued me. He must have known I had been at the house with Gert."

"What did you do with the letters?" Jaime queried.

"All bound together, I buried them in the crawl space under the white clapboard house's bathroom. I thought leaving the notes under the space where she ended her life was fitting. And when your stepdad died in that same room, well..."

By this point in the early evening, we were all exhausted and in need of food and rest. Dining in the hotel, we chose not to discuss the information Mother had disclosed. She was actually relaxed and pleasant for a change; maybe the release of the events from her soul was what she needed.

After dinner, I walked Mom to her room, just the two of us. We agreed we should retrieve the letters from the house and burn them. We would do that the following day. Saying goodnight to her, I moved towards the elevator. Standing at the door waiting for the elevator, Mom called out to me.

"I've always felt it was my fault you are gay. Somehow I was being punished for what I helped Gert do. I hope you understand why I didn't want a child like Gert."

Blowing her a kiss as the doors opened, I said, "As much as it caused me pain in my life, I can tell you, with all honesty, I get it."

Meeting Jaime in the lobby, we exited the hotel and hailed a cab to transport us to South Jennings Street. We needed to see Big Mama. Serious alcohol was required to wash down the giant pill of crazy we had just been handed.

Extremely hungover the following day, I stumbled to Mom's hotel room. The door was slightly open; housekeeping was inside performing their daily task. I knew where she was and cursed her for going without me. I woke Jaime, and off to the white clapboard house we went. Rounding the corner onto Marsalis St., I spotted her car in the driveway. I was incredibly sick to my stomach from the alcohol consumption the previous night, the kind of hangover where certain smells make you want to puke. It was that heightened sense of smell that indicated where Mom was. Jaime and I walked through the side gate; my mother stood on the concrete path to the little house. The grill was fired up and ready to go. Holding the letters to her chest, she said a little prayer. I think she said it for Gert or perhaps asking for forgiveness in her part of it all.

I cleared my throat to warn her of our presence. She turned and smiled and laid the letters on the burning briquettes. The dry, brittle parchment paper gently changed colors from ecru to sepia until they were aflame and left charred, falling through the grate.

Watching them burn, it dawned on me. "Jaime, what about the love letter?"

He ran to the little house and pulled it from the book on the shelf. Handing it to my mom, she placed it in the fire.

"Why was that letter not with the others?" she inquired.

Jaime explained he had found it in the book with the photo of Gert's sister and brother-in-law.

"I don't recall that being in the book. Odd. Well, it's over now. Demons have been exorcised, and we can now all rest."

Chapter 9

Letting Go

Mom returned to her life in Florida while Jaime and I returned to ours in the white clapboard house.

The burning of the letters and disclosing past events appeared to subdue the demons. Perhaps Mom's idea to eliminate the letters had been correct; no more red-eyed couple in the little house, no more dreams where I couldn't breathe, or me waking to bruises unknowingly inflicted. For now, all seemed to be re-solved on the supernatural front.

Even though much time had passed, the majority of my family still didn't speak to me. Rumor had it they felt I had manipulated Mom into letting me live in her house. From my perspective, the issue was sim-ply that I was holding up money perceived to belong to them. I suspect none of them knew the challenges Jaime and I dealt with in that house. Perhaps my oldest sister knew, but she had grown as distant as the rest.

The holidays were once again creeping upon us, and Jaime was still not working. His demeanor made him less and less attractive with each passing day. He did not want to engage on an emotional level, or on any level for that matter. His libido had always been high, and I was very grateful for that. But now, as time had passed, he stopped participating, at least with me.

We readied ourselves for Thanksgiving celebrations in the recently remodeled house on Marsalis St. The kitchen was beautifully finished out, the garage converted to a formal dining room, the new second bathroom installed, and the original one partially complete. Close enough to being finished to suit us, we decided to host a holiday dinner for friends.

Thanksgiving day arrived; food and friends were abundant. It was just how I imagined the Pilgrims and Indians managed when they got together for the first time. Strangers doing their best to figure everyone else out. This year, the hosts were the two most significant strangers in the house trying to figure each other out. Our relationship had continued to falter, and in all honesty, our sobriety was vacillating as well.

As Thanksgiving passed, the mood around the house was somber at best. December, now just days away, was traditionally the month we celebrated most. I feared this year would be significantly different from the ones before. Our biggest issue arose the Monday after Thanksgiving when I informed Jaime I was going to England on business. He was irritated about the trip, and I could not understand why. He had made the point clear long ago that work took precedence over all else. When he chose to move to Cali without discussing it with me, the mold had been cast regarding work and family priorities. I was only going for ten days, but he acted as if the trip was indefinite. I began to understand when through a drunken slur, he accused me of abandoning him.

Packing for my trip, Jaime interrupted me by entering the room wearing nothing but an erection. It had been so long since we had engaged in coitus I wasn't going to oppose the interlude. He was unlike he had ever been, totally wild, asking me to do things he had never requested before. My assessment; he was attempting to guilt me into staying home. After we both erupted with pleasure, he made the request that I not go. I explained to him since I was the only one in the household producing an income, the proposal wasn't an option.

The plea denied, he got up from the floor where we had ended up and left the room. The recently added-on bathroom connected to our room and was within steps, but for some reason, he went to use the original bathroom still not complete. This was very vexing to me, and I could only assume he thought I would use the shower in our bathroom and was being nice while avoiding me.

Completing my shower, I wrapped my towel around my waist and returned to finish packing for my 5:25 PM flight to Heathrow the following day. I heard the water in the other bathroom still running; this struck me as odd. Concerned a fitting in the unfinished room had come loose, I headed towards the noise to investigate.

Opening the door to the bath, I found Jaime standing in the tub with scalding water raining down on him from the shower head. His arms stretched upwards like he was being pulled towards the ceiling. His luscious olive Latino skin was bright pink from a slight scald. I reached for the valve to turn the water off. "Don't you dare touch that faucet!" radiated from his mouth.

Stepping back from the tub, I peered into his eyes; he wasn't there. I recognized the look; I needed to get his attention, so I made a fist. I punched him in the stomach using all the strength I could manage. Folding over in pain, he plummeted to the tub base, screaming for me to turn off the water. Sealing off the faucets, I reached for him.

"Why did you try to scald me with the shower? What did you do to the faucets?"

"I didn't do anything. Let's get you out of the tub. Are you seriously burnt anywhere?" Assessing him from head to toe, I observed the pink was gone from his skin, and there were no signs of blistering. I grabbed a nearby towel and pulled him up from the tub.

"Why am I naked? What am I doing in the shower?" His bark revealed he was full of anxiety.

"We just had sex, and you came in here to clean up."

He grabbed the towel from my hand and tore out of the bathroom. "I didn't ask you to have sex. Oh, Dios Mio, tell me we were safe!"

"Safe? What do you mean? We had sex like we always have."

"Oh shit. What the fuck?"

"Jaime! What the hell is going on here?"

"We haven't been having sex because I found out I was positive."

"When? And why haven't you told me?" The shock in my voice was apparent to him.

"Since your last physical showed you were negative, I knew you would know I had been screwing around if I told you."

Following him through the house, I worked out what he was saying in my head. "How long have you been sleeping around? Or is it with just one other person? Why would you fuck someone else after you proposed to me? You told me we were in a monogamous rela-tionship. You low-life mother fucker!"

"This is why I didn't tell you. I knew it wasn't going to go well." Tears began to fall from his eyes.

"You were right about that! I have supported you and all your bullshit, and ———— you know what? Just shut the fuck up. I need to get ready for my trip." I left him standing there in his towel, retreating to the bedroom to finish packing. My rage was so intense I allowed the actions of what Gert did to play in the conscious forefront of my mind. I was contemplating how to kill him. The fury within me grew and grew; wholly focused on my anger, I didn't hear him enter the room.

"Your cell phone is ringing." He sheepishly handed me my phone and turned to go. The phone timing was impeccable, my thoughts of murder subsided, and my rage slowly came under control. "Hello."

"Thank goodness, this is the right number." On the other end of the call was Andy.

"Hey there, listen, now is not really a good time. Can I call you back tomorrow?"

"Yeah, I guess. But hey, real quick, I just called to tell you that my dad passed a little while ago."

"I am so sorry to hear that. How's your mother doing? How are you?"

After a long pause, Andy replied, "Fine." With a deep breath released, he said, "Call me later when you can talk." The phone went silent. I immediately hit the redial button.

"Hello."

"Hey there, this is important. I have time now."

As he wept, he explained the reason why he called; his dad had requested I sing at his funeral. It was difficult for me to say, but I told Andy I was leaving for London the next day for work and wouldn't be in town.

"That's perfect," he responded between tears.

"I am so sorry I can't be there for you."

The voice on the phone changed, "Henry?"

"Hello, Mrs. Dench. How are you holding up?"

"I am doing ok, all things considered. It was expected, so I am as prepared as I can be. What Andrew meant by 'Perfect' is the funeral is being held in Cambridge at the family crypt. Services are Saturday morning. Is it possible you can manage it?"

"I will most definitely manage it."

"I am going to put Andrew back on the phone. This has been really hard for him; I need you to help him through it."

Andy returned to the phone. "Thank you. I hope this won't be weird for you."

Missing him and his family over the years, I hated the fact that it took death for him to call me. I worked up a smile and said, "Absolutely not. I've missed you." There was no response, and once again, the phone was silent.

Having recaptured my sanity, I finished packing my suitcase and moved to the bedroom door. My primary bag was ready; I would pack my toiletries and carry on the next morning. Dropping the case by the door, I exited the bedroom to find Jaime. Walking into the family room, I noticed the back door open and the light in the little house was on. He had retreated to his make-shift office.

Taking a deep breath and looking around for the red-eyed couple, I trotted down the stairs and up the path leading to the little house. Rounding the corner to his small office, I found him on his laptop typing away. "Sorry to interrupt, but we need to finish the conversation from earlier."

He closed the laptop lid and leaned back in his chair, waiting for me to speak. His posture was cold and impersonal.

"I am sure you are dealing with your diagnoses and the ramifications of cheating on me; those are your issues, and you need to find some resolution in your soul. I truly never suspected you were sleeping around; pure ignorance on my part for being so trusting. When I return from England, I will get tested and hope for the best. If I test positive, you always need to remember that it was you who infected me."

He looked up at me cold and hard. His eyes were so black there was no distinguishing the iris from the pupil. "By the time I get back from the UK, I need you moved out of the house. Don't know where you will go or what you will do; I don't really care at the moment. I don't want bad things to happen to you, but honestly, my perspective may change."

He flipped the laptop back open. "I am searching for moving trucks. I already called Big Mama and asked for some money."

"Did you tell Big Mama the whole story? What is really going on?"

"Not his business."

"Oh well, he is a smart man; I am sure he will figure it out. Needless to say, you need to sleep somewhere else tonight. You are not crawling into that bed next to me ever again."

I left him there in the little house, making his plan for extraction. Back inside the main house, I closed the bedroom door and crawled into bed. I pulled the covers up over me and worked to find a comfortable position. My pillow was soon soaked through from the tears I cried myself to sleep with.

I woke from a restless sleep early and finished gathering necessities for the trip. Double-checking I had everything I needed, I made my exit away from Jaime. I put my bags in my car and headed to Andy's house. I didn't know if I could get past the guard, but I was going to try. I stopped at a donut shop for coffee and some sugary comfort food. Consuming the four chocolate-covered doughnuts, I summoned the courage necessary to see the Dench family.

I drove up to the guard's pavilion with purpose, my story all ready to beg for my entrance. As I arrived at the gate, the guard waved and opened the iron barriers. He called out as I passed by. "Mrs. Dench hoped you would stop by."

With a wave, I acknowledged his comment. I didn't know if she was expecting me or if the attendant had confused me for someone else. I parked in the circle drive and headed up the front steps. Waiting to ring the doorbell, I concluded the visit was a mistake; I should wait to see them overseas. While pausing in front of the iron doors, I heard, "We are on the back lanai, come on back."

I knew the voice but wondered if I would recognize the man. I let out a slight gasp when I saw Andy; he was even more handsome than my mind's eye recalled. I felt clumsy walking towards him. It had been over ten years since we had seen each other, and I felt like it was a first date.

Reaching the bottom step before I did, he reached out his hand. My initial response was to shake it; he took my outstretched hand and tucked it under his elbow. We proceeded toward the courtyard where his mother waited.

"I had hoped you would stop by. Andrew said you were en route to London today." Mrs. Dench, eloquently dressed in a simple black satin dress, greeted me from her perch.

"Evening flight; I wanted to see you. Check what requests there were for the service so I could prepare." Andy gripped my hand tightly; I knew he was doing all he could to keep from breaking down.

"I see death every day at the hospital and thought I had hardened against it, and even though I know he isn't suffering anymore, I can't bear the thought of no longer getting his morning text wishing me a good day."

I pulled my hand loose from his and put my arms around him. Both of us felt so much pain at that point, but my focus was on him.

"He asked for you to sing Peace in the Valley, the song you sang at Mrs. Day's funeral."

"I will be most happy to do it."

His mother, ever the gracious hostess, motioned for me to take a seat. "Sit, have coffee or tea with us till you have to go." I sat on a striped divan next to Andy. I admired how his mother had not aged a bit since I last saw her. Maybe slightly, but it was minimal. If she had work done, it was indeed the best.

Morning coffee led to lunch while visiting with well-wishers dropping by. When it was time for me to go, I said goodbye to each of them and made my way to my car. Information for the services tucked into my diary, I drove back to Marsalis St. to leave my car. I hoped the shuttle to the airport would arrive on time. Jaime's car was not in sight; I made a clean getaway.

My flight overseas was quite lovely; it was a company perk that business class was allowed if you flew for more than six hours. I made sure to book a direct flight from Dallas to Heathrow to ensure the perk was utilized.

The first day in London was a whirlwind; airport, customs, hotel, client site visit, dinner, and finally, back to the hotel for much-needed sleep. The second and third days were a repeat of the one before. On the fourth day, I was scheduled to take the train to Cambridgeshire.

The train ride from London was quaint. A slight snowfall had occurred Thursday night in the countryside, leaving a thin blanket of white covering the rolling hills. The one hour and twenty-minute ride arrived in the university town on time. I exited the train to find a chauffeur holding a placard with my name on it. "Mr. Andrew will meet you at the hotel."

The elegant man dressed in black requested my luggage, and off we went to the car park. The S-Class Mercedes was black from stem to stern. After placing the bags in the trunk, he opened a rear door for my entrance onto the supple leather seat.

Pulling away from the station, the driver updated me on scheduled events. "There will be cocktails at Dench Manor at six, with dinner following at seven. Do you have suitable attire? Mr. Andrew said not to worry if you didn't; he would have the shop come to the hotel with some options."

"I have a dark suit and tie. Is that acceptable?"

Without a response to me, he retrieved a car phone and advised the person on the other end to gather Size 40 Regs and deliver them to the hotel for a fitting. I panicked internally as I didn't have the money to purchase clothes. I was struggling financially to support Jaime and pay the remodeling cost of the white clapboard house; this unexpected expenditure would be an issue. I had a corporate credit card but knew its use for personal shopping was frowned upon.

We circled around the fountain in front of a hotel, the car coming to rest at the steps leading to the entrance. The trunk opened, as did my door; I assumed we had arrived at the hotel where I was to meet Andy.

It was Andy who opened my door; ever the gentleman, he escorted me up the stairs toward the lobby. My travel cases, along with the chauffeur, were no longer in sight. Passing through the revolving door, we crossed the lobby straight for the elevators. "Don't I need to check in?"

"Oh no, everything has been taken care of. It's our gift to you for being here."

Exiting the lift, my room was immediately on the left. Andy inserted the key in the lock, and voila, a beautiful one-bedroom suite was in front of me. A funeral was a terrible reason to experience this luxury.

"My family owns the property along with a couple of others here and in Wales. The party tonight is at Dench Manor. We don't use the term wake; we aren't Irish. Dad was the last family member to own shares in the manor, and now that he is gone, it will be sold or converted to another hotel. I have very few memories of it; my mom and dad were living in the US when I was born. I have visited a few times, but not really my thing. There is some question about my shares of the estate; my mother said I shouldn't worry about it. I don't need the money, and I would rather see it support some charity. Truthfully I don't want to have to worry about what to do with it."

Realizing he was rambling to avoid any deep connection, I interrupted him. "Your parents instilled a strong sense of self in you but not any arrogance; I like that."

"You know my dad didn't carry that air about him either. He said the years he spent here were cold and unloving. The falling out with the family over the lesbian sister left him bitter toward his parents. He told me many times he was better suited to living in Texas. I am so glad he did; I would have never met you otherwise."

A man entered the living area carrying crystal flutes full of champagne. Announcing my bags had been unpacked; I was given directions to call him one hour before I needed to leave; he would repack them for me. With a glass of bubbly in my hand, I countered Andy's last statement. "Forgive me for bringing this up, but aren't you the same guy who dumped me because my family had a dirty secret that would break your dad's heart?"

"Can we talk about that when we return to the States?"

Acknowledging Andy was using all the grandeur to divert his breaking heart, I agreed. I made my way to him and placed an ever-so-slight kiss on his lips. "Yes, let's focus on your dad and the family for now."

Turning around, I found another strange man standing in the suite's living room. Andrew greeted him and instructed him to fit me for the evening event. "Preferably wool, as the evening will most likely be cool."

Three evening suits were presented; they all looked black to me but were, indeed, various shades of dark blue. I tried each one on and waited for Andy to pick the one he preferred. Putting the suit he chose back on, the shopkeeper made his markings and was gone with a commitment to return within the hour. Standing in my briefs, holding a glass of champagne, I noticed Andy looking me over. "I don't recall you being that handsome."

His flattery created an uninvited bulge in my briefs, causing Andy to blush. "Perhaps you would like to shower and shave." With that statement, he turned to leave, saying, "I will meet you in the lobby promptly at 5:45."

Dench Manor was unlike anything I had ever experienced. The use of the word grandeur did not even begin to describe it; a servant for everything. Old-world, really old-world money; the level of status that allows you to never question the next meal's whereabouts.

The evening event was festive; fantastic talks about art, food, and music were abundant; the only thing missing was the conversation about his dad. It was as if everyone knew the secret about him being Gert's son. All the formality was only for proprieties sake.

The services the following day were quite the opposite. There were four chairs in the family crypt, all sitting neatly in one row; one for his mother, one for Andy, one for a distant cousin, and one that remained unoccupied. Directed to stand at the back of the crypt, when prompted, I should sing the song requested, A Capella. The entire event was over in twenty minutes.

Leaving the crypt, I wanted to ask Mrs. Dench the purpose of the soiree the night before and no attendees today; I thought about it carefully and concluded it was a question better left unspoken.

I was to spend the rest of the day with the Dench duo. The history of Dench Manor was explained to me before leaving the crypt; its importance to England's commonwealth was greatly valued. The evening that followed consisted of a lovely dinner at a local restaurant and back to the hotel for bed.

Sunday morning arrived, and I found myself at breakfast abandoned. The unexpected departure for the US by the Denches caught me off-guard. A note of thanks, without explanation of their leaving, was delivered by the hotel manager. The beautifully hand-written letter on the hotel stationary thanked me for attending and singing as requested. Upon handing me the sealed envelope, the manager commented that Mrs. Dench had settled all accounts. I was stunned by this turn of events. Why had they been so kind and genteel the day prior, then disappeared without saying goodbye?

The diversion from dealing with Jaime was appreciated; living in this world of refinement allowed me to escape my life for a bit. That said, Andy's unexpected departure left me feeling sad and deserted.

After a comfortable ride back to the train station, I was once again en route across the English countryside, off to additional meetings for the rest of the UK tour. I hoped the strength to survive would come upon me sooner than later. It turned out to be a whirlwind, which kept me focused on work and not on either Jaime or Andy.

All the customer commitments met, I headed for Heathrow for the long flight home. Thank god for the direct flight on which, I hoped, I could rest.

Arriving at the gate for my flight, the attendant observed my passport, clicked some buttons on her keyboard, and looked back up at me, "Sir, you are supposed to be in another area." I was preparing to start a row when she motioned for someone to come over. A porter walked over to where I stood and picked up my bags. He then asked that I follow him. Not knowing what was happening and being totally exhausted, I complied.

Along with my luggage, the porter retrieved my passport and ticket from the gate agent. We moved into a glass corridor, walking past the people patiently waiting for their turn at airport security. Reaching a different security desk after bypassing the masses, another clerk immediately greeted me and asked that I follow her. I realized I was being escorted through the airport, and I had no clue as to why. Arriving at a glass elevator, the doors promptly opened;

my escort proceeded with instructions. "All first-class customers are boarded through this area. Hand your documents to the clerk up top. They will take care of you from that point forward."

Retrieving my passport and ticket as the doors closed, I stood dumbfounded as the lift rose two levels. The doors parting, I heard, "Good morning Mr. Notenburg. May I have your passport?"

With a few clicks and smacks of a stamp, I was led to a private waiting area and told to make myself comfortable. They would retrieve me when it was time to board the plane. I opened my ticket folder to find I had been upgraded to a first-class concierge service. Another perk of the wealthy, I concluded.

Boarding the plane, I took my seat in 3A, where my jacket was swiftly retrieved from my hand and replaced with a glass of champagne. I began to settle into my cube while the porter introduced himself and advised me to make myself as comfortable as possible. Once settled, he handed me an envelope with my name on it, very Mission Impossible-like. I opened it to find another handwritten note from Mrs. Dench. "Thank you for being there. Enjoy your flight home, and know all will be as it should very soon."

Holding the note in my hand, I couldn't help but think the paper was familiar; something about its texture and color awoke a memory.

Excellent food paired with fantastic wine took my palate to new heights. This was a fitting goodbye to Mr. Dench; he was the one who taught me to appreciate such things. My stomach full and my inhibitions sufficiently sedated, I fell into a deep slumber. It was the first time in forever that I slept without dreams or cares. The porter woke me just as we reached the outer banks. Breakfast was served before I returned to life as I knew it or would discover it to be.

Going home on the airport shuttle, I wasn't sure what to expect when I turned the corner on Marsalis St. No moving vans, no cars, nobody; Jaime had packed his things and was gone just as I had requested. Some of the furniture we had purchased together through the years remained; in all honesty, I wish he would have taken everything that was "ours" as they were one more reminder of the time we spent together.

I unpacked my suitcases, did laundry, prepared some dinner, and worked up my courage to face another week at the office. This would be the first night I had ever slept in that house by myself; I prayed I would wake up the next morning. One uneventful night followed by another. The week passed without any paranormal events.

February rolled around when I finally decided to visit Jaime's office in the little house. Going in, I found everything exactly as it was when I left, sans his laptop. It was all my mom's stuff, so at least he had the decency not to take what wasn't his. I walked around the beautiful desk he had restored and sat in his chair. A soft touch of his scent remained in the room. I missed him but knew I couldn't return to him after being lied to and cheated on. Even with my low self-esteem issues, knowing he risked transmitting HIV to me because of his selfishness, I wouldn't return.

Sitting in his chair, I said a little prayer of thankfulness; my HIV test results had returned negative. I would have another test done the following month just to be sure. I turned the desk chair to leave this place behind. I would lock the door and let whoever lived here next deal with these rooms. Leaning forward to leave the chair, I saw his ring sitting on the bookshelf. The ring he ordered from South America for our marriage was left behind; I couldn't believe he had left it sitting there. Picking it up, I began to wonder where he had put mine. I quickly began to open drawers, moving paper clips and rubber bands, lifting rulers, and looking everywhere to see if I could find it.

I turned to open the file drawer; the cigar box he had presented the wedding bands in awaited me. We never smoked the cigars which accompanied the rings; well, I hadn't smoked mine. Jaime knew how to choose good cigars, and I thought, what a great sayonara to this room and him. For a moment, I was pensive. Then it came to me: what the hell, let's enjoy that cigar. I anticipated the joy remaining from one of the few things he hadn't ruined for me.

I pulled the box out of the drawer and set it on the desk in front of me. I observed the box for a little while before opening it. A distant voice reminded me of Mom saying she kept the letters from Gert in a cigar box. The bow tie and button remnants delivered to Pa Day were also in a cigar box. What was it with cigar boxes?

Finding a lighter in the main drawer, I reached for the box to open it. Flipping the lid back, I saw the cigars were not inside. Instead, the box contained an unexpected surprise.

A set of letters, bound together with a ribbon reminiscent of the past, was all the box contained. I picked them up, wondering if I had found secret letters from Jaime's lover.

I dropped them back into the box when I saw the writing on the top piece of parchment.

'To N. Love G."

Chapter 10

Predestined Relationships

Two months passed before finding the place I wanted to call home. With all the hoops one must jump through by lenders, the aggravation of pushy real estate agents, and knowing Gert was not gone, this was the longest two months of my life.

With a recent promotion to executive management, a pay raise with a handsome bonus put me in a position to purchase a home all my own. With all the failures from previous relationships fresh on my mind, I decided just to do me for a while. Free to utilize my libido in any way I chose and spend money without dialogue about the expense; I was ready to be single. I no longer wanted to spend energy worrying how anyone else felt, if they didn't like what I wanted for dinner, if I was hogging the covers, or what the bedroom temperature was. I chose to avoid the obstacles that came with being in a relationship.

Reviewing my family's history of bad choices when it came to choosing lovers, it made sense to go it on my own. I also concluded I was broken in some areas; it was time that I spent some time in therapy while experiencing some independence. It turns out that finding a counselor is just like dating; you go through several before finding one that seems to fit.

My new abode had all the amenities I sought; a zero-lot-line property with minimal grass in the front yard and huge flowerbeds. Located on top of a bluff, the hills leading down to the creek were covered with rocks and trees. The back stone patio was tiered partially into the cliff, making it perfect for enjoying a touch of nature in the middle of the city. It was only thirty minutes to and from work and fifteen minutes to the airport. The location and minimum maintenance were perfect, as my new position required a significant amount of travel.

I settled in quickly and started projecting right away in my free time. Painting, making curtains, and moving a wall; all these activities kept me busy and didn't allow me time to get sucked into the fear of being single. My newfound counselor shared his concerns I might be reactive and find a rescue that needed to be saved. He theorized that after Andy, my focus shifted to saving other people, thereby avoiding working on myself.

His analysis was painful, but I knew deep inside it was true. I was following my mother's patterns; high attraction and attention pulled us in, then we moved into rescue mode and then resentment for rescuing them. The poor bastards never stood a chance.

The next months were filled with nothing but house projects, travel for work, and playdates. The pendulum was swinging far right; my being aware of my rescue behavior pushed me into a mindset that people needed to maintain their own lives. While this is somewhat true, the soul quickly dries up if you aren't willing to help your fellow man. Some days people need to be pulled out of the dirt, and it's a good thing to lift them up. After that, it's a habit and most likely not a good one. I needed to find the middle ground, help them up once, maybe twice, all the while being cognizant of why.

It took several months for me to find my way to a happy medium when dealing with people. Coming home from a particularly grueling counseling session one Saturday afternoon, I felt dejected and sad. I went for my usual recovery, planting flowers. The front flower bed of my home was relatively large and in excellent shape. Still, my need to play in the dirt made it easy to persuade myself the soil needed more flowers.

On my way home from the doctor's office, I made a detour to the garden shop; a bag of mulch and two flats of Finca's later, I headed to my castle. I quickly moved into and through the house, changing into gardening clothes.

I opened the front door by the flower bed on my way to retrieve the plants from the trunk of my car. After grabbing my gloves from the pegboard wall just inside the garage, the flats were quickly removed and on their way to their new home. Exiting the garage with my hands full, I rounded the corner of the house and was startled to encounter a man standing there.

Caught off guard when I bumped into him, I backed up a few steps while he immediately apologized for startling me. I introduced myself, and he responded in kind. His name was Bob.

Bob was, by my best guesstimate, in his mid-seventies. He wore a clean but worn pair of overalls and a t-shirt. He had the most beautiful blue eyes I had ever seen a man carry. His hair was slightly unkempt, his face cleanly shaven.

We talked about flowers and different types of plants while I toiled away with the project at hand. I quickly forgot about my irritation with the counselor while visiting with Bob. He told me how he had been in this area all his life and how much it had changed.

The time spent while he revealed the dirty little secrets of the neighborhood went by without notice. He knew who was sleeping with whom, the maid from the house across the street who was stealing retirement checks, and the kid who was brought home in the cop car late last night. I was impressed with his Gladys Kravitz's knowledge of the neighborhood.

Inquiring if he was married, he said he didn't want to talk about it. I saw the sadness in his eyes and changed the subject.

Finishing up my project, I spread the last bit of mulch from its bag. Standing up, proud of my accomplishment, I smiled at Bob. "Ok, now you have told me everything about their houses; what do you know about my house?"

He pushed on his temple for a minute, pondering his response. "You think too little of yourself. You have convinced yourself that the only reason anyone wants you is for sex or what you can do for them."

My first thought was he must know my therapist. "Well, Bob. I think you may be right, but curious how you know that."

"Ah, hell, that's easy. You still love the man that you think got away, but bring all these boys to your bedroom, attempting to silence the ache deep inside you."

I couldn't help myself but smile widely at him. His statement wasn't mean or judgmental; it was merely his perspective and quite possibly spot on. "Bob, with that said, I think I need a beer. Can I bring you one?"

"I don't drink anymore, son. Although a nice cold glass of water sure sounds nice."

I tossed my gloves on the porch and excused myself. Entering the house, I moved to the kitchen to make my favorite drink for hot weather. A beer and coke combo Jaime had taught me. I grabbed a bottle of water from the fridge before making my way back to the front yard. Pulling the front door closed behind me; I realized Bob was nowhere to be found. I looked past the side of the house leading to the patio and saw the gate had been opened. I assumed Bob wandered to the stone patio in the back of the house to check out the plants. Passing by the garage, I moved up the side yard towards the opened gate. Coming around the corner of the house, I saw Bob walking down the steps and off into the gully below the bluffs. "Bob, I have your water here!" I hollered out at him.

He turned around and waved, proceeding on with his journey. I was aware of the trails leading to the homes on the other side of the bluff, but I had never seen anyone in the woods at the bottom of the gully.

Watching Bob off in the distance, I sat down on one of the patio chairs and enjoyed my refreshing beverage. It wasn't long before Bob was out of sight, gone beyond the brush and stone. I took a moment to soak in what he had said; he was absolutely right. I didn't value myself and needed to learn how.

My first Fourth of July in the neighborhood was coming up soon. The annual neighborhood block party was the perfect opportunity for me to get to know more of my neighbors. Each house was to provide something for the event; my contribution was paper plates and napkins. I was being lazy and didn't want anything that required cleaning afterward. This was my first event in the neighborhood, and beyond having met Bob and my immediate neighbors, I didn't know anyone. I paired up with my neighbor Juliette and made the rounds. I was surprised to find I was the only Gay living in the neighborhood. The community was not very old and reasonably culturally diverse, but I didn't meet one other member of the LGBT community that day. I later realized that I was living in suburbia by choice, and although gays did live in the burbs, per capita, the numbers were low.

I asked several people in the community if they knew Bob; no one knew who I was talking about. I described him in complete detail, including where he walked to the day we chatted, but my quest to find out about him failed. No one seemed to know who he was. I thought to myself; he sure knows all your business; maybe you should pay more attention to who lives around you.

As the sun faded below the horizon, I was introduced to Audrey. She was a very elegant woman in her late eighties. Regal and well-dressed for the evening events, she was from an era where outward appearances mattered. She never left her house without being presentable. We struck up an immediate friendship and quickly entered a deep conversation as the sun waned from the sky. She disclosed she had grown up in the area and lived in this neighborhood since it was built. She pointed to a large house with elegant curb appeal just on the other side of the bluff; she informed me that it used to be her home. Her husband was a home builder and developed this part of the city. He built the house specifically to meet her requests. Continuing with details of each and every structure in the neighborhood, she mentioned how my home was one of her husband's favorites in the community. They had planned to retire to that house when the time was right.

"Is your husband nearby?" I politely inquired.

"I don't think so, my dear. He has been gone for about ten years now. I suspect he is roaming around here somewhere waiting for me, but I am not quite ready to go."

"I am sure he will wait as long as he needs to. How long were you married?"

"Sixty-one years; I was quite young when he convinced me to run off with him and start a life. What amazing adventures we had. But now I live with my daughter and her husband right here."

"I think it is wonderful that your children are caring for you."

"Let me tell you a secret." She said with a big smile on her face. "If they want any of the inheritance, they had better!"

We both giggled out loud at her audacity. I patted Audrey's hand and said meeting her had been a pleasure. The fireworks were about to begin, and she was ready to go back home, away from the noise and the crowds. I thanked her for her time and turned to go. "I am going to go now. Will you be all right here?"

"Oh yes, as long as the brakes are on, I am good. My daughter is on her way to push me back inside."

I loved Audrey's sense of humor and the light way she looked at life. It hit me just as I said goodbye to her; she had lived there all her life. "Ere I take my leave, quick question for you. I had a delightful gentleman stop by and visit me recently. I was working in the flower bed, and we had the most lovely conversation. No one else seems to know who he is."

"Honey, I know everyone and everything that goes on in this neighborhood."

I felt slightly dirty from her comment due to the one-eyed wink she gave me when saying it. "He said his name was Bob. He was in overalls with a t-shirt, late seventies would be my guess."

"My dear boy, I told you my husband was roaming around waiting for me. I am so glad you got to meet him." She smiled sweetly at me as Juliette approached to make our exit. I smiled back at her and asked, "Any messages for him next time he stops by?"

"None that I can think of."

I didn't see Bob around for a while, though I sensed he was being playful sometimes. I would find strange objects in the flower beds or pots freshly tended. It made me comfortable in the house to know he had an eye on me.

The last time we crossed paths was the following October. I was taking down the potted ferns that had outlived their beauty on the second-floor balcony. Climbing to the second-floor ledge on a ladder, I was attempting to retrieve the plants when the ladder began to sway. I had overreached for a basket throwing everything out of balance. The planter and I began to travel backward when it was released from its hook. I reached for the balcony rail, hoping not to plunge to the stone floor. I released the fern, hoping I would find something else to grab hold of. Contemplating the best place to jump and hopefully minimize bodily injury, I heard Bob.

"Hold on to the ladder; I gotcha."

I grabbed the top rung just as the ladder's direction gently altered. I looked down to find Bob pulling the opposite side forward until all four legs were again on the stone foundation. With my legs wobbly and my knees weak, I made my way down to the stone-covered surface. I was more than a little shaken and ever so thankful Bob was there to save me. "Thank you so much, sir. I am glad you were around to keep me from falling."

"I won't be around much longer to keep you out of trouble; please buy a proper ladder if you are going to be up there."

"I will, sir. Where are you going?"

"Audrey is going to join me tonight. We can finally be together again and move on to our next destination." Before he finished telling me his wife was going to be with him, I heard the ambulance's sirens as it passed my house. I saw Bob amble off through the brush. He was heading home to be with his wife in the afterlife.

I told friends about the event, and how touched I was that their love had lasted. Many who have known me for a long time have endured my stories of life beyond our bodies with skepticism. My ability to tell a good story would keep their attention but did little to persuade them of what I believed to be the truth.

A year had passed since Jaime, and I hosted Thanksgiving at the white clapboard house. Most of the friends we knew as a couple had been kind and remained neutral about our splitting up. He was no longer in Texas, which made it easier for all of us.

I decided to host another friends-giving: a combined housewarming party and holiday gathering. A social media invitation was generated, and the planning began for the Friday event. Early evening cocktails and hors d'oeuvres would be served; the piano tuned, the menu set, and the liquor cabinet full, the party was on.

I spent the evening visiting with friends, catching up on all the latest gossip and whatnots of Fort Worth. Living just far enough from the city center, I didn't keep up with the local news, so to speak.

Making my way for a refreshing beverage, I saw a man I had never met standing at the bar in my family room. I assumed he was a guest of someone I had invited but wasn't entirely sure. He had the body type that I drooled over in my dreams, not overbuilt but fit and, as Goldilocks put it, just right. Pushing up close to him at the counter while I requested another drink from the bartender, I asked. "Are you having fun?"

"Just got here. Don't really know anyone."

"Have the host introduce you around. Don't be shy." My friend, who was working the bar, smiled at me; he knew my propensity for causing a little trouble whenever possible.

"I don't know the host."

"Forgive me for asking if you don't know the host; how did you wind up here?"

"A guy I am dating said he had to stop by to see his friend for a few minutes. He disappeared when we came through the door, so I did what any gay man in strange surroundings would do; I made my way to the bar."

Putting my hand out to shake his, I asked, "What's your name?"

"Clay."

"Great name; I have a nephew with that name. And may I say, you are as handsome as the name?"

Laughing out loud, he rebuked, "What the hell does that mean?"

"Artists use clay to mold and shape beautiful things. From my perspective, the artist outdid himself with you." The bartender handed me my drink and smirked at me, "That was pretty good!"

Clay began to blush slightly.

"Thank you for that. I am a little embarrassed by the reference, I must admit, but thank you for the compliment."

"My pleasure. Now, do you spot your boyfriend anywhere?"

"Not my boyfriend, third date."

"Well, in that case, we need to introduce you to some people. And since I am the host, I know everyone here." With a Cheshire cat grin, I continued on, "Well, now I do! Let's make the rounds; you might find your date or another man you want to get to know."

"I believe I already have." He said with a gentle upturn of his lips accompanied by a wink.

Clay and I didn't leave each other's side that night, beyond nature's requirements anyway. I made sure to introduce him to everyone at the party. Eventually, we found his date curled up in the lap of another man. "Marc, Did you forget you brought someone with you?"

"Hi, Hankkkkkkk. I saw you were entertaining him, so I wasn't worried. Hug, Hug, Kiss, Kiss."

Clay had already blown Marc off as a long-term option; that statement closed and locked the door.

"Hey Hankkkkkkkkk, I hear rumors you had another ghost encounter," Marc made sure to speak loud enough the entire room could hear him.

I enlightened the crowd with the tale of Bob and his saving me from falling off the ladder before returning to his wife. The response was typical; some loved the story, and others said I was making it up. But Clay was different; he continued to ask questions about the encounters I had had. He was intrigued by all of it.

The last guest finally exited the front door and into a ride-share around 1:30 A.M. It wasn't until I shut the front door we realized Clay had been dumped. Marc had left with someone other than his date, leaving Clay with me.

"I enjoyed your company so much I didn't even miss Marc."

I heard a trash bag open and bottles clinking into it, falling one by one as they were pushed from where they stood. The bartender had begun to clean up. I didn't want Clay to leave, but I also didn't want to play driver to take him home.

I called out to the bartender, "If you will clear the bar and put all the liquor away, we can call it good for the night."

I turned back to the kitchen to see Clay dressed in an apron, cleaning. Well, my heart leaped. This good-looking man who didn't make fun of my ghost stories was cleaning without my asking; there just might be something here. Within thirty minutes, the dishwasher was full and running; the trash was contained and placed in the garage. I paid the bartender his fee for the evening, said goodnight to him, and was ready for bed.

While waving goodbye at the bartender from the front stoop, Clay approached me from behind and put his arm around my chest. He pulled me tight against him; standing there, he held me close for a moment. No words, no need to speak, just simply body against body, taking each other in. "I have summoned my Uber; it should be here in five."

"It was a really nice surprise to meet you tonight."

"I agree. Can I possibly have you for the rest of the weekend?" His arms still stretched across my chest; he asked the question so softly into my ear I was literally melting. Well, figuratively, but you know what I mean.

Before I could answer, his transportation home pulled into the driveway. He released me and walked towards the car.

"My number is on your nightstand. Text me your answer."

No sooner than he could have buckled his seatbelt, my front door was closed, locked, and he had a "Yes" in his messages.

Clay and I clicked on almost every level. Our interests were varied but not so far from one another's that conflict might arise from them. We were both interested in the other but were not needy or jealous. It seemed an excellent fit. We spent as much time together as possible over the following weeks.

Two weeks prior to Christmas, Clay asked if I would be interested in accompanying him and his son on a trip. They were going ghost hunting in East Texas with some friends. It was an annual pilgrimage and an opportunity for me to meet his son. I didn't know how I felt about the idea; a trip with his kid suggested the relationship was at a different level for him from where I was. I had not made any plans for Christmas; this would be the second one without Jaime, and it still felt off. It had been over a year, and I should have been done with my emotions regarding him, but I wasn't quite there yet. We needed to talk about his invitation.

I waited until we had dinner scheduled before I brought up my concern. I didn't want him to feel ambushed or think I wasn't interested in him, but it was imperative we were on the same page. Sitting on the couch with pre-dinner cocktails, I broached the subject with him. It was one of the best conversations I had ever had. He understood where I was coming from, and he explained he thought it essential to find out if his son and I could get along before investing more time in developing our relationship.

Clay told me how deeply he hurt his wife by not being honest with her; he vowed never to be that guy again. It was after she became pregnant that he came out to her. She always suspected he was gay, and since they never intended to have children, it was something she felt she could live with. Fate had a different plan for their lives. They agreed to co-raise their son, and each moved on with their lives independently.

"I love my son and, in a way, still love my ex-wife. We fit somehow. It's not conventional, and neither of our families gets it, but it works. Most men are threatened by the arrangement and won't even consider having a relationship with me. This ask is a big risk for me. I really enjoy your company and how I feel when I am with you, but I need to take things slowly to see if it works."

It was my turn to reveal how I got to where I was in life and my concerns about another relationship. We concluded the road forward was full of potholes; we would avoid as many as possible by proceeding with our eyes wide open.

"As long as we are putting it all on the table, I need you to know that I am HIV positive. I hope that's not a deal-breaker. My son does not know; I don't want him to live a life concerned about how long his father has to live. I am healthy and care for myself, so until it's time to tell him, I choose not to."

"Thank you for telling me before we have sex. So, we will practice safe sex and do whatever is necessary to keep you healthy; for your and your family's sake."

On our way to the ghost hunt in Jefferson, TX, his son filled me in on his hopes of meeting a ghost and interacting with one. He was fifteen years old and was intrigued by the possibilities.

I held back from telling him what I had been through, with the exception of the story of Bob. This was a safe concept for a teenager; I didn't want to scare him. Clay was most appreciative that I kept it low-key.

I learned a lot from his son; he was very well-versed in his knowledge of the supernatural. We discussed various means of communication, unwanted attacks on the living and spiritual guidance for people, the differences between the two of them, and how each one might summon an entity. It was quite intellectually stimulating.

We arrived at the hotel on the main street in Jefferson, a beautiful old home that had been restored into a B&B. I was intrigued by the hamlet we had entered; very few modernizations had occurred since the 1950s. The townsfolk liked it that way, the history was what brought the tourist, but it was also what kept the spiritual encounters active.

Checking in, the owner began a quick historical rundown of the home. Clay and his son had been there numerous times; the information was well-instilled in their minds. While I was being educated, they offered to take the luggage to the room. I thought it odd we were sharing a room with his son, but it didn't seem to phase either one of them.

"The house was originally built by a man and his wife who migrated here from Europe." The owner reached for a photo album on a nearby shelf while continuing the history lesson.

"After being involved in an event which frightened him, the man and his wife left the South of France and headed for Texas. In agreement to make up for the upheaval in their lives, the husband built this beautiful home for his wife. They bore two sons; one remained here in Jefferson, the other moved out west."

Flipping through the pages of the one-hundred-plus-year-old book, a picture of the family appeared. Looking closely at the image and then back at me, she said, "My goodness, you are a ringer for Henry." I looked down to see what she meant, and there I stood in the photos. The name written in the book was "Henri De Lyon et Famille."

After I collected my thoughts, I responded. "I suppose I should; he was my great-great-grandfather."

"Well, why have you not visited us before now?"

"My mother didn't like to talk about her family. I know minimal history beyond them coming to the states and spreading out through Texas."

The hotel owner continued on, confirming the brothers parted ways after Henri passed. She shared stories of his involvement in moving enslaved people to freedom on his cargo boats and many of the ways he helped those less fortunate. Hearing these details about my family that I never knew was nice. During the revelations, Clay reappeared to find out what had happened to me. I quickly shared with him that he had been visiting my family home for years before we met. Smiling at us, the woman behind the counter said, "Perhaps this was all predetermined by the spirits."

We chuckled and continued listening to stories while flipping through the photographs. It was eery how much I resembled my great-great-grandfather and even odder how much my mother resembled his wife.

After twenty minutes of participation, Clay retrieved his son from our room. He sensed his son would enjoy the conversation based on his desire to meet a ghost.

The hotel owner asked, "Do you ever connect with the dead?"

I smiled, contemplating how to answer in front of Clay and his child. Forming my answer, the interior bell hanging on the front door clanged as people entered. Saved by the bell. Clay's friends, whom he met there every year, entered the lobby. This was the one time of the year each family could get away from their busy lives and spend time together.

Introductions and greetings were made. Clay's friends had decided to connect at Henri's before we walked to a nearby restaurant for dinner. Clay's son quickly revealed all the new information garnered that afternoon, as well as my relationship with the hotel. Clay's friends carried an unusual interest in Phenomena and were overly interested in EVPs, and apparition captures. Clay's son was anxious for me to share my story of Bob with them.

"You were about to answer me if you talked to the dead." The hotel owner interrupted the introductions wanting to know.

I deflected the question with a question. "Why do you ask?"

"Your ancestors had the gift, which is why this house is so active. Perhaps that is why the town is so active. It usually skips a generation, so by my calculations, you should have the gift."

"I have had encounters during periods of my life."

"Then expect to be visited by the ghosts of your family during your stay."

Clay and his friends, giddy with excitement, only agreed to go to dinner after I committed to telling them what I had experienced. Attempting not to pull focus on me, I shared small stories and events that had occurred through the years. This was Clay's trip with his friends; I didn't want to become the main attraction.

After moving on to the restaurant for dinner, the adults consumed three bottles of wine while laying out plans for the next three days' adventures. Antiquing and ghost tours were scheduled for each day before we would return home.

I was a little excited and somewhat trepidatious about the possibility of interacting with past relatives. This was something new for me; I had not been around people who invited the phenomena in. In all reality, they had not experienced what I had, so I was reasonably sure they wouldn't be so welcoming if they knew the perils to be had.

The room we shared with his son had two queen-sized beds in it. Clay and I took the one on the left, nearest the hallway, and his son on the right by the windows. Everyone performed their nightly rituals; I visited the bathroom last while Clay and his son engaged in their bedtime custom; they read to each other.

Settling into bed, the two men across from me finished the chapter they were reading and said their goodnights. Even though his son was fifteen, Clay ensured the bond between him and his son did not wane. He was an amazing dad. He treasured his son, but he also didn't allow for nonsense.

Snuggling up to me in the bed we shared, we struggled to find a comfortable position. This took a few minutes as it was the first time we had slept together. We traded off on being the big spoon and finally determined Clay's height made it easier for me to be the little spoon. I didn't mind at all. Finally situated and on my way to slumber, it began; the knocking, the pushing, and the impossible-to-ignore thumping of his hard-on against me. He whispered an "I'm sorry" to me, and we finally managed some sleep.

I slept soundly in his arms; the one thing I had not gotten used to about being alone was not having someone next to me at night. I still wasn't used to sleeping solo.

I woke during the night hearing pots and pans banging in the kitchen. Our room on the ground floor was located directly across the service area; I was quickly annoyed by the noise the staff was making. The irritation quickly diminished when the smell of French press coffee wafted across my nose. I peered behind me to find my companions were both still sound asleep.

Gently crawling from the bed, I found my slippers and moved towards the door. I was craving the coffee; the aroma was rich and slightly decadent. Exiting the room, I noticed the hallway was dark. The lights in the kitchen weren't on, and the only light casting shadows came from the nightlights on the stairwell leading to the second floor. The chime of the clock struck once, suggesting it was merely 1:00 A.M. I moved into the corridor so I could see the clock. The face on the clock showed 3:30.

I returned to my companion in bed, somewhat confused. Sleep came quickly after I was back in Clay's arms. The next thing I recalled was hearing Clay tell his son to be sure and wash his hands when he was done with the toilet.

Everyone was dressed and ready for a day of antiquing; we found our way to breakfast with friends and family. I was not even seated when the question was posed, asking if I had any experiences during the night.

I shared every detail of what happened the previous night; personal interactions were omitted, of course. Everyone was excited at the prospect of what else the day would bring; who knew what I might find in the antique store or on the ghost walk. The time ambling through the shops and chatting about life was very relaxing; it felt very natural to spend time with these people. They engaged me in their conversations, and my opinion was often requested.

After dinner and wine were consumed that evening, we began our ghost-hunting exploits. This was, simply put, a great show presented by a well-trained host leading people around the historic city. None of my paranormal senses were aroused during our tour of the centuries-old city. The suggestions of the supernatural arose a confident expectation in the group, which in itself, created a sense of anticipated surprise. I played along with the tour guide, not wanting to disappoint my mates. Three hours had passed when the tour arrived at our companions' hotel. It was a short walk back to my ancestral home, but not knowing how long they would chat, I excused myself to find the restroom. The gang stood talking while I hurriedly made my way to the toilets in their antebellum hotel lobby.

Finished relieving myself, I stopped at the sink to wash my hands. Reaching for the soap, a man exited the toilet stall right behind me. Dressed in period clothing, I assumed he was one of the tour guides. I finished washing my hands and reached for a towel to dry them. Looking up into the mirror, I realized he was nearly on top of me. I pardoned myself and stepped sideways, allowing him to reach the wash-basin. He smiled at me, and in a thick European accent, he said, "No need." He marched forward into the mirror and was gone.

Clay and his son were unaccompanied by his friends when I returned to the lobby. I told them what happened in the men's room; the story caused his son to shriek excitedly and run to the bathroom. He inspected every nook and cranny in the men's room. He really wanted to see an actual spirit. After his exploration ended in finding nothing, we went across the street and into our hotel room.

Once again, cuddled up next to my weekend companion, I slept through the night only to be awoken by Clay and a hot cappuccino. He had wandered down to the bakery with his son to let me sleep a little while extra. His son was in the shower when he woke me from my beauty sleep. He did this purposefully to give us a few minutes of alone time. His delivery of a moist kiss to my lips caused me to rise to the occasion. Patting the covers to hide any improprieties should the bathroom door open unexpectedly, he smiled at me. "I didn't want to tell you this in front of the others, but I found your ghost from the other night."

"What do you mean, found?"

"Hang on." He left the bedroom, and a few seconds later, I heard the pots and pans banging.

Grinning from ear to ear upon his reentry to the room, he said, "It was the ice machine on the other side of the wall." We laughed at the situation, and I was beginning to fall in love with him. The fact he told me in private and didn't embarrass me in front of newfound friends spoke volumes about who he was as a person.

At breakfast, the focus was on me once again; Clay's friends wanted to know what happened overnight. Smiling at him, I said to the group, "Actually, Clay has become the real ghost hunter."

I told them about the ice machine noises. We laughed until our stomachs ached. What a great time we were having, and no one had surprise bruises or other unexpected injuries. Midway through breakfast, Clay's son asked, "Dad, why did you keep pulling on my toes last night?"

"I never touched you last night."

"You got up to open the window, and then on your way back to bed, you pulled my toes."

"The windows are sealed shut. I noticed when I checked the locks before going to bed last night; he couldn't have opened the windows." I said, defending Clay.

"I swear he pulled my little toe each time he passed the bed."

"Clay, did you get out of bed last night? I didn't hear you if you did."

"I never moved. The windows were closed when we got up for coffee." Clay's son acknowledged he hadn't touched it, and I confirmed it was closed when we left for breakfast.

Back at the hotel and entering our room, the window was now ajar. The three of us stared at one another, not understanding. Heading out for the day's adventures, we were greeted by the hotel owner. "I trust the stay is satisfactory. Is everything good? Any surprises?"

Clay spoke up, "Just one thing, the window in our room was opened slightly this morning when we returned from breakfast."

"Oh, Henry always opens it when he has his morning smoke."

"I don't smoke, and I don't recall telling you my name was Henry."

"I was referring to Henry De Lyon. So you're the one that got the name?"

"What does that mean?" I didn't know what she meant about the name. I knew I carried the legacy name in the family but didn't understand the implications she was making.

She walked around the reception desk. Laying the linens she carried down on the marble countertop, she opened a small compartment in her desk. Retrieving a letter, she claimed it was found lying on the hotel lobby bureau around forty years ago. "We don't know who wrote this or how it arrived. My parents had purchased the home and were in the process of converting it when this was found sitting on that console by the front door."

She began to open the letter when the doorbell clanged, causing each of us to let loose a squeal. She asked if I wanted to read it privately or if she should read it out loud. Seeing Clay's friends had joined us, I implored her to read it aloud. Clay brought his friends up to date on the morning's events since breakfast. Eagerly, we all took a seat as the hotel owner began to read the letter.

"One day, a man will visit you. He will carry both his great-great-grandfather and grandfather's names, Henry. He will also carry their gift of communicating with those from another dimension. He will not be aware of his abilities or why fate has delivered him to this house. He will know the history of the De Lyons and why they crossed the sea to settle here. The evil our forefathers unleashed required a separation of kin. My husband and I will spend all our energy protecting the younger Henry, both in life and in death. Henry De Lyon's gift has passed on through his family lineage."

She pointed to me as she continued to read on. "The third Henry will live his life in danger from evils of the dark, nocturnal bruises will reveal the hands of Hades attempting to retrieve him four times. Three times he will be saved from the demons; the outcome of the fourth encounter is unknown." Looking up from the letter, she smiled at me. "There is no signature on it."

I reached for the letter to read it myself. Absorbing the words, I could sense everyone in the room staring at me. The hotel owner retreated to the desk where she stored the letter, closed the drawer, and said, "I am going to make tea and set up a tray of biscuits. I think Hank has more he wants to share."

The reference to tea and biscuits brought out a touch of an English accent. "Ma'am, is your family name Dench by chance?"

She didn't respond as she exited towards the kitchen.

Chapter 11

I held the letter tightly in my hand, recognizing the paper's texture and color; it was the same stationary paper at the Dench Hotel. Delving into every nuance, I was trying to make sense of it. When I turned the letter over, I found a clue; 1962 had been embossed in the lower left-hand corner. Apparently, the marks were incredibly faint from a very dull pencil and almost appeared to come and go at will.

It was the clinking of the teacups on the trolley that broke my trance. Tea and biscuits had arrived. "The date on the letter says 1962, is that when it was delivered?"

"I never noticed that before." A look of concern crossed the proprietor's face. Handing a cup of tea to me, she let her hand rest on mine before moving on to serve the other guests.

Pouring milk into her cup before adding her tea, she settled into a comfortable chair directly across from me; the hotel owner thoroughly observed the group before speaking. "This is my favorite chair."

Then she announced, "I have a gift too. I am a psychometrist."

Clay looked at his friends and shrugged his shoulders. His son concluded no one knew what the term meant, leading him to provide an oral lesson to the group. "She sees things when she touches a person; generally, it occurs when she is being compelled to reveal information the person needs to know."

"Very good, you are mostly correct." She said, agreeing with the young boy. "It's the compelling part I am not sure of; my experience has been the visions only occur when I ask a question of the person I am touching."

"Is that why you left your hand on mine when you served me the tea?"

"Tis indeed, you asked if my name was Dench, and yes, it is, but only by marriage. I married a distant relative of the Dench clan. My maiden name is Fox. Do you know anything about your family history?"

I shook my head no, it had never really been of any interest to me, and my mother rarely spoke about the past.

"Do you know when the De Lyons came to the US?" she queried.

"I believe it was around 1855."

"That is correct. Do you know anything about the Five Practices of supernatural phenomena?"

I acknowledged my lack of understanding with a head shake in the negative.

Clay's son gleefully interjected. "They are the practices established in 1800s Europe. The intent was to develop a science practicum around the two world's planes; the living and the dead. The practices were performed by five participants; Physician, Psychologist, Psychiatrist, Occultist, and Spiritist. Seances held by these groups attempted to communicate with the beyond; they intended to reveal knowledge to all mankind. Most practitioners were viewed as charlatans merely seeking money, but some appeared to have actual encounters with people not visibly in the room where the seance was being held."

Each member of the room, including the hotel owner, looked at Clay's son with great concern. We were not entirely sure if he was channeling a spirit or not. Realizing we were staring at him, he retaliated, "What? I like to read!" Confirming he was still just a fifteen-year-old boy with a slight obsession with the occult, everyone relaxed.

"He is right. The men who attended these meetings believed they could harness information from ancient worlds to help their causes. This would become a huge fascination for the Nazis. In Bordeaux, France, in 1854, five men gathered at the home of my husband's-grandfather. Each with a specialized practice they were developing. Letters between the group were uncovered in the 1930s detailing the seance that had been planned. It was the beginning of their quest to determine if their hypothesis was tangible."

"Only two people would live to reveal what occurred that night. They were the only men to leave the room alive. Servants found the other three men dead at a round table in the ballroom the following week. Interviews with the staff afterward revealed they had been on holiday; the owners were not due at Dench Chateau until the next week."

"The three men found dead were all strangled within seconds of each other. Details from the doctor who examined their corpses noted severe bruising on their torsos and extremities. The two men who escaped that night knew what happened; one would return to his home in Cambridge at Dench Manor. The other headed to Fontvieille, France. He immediately gathered his wife and son to begin their journey by train and boat leading them to Jefferson, Texas."

"We know these details from the journal kept by Viscount Andrew Dench. He clearly identifies each of the men who attended the seance, acknowledging their specialty within the five practices. His role was as Physician, and your great-great-grandfather was Spiritist."

Scratching my head, listening to this was overwhelming to me. I knew instinctively it all to be true.

She proceeded, "Something that didn't belong in this world crossed over that night. Viscount Dench made references to the evil spirits in his journals. He believed the demons followed him home. Many odd things happened through the years to the Dench family. As recently as the date on that letter."

My arm hair stood perpendicular to its follicle, indicating an event was about to occur. "What did you see when you touched my hand?"

"I saw a man who nearly died twice at the hands of nocturnal demons. The handprints on your back and legs indicated several spirits were present. I saw a man who saved you once and a woman who saved you another time. The woman was your mother; the man was your lover." Stillness consumed the room.

"What else did you see?"

"I have more to tell you about the Dench ancestry."

Unexpectedly, Clay's son interrupted. "Are you the daughter of Kathleen Fox, the Spiritist who was documented speaking to the dead in the 1920s? You look like a picture I saw of her in a book. A lot like her!"

"We share the same bloodline, and Thank You for thinking I am that old." After providing a touch of comic relief to the moment, her gaze returned to me.

"The Dench family dynasty recently ended; I fear something dangerous is about to happen to you."

"What are you referencing?" The trepidation in my voice was unmistakable.

"The empty chair at the family crypt. The chair you assumed was for you at the funeral in England was not for you; that is why you were directed to stand at the back of the crypt. The empty chair was intended for my husband." Lifting her cup of tea for a sip, she stared at me.

Clay and his friends had reached the pinnacle of being freaked out by this point. Listening to the hotel owner reveal things they had no way of knowing and my acknowledgment of it all overwhelmed them. I completely understood why it would. The energy in the room was palpable, filled with a charge seemingly ready to ignite.

Clay abruptly stood and spoke, "I need to take a break from this conversation. What do you all say we go have a cocktail and let the two of them continue? I don't think any of us need to know this."

Escorting them to the front door, I smiled at Clay and apologized for this unexpected turn of events. He did not respond as he reached for his son's hand while they moved beyond the door. Returning to my seat, I refilled my cup with cold tea. "Why would you have been there at the funeral?"

"My husband and Andrew's dad were fairly close; they spent most of their lives in close proximity. They were at Oxford together before he moved to the US. They were confidants in every way. Andrew's father hid a secret from his wife and child, and that is why he left."

"I know; his mother was Gert. He was taken away from her and raised by her parents shortly after his birth."

"How did you know that?" she queried.

"My mother told me."

"How did Norma know?"

"I am not sure exactly." It caught me off guard that she knew my mother's name. Thinking about it for a second, I reasoned mom's grandmother was a Fox; perhaps they crossed paths at a family reunion. If she, indeed, carried the Fox lineage as she claimed.

"Andy had a picture of Mom and Gert together. He and I were dating when the first brutal encounter happened; he is the lover you mentioned from your vision, the one who saved me."

"Yes, I know; I recognized him in the vision. He looks a lot like his father."

"He broke up with me after that, saying my family had something from the past that would break his dad's heart, and he couldn't risk me being the one to bring it up."

"He must be referring to your mom and Gert."

I raised my eyes to meet hers. "So much for keeping secrets."

"What you don't know is what happened to Gert after she announced her love for Norma at the wedding. Gert had been in and out of mental institutions throughout her life. During her periods of lucidity, she was released. She managed passage to the United States during a release period. The family could not force her to return without risking her psychosis becoming public knowledge. That is when Lily and Edgar moved over to take care of her. Her profession of love for Norma was all that was needed to remove her from the States. Arriving at the Dench Chateau, your grandfather met with Baron Dench in an attempt to exorcise the demon they believed to be consuming her."

Allowing time for me to absorb the information imparted, she stopped talking briefly.

"Viscount Dench's journals were passed on to his airs; they all knew what happened in 1854. Exact instructions for removal of the demon were written down, should it return. The Dench family reached out to your grandfather, requesting his help. Your grandfather was a spiritist, just as his grandfather was, and as are you. He agreed to meet with them; all involved were convinced Gert's demon could be sent to the realm it came from. The end result was they drove her to insanity. Her only psychosis, if you will, was to be in love with a woman. Gert didn't possess an evil demon until they altered her spirit. After the experimentation on her, they sent her to a sanitarium in the US where she was intended to remain until she died."

"Why was Andy shut out of the Dench fortune?" I was curious about her insight as she appeared so well-versed in the Dench family secrets.

"Andrew's dad found out about his mom when he was at Oxford. He confronted his parents/grandparents shortly after that. When all was revealed, he was given part of the family fortune as hush money. In a legal agreement to keep quiet about what he knew, a sizable fund was set up for him. The stipulation he never spoke of his mother to anyone allowed him to continue using his title even though he technically didn't have one. Soon after the agreement was complete, he moved to the United States. He was told she had died since he last saw her and was buried in Big Springs, Texas. We can only assume that is why he chose to come to Texas."

"Then why the lavish party for the funeral? I don't recall seeing you there."

"It was all a farce to minimize further questions about the Dench's ancestral line." She did not answer the second part of my query.

Quietly proceeding, she said, "There is some connection between our families on the spiritual level. Maybe some unresolved conflict from the past is why Andy and you keep coming back to each other."

My stomach began to rumble from the lack of food. Oddly enough, I had not been seeking comfort food through this intense revelation. "I need to get something to eat."

"I understand. But before you do, can I hold your hand for a moment?"

I leaned forward, my hand moving towards hers without cognition on my part. Her eyes closed while she held my hand; she looked to have entered REM sleep, her eyeballs very active behind her semi-closed lids. Slowly opening them, her pupils adjusted to the light in the room. She met my eyes full-on.

"You must cleanse the white clapboard house. Andy must accompany you to protect you from Gert. She can't hurt him. I will send you home with the information you need for this task. It is the only way for you and,,," She paused, searching for words, "for you to find peace."

The doorbell clanged just as she released my hand. Standing up and retrieving the teacups and saucers, she loaded the trolly, retreating to the kitchen. "We brought you some food. Thought you might be hungry." Clay placed the styrofoam container in front of me. "I am going to get him settled into bed. You eat, and I will be back."

The two new men in my life strolled down the hall towards the room. Without hesitation, I opened the container and began consuming the cold spaghetti and meat sauce. Closing the lid on the empty container, I tossed it onto the wooden table in front of where I sat, waiting for Clay to return.

Upon his entry to the room, his mood was easily read; I sensed the forthcoming conversation would be unpleasant. He leaned towards the coffee table, reaching for the empty container. Proceeding to find a trash bin, he was silent. Stretching my arms and legs, I waited for him to start the conversation.

I heard Clay close the trash bin and move toward me. I turned to let my eyes follow him; his walk was somber, and my instincts were right on target. When he sat across from me, I reached for his hands. He avoided my reach by sliding back into the chair. "He was asleep before we finished another chapter. I think he was tired."

"I hope he gets a good night's sleep. Don't be tugging on his toes." I was attempting to introduce some humor to the situation, but as had always been my misfortune, my joke didn't land well.

"This has always been fun and games: a nice little lark with the excuse to hang out with my friends. I never liked that he started digging into the various arts and sciences, if you will, of the afterlife. Hearing him outline the five practices and knowing who her parents were and what they were known for, it's all gone too far." Clay's tone was somber and slightly harsh.

"I understand."

"I am not sure you do. I can't afford to expose my son to what's going on in your life. At first, I found it interesting; well, I found you interesting, and this was just one of your quirks."

"Yes, we all have them," the disdain in my tone triggered Clay.

"What's that supposed to mean?"

"Just like your HIV is a quirk of yours that I would learn how to manage, this is my quirk."

"How dare you bring that up, and how dare you make that comparison."

"The comparison is that both of these things are outside influences and are a part of who we are. We didn't ask for them, and I am fairly confident neither of us wanted them. But they are ours. Like my therapist once told me, we all have our own little bag of shit we carry around with us, and no, it's not pretty and probably smells bad, but it's ours, and we have to learn how to manage it."

"I get your point, but it doesn't change the fact I don't want you exposing my child to any of this."

"You know, Clay, this is not what I expected from you. It's better this unfold now; hopefully, we will both recover from the hurt faster this way. I appreciate your commitment to your family; I am jealous of it since it's something I never had. I would never come between you and your son. How do you propose we manage the rest of the trip? Do you want me to get my things and go?"

"No. I will sleep in the other bed and tell everyone I had an unexpected call and have to get back to town. I will drop you off prior to taking him home. No big scenes needed, right?"

"If he asks about things you don't want him to know about, then what?"

"I'll steer the conversation to something else."

Agreeing to keep things civil even though we were both hurting, we headed to the room. Quietly slipping through the door and into our respective sleeping areas, I heard his son. "Dad, it's not his fault he is a sensitive."

Although I don't think he understood the impact of what he said to his dad, I smiled, knowing he had my back. Laying there, I pondered if the men I was named after had conjured spirits here to this very place.

The drive home the following morning was quiet. I sat in the back of the car, making the excuse I wanted to stretch out across the seat. I replayed last night's events with my distant relative from the evening before. It bothered me that she misspoke twice, and I wondered if I should have corrected her. My internal processor advised me to leave it be, but I couldn't help but wonder why she didn't mention Lily and Edgar's murders. Something else was off; if the fourth chair at the funeral was for her husband, why wasn't he occupying it? Where was she to observe I stood in the back?

Clay and his son were both relatively quiet for the two-and-one-half-hour drive home. Clay choosing not to make dialogue, and his son engrossed in reading the next part of his book.

We pulled into my driveway, and I exited with little fanfare. The trunk popped open via the remote button at the driver's seat. I retrieved my bag and gently closed the trunk with no emotion attached. As I walked towards the house, the passenger window rolled down as his son called out to me. "Don't forget your book. It was an interesting read."

"Where did that come from? I don't recall having that book."

"Mrs. Dench asked me to give it to you when we checked out."

Thanking him for the book, I took it and waved good-bye to them. Wishing them their best future life in my head, I watched them drive away. I raised the spine of the book to see what it was. After reading the title and author, I realized I had become so focused on another relationship ending that I forgot to follow up with my supposed distant relative on her recommendation. There in my hands was the book she had promised. "Cleansing a House" by Henri De Lyon.

Chapter 12

House Cleaning

Struggling to discern a clear path for the task clearly in front of me, I put the book away in a cupboard and went on to live my life. I had no reason to go back to Marsalis St; the white clapboard house could keep its unwelcome guest and remain empty of human life as far as I was concerned.

Not long after my trip to Jefferson, my mother passed away while she lay quietly in her bed at her home in Florida. Her exit further cemented my resolve to never return to the white clapboard house. The family gathering to mourn her was ruthless; within an hour of dirt being piled onto her coffin, the question was asked. Who was getting what?

Fortunately, my mother prepared a will to ensure there was no question of her wishes for dividing her estate. In a family of people who could benefit from some financial assistance, she split her assets evenly between her living children. A bank in Florida owned her home via a reverse mortgage; all that remained was the house on Marsalis St. and her personal effects. Her wishes were clear; each living child would receive an equal share of the profit from selling the white clapboard house. The family had great contention about this; thus, the battle of wills began as every child had an opinion.

As for me, based on my experiences in the house, I didn't want anything to do with it. Even my dad got in on the action saying he had been deprived of his share of the house when he divorced my mother. A judge quickly dismissed his claim leaving his children to pay additional fees assessed by attorneys.

When the annual taxes came due shortly after her demise, it was made clear the fees due were the responsibility of each child equally; it was quickly decided the property would be sold as soon as possible.

My oldest sister and I, the only siblings living nearby, were assigned the task of preparing the home for sale. Knowing her objections about entering the house, I agreed to have it cleaned and staged for marketing. The house's remodeling had been completed by the time I moved out, leaving only minor touch-ups to be done. Of course, the other cleaning needed to be completed, but I had not found the wherewithal to tackle that process.

I contracted a local real estate agent to get the process started. The siblings agreed upon a low market price in hopes the property would move quickly. A cleaning crew was brought in, and everything shined to sparkle by the time the For-Sale sign was posted in the front yard.

Over the next six months, numerous showings occurred; but not one offer materialized. Potential buyers stated they weren't comfortable in the house. I suspect it had something to do with the disclosures we were required by law to make. Lead paint, possible asbestos insulation, people dying there - multiple times. Apparently, these were issues most buyers weren't willing to overlook.

After several family discussions and heated arguments, it was agreed to reduce the sale price. The price per square foot was so low that there wasn't any reason for it not to sell. Then one afternoon, that all changed; I received a call from the realtor that he was canceling the contract due to having an unpleasant experience in the house. He never divulged what the experience was, but he was done and refused to represent the property. His network must have been far-reaching, for no matter whom I contacted, they declined to list the property; even trade flippers didn't show interest.

Managing the sale of the house and my angry family members, in conjunction with my increasing work responsibilities, was beginning to take a toll on me. The constant barrage of expectations every time my phone rang pushed me one step closer to the edge. One evening, while searching for a new bottle of gin at home, I unwittingly opened the cabinet where the book written by Henri De Lyon resided.

Along with removing the bottle from the cabinet, the book made its way to the countertop. With a fresh cocktail in hand, I began to read through the guide to spiritual house cleaning. In my inebriated state, the book appeared laid out precisely with basic steps one must do. The six G&Ts I consumed while perusing the pages did not convince me this was my responsibility; after all, no one in the family believed my stories. I had also been accused of making this all up so I could keep the house for myself; I could have cared less if the property ever sold.

After a night of fitful sleep, I returned to the book over coffee for a semi-sober review. Wondering if I should man up and take care of it, I decided to find another opinion. I recalled a woman I met when I lived with Jaime, a Curandera who owned a shop just north of downtown Fort Worth. I searched the internet for her number and made an appointment to discuss the past. Basically, I was looking to find some assurance I was doing the right thing.

Meeting with her, I outlined the house's activity and the advice given to me by my relative. The entire time I spoke, she kept repeating a prayer for me. After an hour of her time, she recommended I do the cleansing. "Energy is strong with you, but I cannot tell if it is strong enough to fight these spirits. But, my little güero, you must try, or this will haunt you for the rest of your life."

She left the table where we sat and moved through her shop, collecting the items required for the cleansing. I paid for the supplies with a credit card and thanked her for her time. I reached out to shake her hand goodbye. Taking my hand, she held it before smiling at me; she was doing a reading. "The light seeker will return to you and stay with you all the rest of your days."

With supplies in hand, I returned to the white clapboard house on Marsalis St. the very next day. In my possession was sage, a lighter, sea salt, and the book containing the prayer I was to read aloud. I initially moved past the white clapboard house towards the little house beyond it. Every nerve tingled, on high alert, as I scurried down the concrete walkway. Intent on retrieving a piece of paper from the book containing the red-eyed couple's photo, I entered the small dusty office. I don't know why it was important to me, but I felt it necessary to have the same parchment paper from England in my possession.

Before beginning the ritual, I copied the prayer (or spell, depending on your belief system) on the piece of paper I had torn from Lily's book. I had not seen the red-eyed couple since I returned to the house to prepare it for sale; I hoped I could still count on them for assistance.

The cleansing guide recommended carrying something on your body that belonged to a spirit with good intentions; the picture of Lily and Edgar was the only thing I could think of. Copying the prayer onto the parchment paper, I recited it several times before migrating towards the white clapboard house.

I managed my nerves and gathered my cleansing aids. With caution thrown to the wind, I began my exit from the little house. Turning towards the front door from Jaime's former office, my left foot kicked something on the floor. I heard it clink as it slid across the dark green tile. I felt obliged to scan the floor, searching for the mystery item. Finding it, I crossed the room and stopped just above it. I kneeled down on one knee reverently. I retrieved the pearl button from the floor and placed it in my pocket next to the picture. Three good luck charms in my possession; this was a good omen. It was a sign the red-eyed couple was nearby.

I entered through the back door of the small seven-room white clapboard house. Systematically moving room by room, I began the ritual. The process was the same for every room, a series of three steps repeated in every corner of the room. First, the Southwest corner, then the Southeast corner, and so on.

> **Step one:** Blow the smoke from the burning sage into the corner.
> **Step two:** Throw a handful of sea salt into the corner.
> **Step three:** Repeat the prayer of expulsion.

Starting with the family room and then the back bedroom where I had played as a child. After the new bathroom, once a bedroom, I moved to the kitchen and on through to the living room, followed up by the dining room. In every room, I repeated the steps. When all four corners had been addressed, I moved on to the next room. My adrenaline was pumping through my veins, my fear building with two rooms left. Nothing queer had occurred thus far, and I felt confident Monsieur De Lyon had provided excellent instructions for the task at hand.

I moved into the room where Gert supposedly killed herself. The same bathroom where my stepfather died, the space above the soil where Mom buried the letters from Gert. My anxiety increased as I stood at the door of this room. The air had become thick, making it challenging to capture a deep breath. My logic suggested it was all the sage I had inhaled; my senses implied otherwise.

Addressing each corner of the small bathroom, I began hearing the pushback from the other side: guttural noises and occasional nonsensical words spoken. Even with the noises, my emotions were in check; I focused on completing my mission. I allowed myself to hear them and be accessible to what they might be telling me; perhaps the reason I participated in these events would be revealed.

I began to blow the sage into the third corner; it went through the wall and disappeared as if no barrier existed. Previously, when the salt was launched into a corner, it fell to the floor while I uttered the spell; this time, there was no pinging of salt against the wall or on the floor; it was gone. I began the prayer as I backed out of the room. From my peripheral vision, I spotted the red-eyed couple in the hallway. This gave me the strength to continue and reason for concern as they had never ventured into the white clapboard house before.

Moving into the hallway, I completed the last corner of the bathroom. I turned towards the front bedroom; I began to move down the hallway to the room of the first attack. Taking a breath and looking for some courage, I heard my dead brother's voice. His speech was not labored by his large tongue as it had been when he was alive. Dressed in the grey sweatpants and purple shirt he always wore when he was alive, he appeared and spoke, "She is not happy with you."

I went back in time to when he said that exact same thing years before. I approached the door to my parent's former bedroom, arriving at its threshold; my brother stood there looking at me. His face was sad, "Please go before she hurts you."

Not sure if it was really him or not; I just stared. I felt the red-eyed couple pass by me as they took him by the hands and led him away. I watched as they disappeared through the wall to some beyond I could not view. Now it was only me.

Standing in the middle of the room, I treated the Southwest corner. I blew the sage's smoke into the second corner, and while reaching for the salt, the smoke blew back past me. I lifted the salt, preparing to hurl it into the corner with all my strength. My arm propelled forward as fast as possible to ensure the salt fully launched. As my hand full of salt passed my ear, my arm rounding forward, my entire body was pelted with salt rebounding from the previous room. The force of the dried saline pierced my clothes, tearing my skin. Blood began to trickle from the abrasions, the burning sensation of the salt bringing tears to my eyes.

I began shouting the prayer as loud as I could. "In the name of all that is holy, all that is within Christ, you are commanded to leave this plane. With all that belongs to God and of this world, I command you to return to your realm."

While screaming the prayer, I could feel them grabbing me. They would not yield. My legs gave way to the tugs at my ankles, the force knocking me off balance and pushing me forward. Falling towards the Southeast corner of the room, my knees cracked out loud as I landed solidly on the hardwood floor.

The room was growing dark, a fog enveloping the area around me. I continued shouting out the prayer. My voice became more substantial and prominent; the room filled with prayer as salt pinged my body in tandem with the burning sage filling my lungs. I knew this feeling taking over my body; I had felt it before. My soul was leaving my human form.

I pushed myself up from the floor, leaning back against my ankles, my body growing weaker by the second. I felt the cold enveloping me, voices calling out my name. Amid the darkness, I caught sight of a small orb growing larger in front of me. The last thing I saw were five individual points of light extending out and surrounding me.

The next memory I would make would be of a man sitting across from me, an identical twin looking back at me. The only difference was his facial hair and period clothes.

"Henri, réveiller pour moi s'il te plaît."

"What?"

"Votre arrière arrière grand-père est ici."

"I..., where am I?"

My great-great-grandfather was now with me. "My child, you are in between planes right now. You will return soon."

"Are you Henri De Lyon?"

"Oui. You must not give up. You must return and finish the fight. But you can only win with your light
seeker; he must be with you to finish this."

"My light seeker? What does that mean?"

"It will become clear in time, mon petit-fils. Take the
letters far away from here; he must not get them."

"What letters? What are you talking about?"

Suddenly, all was quiet. Then a very faint beeping
noise began. A radio alarm or microwave sounding
its bell, I thought.

"Hank, relax; I'm here with you."

The repetitive chirp became louder every few seconds. The darkness began to fade back to light as I
searched for Henri.

"How's Henry doing today?" I smelled the familiar
tea rose and sandalwood; I knew I was safe once
again.

"He is recovering slowly, but I think we are on the
right track." Opening my eyes, I saw a white coat
worn over scrubs at the end of the bed. A doctor was

reviewing my chart and speaking with Mrs. Dench. "Oh look, I think I see his eyes opening."

The doctor immediately moved beside the bed and began assessing my pupils as my eyes adjusted to the light. "I do believe they are. How are you, my love? I have missed you."

Looking around and gathering my thoughts, I realized I was in a hospital ICU room. The chirp I was hearing was from a monitor conveying vital statistics to a nurses' station somewhere nearby. "What am I doing here? Andy, is that really you?"

"Yes, it is. Just relax. You are in pretty bad shape. What is the last thing you remember?"

Shaking my head from side to side, I said, "A bright light with five people, I'm not sure."

"EMTs think you might have been involved in an attempted carjacking? Do you remember anyone attacking you?"

"I was being..., I was at my mom's house."

"Well, that seems to make some sense."

Andy took my hand to comfort me as I attempted to get up from the hospital bed. "Rest and try not to move much. You were found in your car, severely beaten, and holding a picture."

I shifted my focus from Andy to his mother. "Mrs. Dench, nice to see you, but what are you doing here? The last time I saw you was in Cambridge."

"Yes, it was. When you are better, we will visit and catch up on things."

"Such as telling me why you left without saying a word? I mean, thank you for all the beautiful gifts, but..., and how did you wind up being my physician?" My responses to them were rude, not from meanness but out of confusion about where I was and why they were there.

"I am not your doctor. I came by to check on you before my rounds, and look; you woke up."

"What Andrew is not saying is that he has been here with you every moment he hasn't been with his patients."

I began to cry a little out of pain, both physical and emotional. "I am so confused."

Andy reached across the bed and pressed the call button. "Nurse, Mr. Notenburg is awake; he appears to be in pain. Contact his doctor and request a sedative?" Dropping his hand from the call button, he laid it on my chest. Smiling at me, he brought me up to speed as to why I was in the hospital. "I am so glad you made it back to me."

I shifted my glance from Andy to his mother, not knowing how she would respond to what her son had said. Her smile was genuine and heartfelt. "Let's get you well, and then we can talk through this. There is a lot you don't know."

"I may know more than you realize; maybe that's why I was knocked around so bad."

Both Andy and his mother shifted their stance, glaring at each other before turning back to me.

"Perhaps you do." Andy retrieved a notebook sitting on the window seal. "Do you recognize this?"

He pulled a picture from within the book and held it up for me to see. It was a photo of him with me in European clothing circa 1850. Included in the photo were three other men, each of them dressed from the same era. I knew every man in that photo, my mind reeling from trying to discern where the picture would have come from.

"This was in your hands when the EMTs collected you. Even as badly beaten as you were, they couldn't get you to release it. Once you were sedated, they still were not able to pry from your hands. With the medication flowing into your IV, you startled one of the techs. She said you grabbed her hand and gave precise instructions before releasing it. 'Deliver this to Dr. Andrew Dench; he will know what happened to me.' Making my rounds that morning, the ER director paged me to report to emergency immediately. When I arrived, I saw you on the gurney; I remembered the last time I saw you, black and blue like this. The director handed me the photo and told me what you said."

Just as Andy finished telling me where the picture had come from, the door of the room opened. A physician and his aide entered the room and began checking my stats, inundating me with medically focused questions.

Andy excused himself from being in the way and joined his mother, who had already exited the room. I saw Mrs. Dench wave to me as they walked down the corridor.

"Dr. Dench said you wanted a sedative. Do you?"

"I think so. I am in a lot of pain; maybe sleep would be good." A solution injected into my IV allowed me to slumber, just as I had requested.

Chapter 13

Waking the next time, no one was around; one machine beeped a rhythmic ping repeatedly. During my time spent resting, my physical being recovered; this was my personal assessment due to the lack of machines connected to my body. It seemed as if all my organs were functioning without mechanical assistance.

Vaguely recalling the state of affairs from the last time I was awake, I quickly scanned my arms and noted the bruises were all gone. I lifted my gown at the neck; looking down my torso, the skin appeared perfectly healthy. I couldn't help but wonder how long I had been asleep. I reached for the call button while raising the bed. I needed to know where I was and what was going on. An aide walking past the door saw me moving around and poked her head into the room. "Glad to see you are awake."

In her delightful islander accent, she followed with, "You have been our mystery child. We started to call you Snow White, waiting for you to wake up."

I tried to smile. "How long have I been out of it?"

"Six days. You just hold tight; let me find your nurse and let her know you are coherent."

"Thank you." I scanned the room; it was barren except for one set of red roses on a shelf. I had no way of knowing who they were from. Attempting to move from the bed to find out, I quickly discovered I could not move my lower extremities. While moving blankets and sheets around to investigate, I was interrupted.

"Hello, Mr. Notenburg. I am Dr. Kim. I have been observing you during your stay with us. How are you feeling today?"

"I am a little groggy and am definitely hungry."

"That is an excellent sign. You are a mystery to us, Mr. Notenburg; we have never had a patient heal from extensive bruising like yours in six days. Do you have any recollection of what happened to you or where the bruising came from?"

"Dr. Kim, I do, but you would most likely send me to the psych ward if I told you."

Dr. Kim looked at me while raising his brows; my senses suggested I allow vagueness to be my guide. "I am messing with you, Dr. Kim. I don't have a clue. I was at my mom's house, and then I woke up in the ICU." Smiling at the doctor, attempting to be as convincing as possible, I asked, "Why can't I move my legs? Is there something wrong?"

"No, you are strapped down and catheterized. We will get someone to come and remove it. It doesn't appear you still need it."

"Thank you so very much. Do you know how I can find Dr. Dench?"

"We will call him and let him know you are awake. I am sure he will come as quick as he can."

The young doctor smiled at me and shook his head, confused I was not able to provide any insight into the recent events. Dr. Kim gave the nurse orders to unhinge me from my devices. "We will run a few additional tests, and if all is normal, you can leave today."

"I would like that."

The nurse began the luxurious job of removing my catheter and collecting samples needed for the required tests. I would have preferred Andy stay away about three minutes longer than he did. Even though I was thrilled to see him, I would not have elected for him to see the tube being retracted from my penis. There was nothing private about me any longer where he was concerned. "It is so good to see you awake! How are you? Ready to go home?"

"Yes, definitely. But first, I need to say something."

The nurse took the hint this needed to be a private conversation; she quickly gathered her tools and samples. Leaving the room, she closed the door on her way out.

"I am enjoying the attention and the way you look at me, but I have to be honest with you. I am slightly surprised by the behavior when we haven't crossed paths since your dad's funeral."

The closed door did not stop staff from entering the room and moving around us, making it impossible for Andy and I to have the conversation I felt I deserved. A bag removed from the locked closet just beyond my bed contained my phone, wallet, and the clothes I last wore. Being weak from the lack of actual nutrition, I handed my phone to Andy. "Would you turn that on for me? I am sure work is going nuts, wondering where I am."

"All is under control. Your office was contacted and notified that you had been in an accident and would be in touch as soon as possible."

"How do you know?"

"Because you were a good boy and had your emergency information on your phone. I notified your attorney, and she quickly put everything in order. I am curious why your attorney is listed as your next of kin?"

"It is far more productive to have a non-emotional attorney manage my life than an overwrought sibling with ulterior motives."

"I get ya. But what about...?"

"There is no one else. I assume you already knew that, or why would you have called me 'love'?"

A tray of food arrived and was placed in front of me; next to Andy, I don't think I was ever so happy to see something. With the delivery of the food came a message from Dr. Kim. I was told once I ate and drank some liquids, if I could pee on my own, I could leave. Several glasses of watered-down iced tea were consumed, and even though it burned like hell from the irritation caused by the catheter, I peed into a urinal for the nurse.

Andy begged pardon from the room; he said he needed to complete his rounds before taking me home. While the paperwork for my release was prepared and reviewed with me, Andy focused on his patients. With the nurse's assistance, I dressed in my torn clothes before being wheeled down to the registration desk. Fees for services rendered required my attention before I would be allowed to leave.

The young man working the toll booth, as I like to call it, did some clicking on his computer. He then looked at me and said, "You got some damn good insurance, girl; that will be $100.00."

I retrieved my credit card from my wallet. Handing it to him through the glass porthole, I looked him square in the eye, "Are you assuming I am gay, or is that how you talk to all your guests?"

Pursing his lips revealed a perfectly applied gloss. The fluorescent light bouncing off them subtly, he spoke, "I didn't mean to offend; my respect if I did. But you should know everyone in this hospital knows who you are." Spinning his chair to his monitor, he smiled and gathered all the documents together to process my payment. Returning his attention to me, he asked me to sign the paper receipt.

"Why would everyone here know me?"

Without even a pause or the chance to discern whether or not he should respond, he said, "Child, there has never been a man that Dr. Dench has been so attentive to. And trust me, everyone in this hospital has tried, myself included. So when you showed up in the ER carrying a picture of the two of you together and him spending every free minute night and day next to your bed, well, child, people took notice and began to talk."

I quickly became aware I was being ogled by almost everyone inside and outside the glass partition. I leaned into the porthole and motioned for the young man on the other side to come close. "And you let me leave my room wearing the same dirty ass clothes I showed up in. I am going to get you."

He processed me for about thirty seconds; we then both let out a well-deserved laugh. I wasn't prepared for this, from absolute chaos to having the man I loved since the first year of college next to me. My mind was on overload.

Exiting through the sliding glass doors, there he was. Andy was standing by a car door, holding it open for me. Knowing everyone was watching didn't seem to phase him; I perceived he was making a statement. I moved from the wheelchair to the passenger's seat, and he closed the door. Sliding his long legs into the driver's bay and closing his door, he buckled his seatbelt and looked at me.

"I have your address in the GPS, but if I should go a different way, just let me know."

"Oh, yeah." Speaking my revelation, "You would have found my address on my driver's license. Do you know where my car is?"

"It's at your house; I had it towed there and left in the driveway. I didn't think it was a good idea to leave it on Marsalis St. I lied to the tow truck company, telling them I was you. I don't think they really cared as long as they got paid; they didn't appear overly concerned."

Entering the highway, I was reminded of the younger Andy and his need for speed. Pedal shifters were put to use; we were zooming toward my home. Passing the neighborhood containing the white clapboard house, I asked him to provide an answer to the question I asked earlier.

"How about we get you home and settled? Then we can talk. I am not on call this evening; perhaps we can have some wine and review the last few decades."

Deciding it was best to have him focus on driving so I didn't wind up back in the ICU, I relaxed in the heated seat, taking a moment to observe everything around me. Across town, we sped while I ogled the boy who had become a man. In my mind's eye, when I thought of him, he was still mid twenty's.

I pulled my phone from my lovely plastic hospital bag and began going through messages. In the few days I had been away from work, approximately a week, I had well over 500 emails accompanied by 32 voicemails. The unread text count was surprisingly large as well. It made my heart swell knowing so many had reached out to me while I was in dispose.

My mood quickly shifted as I began listening to the voicemails. The calls were related to work and people wanting answers. At first, I thought my attorney must not have reached my colleagues at the office; then voicemail number five started with a "Sorry to hear you aren't well, but when you get a chance..." The text messages were all the same, little blurbs to get better soon and to call or text about... I was incredibly hurt that my well-being meant nothing more to these people beyond how I could serve their needs. "Welcome to corporate America," I said softly.

"Are you okay? What's wrong?"

"Just a dose of reality."

Seeing the desired freeway exit a short distance ahead, I directed Andy to take it. I would guide him through the back streets to avoid the heavy rush hour traffic. Parking next to my car in the drive, we migrated towards the house. I had developed the bad habit of not keeping house keys on my person. I requested Andy open the garage door from the remote inside my car. In my current state, I forgot about the front door and its coded entry lock.

Finally, inside, I moved towards my bedroom. "I'd give you a tour, but I'd really like to use my own toilet."

Andy chuckled while watching me shuffle down the hallway and turn into my bedroom. "Make yourself comfortable; there's plenty to drink in the bar refrigerator." I didn't need the bathroom; I needed time to let my feelings out due to my colleagues' lack of concern. After twenty minutes of alone time, a knock on the door reminded me Andy was still in the house. "Be right out."

"Just checking; it's the doctor in me."

Moving from the water closet, I headed to the shower, asking if he minded me having a rinse. In reality, it didn't matter whether he cared or not; I needed to wash the lingering hospital odor off my limbs and from my crevices. All clean and in my pajama bottoms, I walked into the family room, heading for the couch. I was surprisingly weak; the journey home, followed by a shower, had utilized the bulk of my energy cells. Crossing the hardwood floors, I felt like a man many years my senior. Falling onto the sofa, I took a deep sigh and gave thanks for being home.

Andy came from the kitchen with a tray full of snack food. A delightful platter of cheeses, grapes, crackers, and, more importantly, a glass of wine. He placed it on the ottoman in front of the couch; it was then I noticed he was in cotton joggers and a t-shirt, both of which fitted him in a very flattering way. He noticed me ogling him, causing him to comment on his attire,

"My after-gym clothes; I always have a set in my bag in the car."

"Handsome. Why only one glass?"

"You need to hydrate before you drink any alcohol."

"I think you know what I have been through this past week. I deserve a glass or two, don't you think."

"I tell you what, you drink these two bottles of mineral water, and I will get you a glass of wine."

I kind of liked him taking control of the situation. Having spent the last several years of my life taking care of everyone else with little repayment, I needed this.

"So what happened in Fort Worth? A repeat of the first time?" he asked.

"Hold up, my questions first."

He responded while reaching for the glass of wine, "Fair enough." Settled in across from me, he pulled my legs up and across his. "First off, thanks for being at Dad's funeral. It meant so much to both my mother and me. I am sorry we left without saying goodbye, but there was a reason. Let me see how to have this makes sense. Nearing the end of my residency, I began drinking significantly. Dad and I were not getting along; I was dealing with the HIV crisis in the hospitals, and the two men I loved were gone. I let you go freshman year, and then Marcus died from complications due to HIV. Every day it felt as if another piece of my life was being altered, and I wasn't handling any of it very well. All this piled up on me, pushing me to cope with life via the vodka bottle."

Andy ingested some wine; I wondered if his drinking was going to be a problem.

"I saw you at The Lumber Company one night just after Marcus died. I was going to talk to you, but I saw you with someone else. You appeared happy, and I didn't want to risk ruining that for you, so I chose to turn and walk away. I found out through some friends that you and Jaime lived together. I resigned myself to the fact you and I were not meant to be."

Andy stopped talking for a moment. It appeared he was attempting to control his emotions.

"I continued to drink heavily, even on the job. It was horrible. I had all these secrets, and I didn't know how to manage them, so I just stayed drunk. The day you called Mom to ask if I was okay was the morning after I wrapped my car around a tree. Mother lied to you about all being well with me; they weren't sure I would live after the accident; she said she saw no reason to upset you until they knew if I would make it or not."

"That's the night I saw you in a vision. You were completely dressed in white; you were attempting to speak to me."

"They worked on me for twelve minutes at the crash site before getting me back. I don't recall any of it. After recovering from the wreck and starting therapy, I slowly began to find myself. During this time, Dad opened up to me about his birth mother. The sister disowned for being gay was actually his mother."

"Gert? I know." I blurted her name out without hesitation.

"How did you know?"

"Let's come back to that." I was intent on our staying focused on him for the moment.

"My dad finally told me his reasons for walking away from his family. After his sister and brother-in-law were killed, he said he felt his grandparents had betrayed him. Taking him away from his mother was cruel; he opted out. A financial arrangement was made that required his silence. He was legally bound never to speak about any of it, especially his mother. Mom and Dad agreed it was for the best they start over again."

Andy continued sharing details regarding Mr. Dench's original plan to settle here. "He talked about the summer he spent in Fort Worth with his sisters, well, really his mom and aunt, how much he enjoyed being around them."

"His plan included moving his mother from the sanitarium to live with him and my mom. With his mom gone from the sanitarium and his aunt and uncle killed before he made it to Texas, he opted to focus on a new life. He confided in me his assumption was his mom murdered Lily and Edgar. When I discovered the connection between your mother and my aunt/grandmother, I was afraid my dad would find out about his mom. That is why I had to let you go; I needed to protect him. When he revealed he already knew all of this, I realized my decision had been all wrong."

"I am with you up to that point. But, okay, hmmm, why did you leave me after the funeral?"

"Walking up to the hotel with your arm in mine, my heart melted. I was so sad to have lost my dad, but then, you and I spent time together; I was so confused. Mother saw it too. She knew you were with someone and told me to make a choice. Either confess my love for you or leave. I didn't know you and Jaime had broken up until we were back stateside. At that point, I thought it best to leave you alone and let you mend."

I sat there with him for a while without responding; he kept his eye on me, waiting for a reaction.

"I think I get it." I stood and steadied myself on the arm of the sofa, "I have finished both bottles of water. I am going to pee, and when I come back, I expect there to be another glass containing wine sitting right there."

Returning to my perch, I was happy to see a glass of Cabernet breathing, its legs waiting to be swirled and reviewed. Receiving a full-bodied sampling of wine on my palate, I savored every drop as it passed into my esophagus. I took a deep breath and began to walk Andy through the past years of my life. The letters discovered with Jaime, the second attack, mother's confession about her involvement in the murders, the warning about four attacks; finally, we were all caught up to date. "It's late, and I am tired. Do you mind if I go to bed?"

"Not at all, and as a doctor, I am going to recommend someone stay and keep watch on you tonight."

"I am assuming that someone would be you."

He smiled at me and confirmed yes with a nod. "I have to be at the hospital early in the morning and need to leave by six. I will just pull the door closed behind me when I leave."

"If you ever leave my side again without kissing me first, I will never forgive you."

"So let it be written, so let it be done."

He tucked me into bed and kissed me on the forehead before stretching out on the settee in the bedroom sitting area.

"Why don't you sleep here, next to me?"

"For medical reasons, I don't want to be responsible for you becoming erect as it will be quite uncomfortable for you, well, for both of us. I also don't want to get too comfortable and sleep past time for work."

Settled into my bed and looking across the room at him, I began to wind down. Random thoughts were invading my mind while lying there. I wondered if Clay's son had understood the implications of this all being predetermined. Was there a grand design encircling us, keeping each other close by to resolve the greater issue? Why did I recognize the men in the photo?

Moving towards sleep, at the juncture between asleep and awake, when our senses are crossing both realms, the men in the orb on Marsalis St revealed themselves. The men who kept me from moving into the next life were the same men at the round table in the chateau. The very ones who connected two worlds, two worlds none of us could have possibly prepared for.

Feeling his lips touch mine, I jerked my head away and screamed. In my deep sleep, I had forgotten Andy was there and his commitment to kiss me goodbye.

"You made me promise not to leave without a kiss."

"I did, and thank you. When will I see you?"

"I am on call for the next three days. I will text you when I can. Call me if anything urgent comes up. I will be back here as soon as I can. I am not letting you go again."

"Please don't; my heart couldn't bear the loss." I heard the front door close, and the deadbolt turn. I looked at the dresser and noticed he had taken my keys; it was an attempt to make sure I stayed home and rested. Working the covers back around me, I quickly fell back asleep. I remained there until the one slit of sunshine poking its way into my room forced me to face consciousness.

Managing to pull myself out of bed, I pushed through my morning routine. Opening the refrigerator, I wondered when he had managed to grocery shop and fill the shelves. Anything I could have possibly need-ed was there. Pushing the coffee grinds to the bottom of the carafe; the French press coffee was ready. After adding creamer to my coffee cup, I passed through the back door to sit on the stone landing. I had a lot of decisions to make; Andy, Work, Andy, mom's house.

I felt a cool breeze blow up and over the bluff, refreshing me. Feeling the air move across me, I thought of Bob and Audrey. I hope they were content in their afterlife, whatever that looked like. It occurred to me that Andy was my Bob; he had waited until the time was right for me to join him. Finishing the delightful cup of coffee, I moved back inside to the comforts of my home.

I saw the picture of the five men from 1853 sitting on the kitchen counter. I perched myself on a stool at the counter and began intently studying it. Remembering my cognition when falling asleep, I stared intently at the men. It was then that I recognized all of them.

The three men who didn't leave the chateau that night were still very active, along with Viscount Dench and Henri De Lyon. It was their essence, their beings, that pushed the spirits back that night on Marsalis St. It was the five of them who took me to my car.

What was my connection to these men? Why were they still fighting against my unknown enemy? I

reached into the kitchen junk drawer for the magnifying glass. After removing a series of useless inane
objects, it appeared. I held it over the photo to study
every part of the sepia-toned paper.

Using the kitchen pendant as a backlight, I searched
for highlights in the background. It was then that I
saw him. A man standing directly behind Viscount
Dench in a dark corner appeared to be a servant.

There were others in the chateau that fateful night.

Chapter 14

The Butler Did It

Andy's time at the hospital kept him busy. We stayed in touch via text whenever he was available; the responses were often slow due to his caseload. I felt confident he wasn't avoiding me this time.

Per the doctor's orders, I remained at home and rested the entire day. I spent most of the time mentally working through the concerns on my mind. As my therapist had recommended, I made a Ben Franklin list to drill into the root of the situation. My list of pros and cons was quickly weighted on the con side; I needed to remove myself from my current place of employment, the white clapboard house, and place my focus on the future.

The time invested in my career had been quite fruitful; I now owned shares in the company and was financially very well set. I had no debt; my home and car were free from obligation. My paycheck paid for day-to-day expenses and a few pleasantries. Thinking through it all, I decided to schedule a leave of absence for medical reasons and spend some time assessing possibilities for what my life could look like. I risked losing the company stock as it was reserved for active executives; I was willing to take the risk.

The risk was minimal from my perspective; if I were deemed ineligible to hold the stock due to a leave of absence, I would receive payment at the current market value. I could survive financially if push came to shove.

I sent emails outlining my intentions, including a meeting invite to discuss my time off. I knew this was the best thing for me. There would be no more juggling kittens in my life.

Andy called during his dinner break; his real intent was to ensure I was resting and caring for myself. We chatted about nothing while he ate his meal. It was as if we were back on the steps of the quad, preparing for the next class.

He finally confessed to taking my keys, claiming he wanted access to the house should I not be responsive to his calls or texts. I reminded him there weren't any door keys on the ring; he reminded me that I had shown him where the door opener was in the car, and he had the keys to the vehicle.

I thought that was sweet and not entirely true. His phone buzzed, causing him to quickly say goodbye and head off to his next challenge at the hospital. I spent my evening relaxing, eating, and watching a movie. I texted him good night after I settled into bed and was asleep before his response arrived.

I looked up from my pillow when that nasty slit of light hit my face again; the clock on my phone showed 9:30 AM. I had slept for nearly twelve hours. I had severely depleted my body's resources with the continuous push over the years; committing to focus on myself had opened a window allowing the stress to float off into the distance.

While gnawing on a bagel and cream cheese at the kitchen counter, I continued searching the picture for clues; I found nothing. I grabbed a piece of paper to lay out the unexplained events beginning when I was five years old, moving through the phenomena I was searching for the missing piece. The thread that tied it all together.

I created another list starting with the obvious person this was all related to, which was Gert.

Gert & Norma

They had a connection: one was in love with the other.

Andy & Hank

Hopefully, interconnected, but definitely involved in it all.

Gert & Norma
Grandmother/Mother
Andy & Hank

It hit me; his grandmother and my mother were involved, and now he and I were involved. This had to do with our lineage.

Viscount Dench & Henri De Lyon

As I reviewed the list, it was now obvious I was on to something; I knew it. I needed more information; I needed to know details about their involvement. They were English, and we were French; how would they have connected in the 1800s? Was there any history further back between the two lines; what about my grandfather and his great-grandfather? The hotel owner's wife claimed they knew each other; she claimed they were the reason Gert went mad. How and why had they known each other? The only place I could think to start was with the Dench family journals.

I had until Monday evening to do what I was being compelled to do. Andy would be tied up with work until then; he didn't need to know what I was up to just yet. I was sure he wouldn't have wanted me to do it and would have asked me not to go. As much as I opposed the forgiveness versus permission argument, I willingly used it in my favor. I had to remain mindful of returning home before Andy left work. I had to be on the road back from Jefferson no later than 2:00 PM Monday.

The parts of my family I personally knew did not have connections with the extended De Lyon family. The Fox cousin who had married a member of the Dench family was my only hope for discovering what our forefathers had started that night long ago.

After a refreshing shower, I brushed my teeth, combed my hair, dressed, and retrieved the spare car keys from the safe. I moved slowly across the garage towards my car, still parked in the driveway; I quickly realized I was still weak from recent events. Settled into the front seat, I pushed the button to start the car, followed by the one to close the garage door.

Jefferson was reasonably quiet for a Sunday afternoon. I parked my car in the paved lot behind the hotel and began my approach to the establishment. Walking towards the front door, I noticed a man in a wheelchair watching me from inside the building once owned by my ancestors. I recalled never meeting the hotel owner's husband; she spoke about him in the present tense, so I assumed he was still alive and that was him in the window.

Another link in the chain, if her husband was of Dench lineage and she was of the De Lyon bloodline, it was another connection.

The door to the hotel was open when I reached it; I looked in prior to entering and offered a you-hoo.

"Hello there, Henry. Come in, come in."

My distant cousin was rolling a trolley with its tea and biscuits into the parlor. "Do sit; we were expecting you."

"Why were you expecting me?" The suspicion in my voice caused her to look up at me and smile.

"My husband saw you park out back and walk around."

"Ohhhhhh." I was caught off guard by a proper English tea prepared that quickly. Calming myself mentally, I noted the time and realized she was probably preparing the afternoon tea anyway.

"I hope I am not disturbing you, but am in hopes you might be able to provide some more information. You know, what we discussed, Viscount Dench and Monsieur De Lyon."

"You would like to see the journals, wouldn't you."

I was a bit unnerved by the fact she was ahead of me regarding my intent. I had not been able to completely make out the man in the wheelchair, but something about him was familiar, oddly familiar.

"I am going to take tea to my husband and retrieve the journals."

I prepared my cup of tea, and upon returning the teapot to the tray on the table, I noticed a text message from Andy.

"Everything okay with you?"

"All is good. How's your day?"

"Fine, weird vibe about you. All okay?"

"Yep. Hugs."

I laid my phone down and wondered what he meant by a weird vibe.

The journals were delivered as promised, my host sitting directly beside me opened them, and we began to peruse them page by page. She would not let me hold them or turn the pages, which I found to be quite odd. I tried a couple of times to turn a page back to a previous section; reacting quickly, she gently patted my hand away. "These are fragile."

Subtle nuances were coming to my attention. Dates in the books went back further than the seances in the Dench Chateau. Entries were made in both French and English.

"Was it common for a Royal to write his notes in two languages during this period, I wonder." I was bating my docent with the books to see what she wasn't telling me.

"I am not sure. I don't speak or read French, and not sure what they contain."

That statement alarmed me; I was becoming concerned for my safety. One requirement in my family had been absolute; elders were adamant each of us was taught to speak and write French at a minimum of a first-grade level. There were very few things my mother shared about her family, but this one ideology was deeply instilled in her.

"I wish I had learned at least a little bit." My comment appeared to relax my host; we continued on with our review of the parchment paper notebooks. I asked if there were any pictures we could look at. I wanted to compare the photo I had with the one they had.

"There are some in a box; let me go get them." Collecting the journals, she left the room to fulfill my request. She made it clear the books would not be examined without her being present. Grabbing my phone, I found several missed text messages.

"I am really freaking out that you are not responding. Answer me!"

"I'm here. What's the matter?"

"Something is not right, I don't know what it is, but I can feel something is off."

"Are you at home and safe?"

His text unnerved me slightly.

> "Not at home and questionable
>> as to safe."

"Hank! Call me now!"

I touched the phone icon on my phone to do as ordered, just as my host returned empty-handed.

"I don't know where they are. Stay for dinner, and I will see if I can find them."

Andy acknowledging his concern for me gave me pause; I decided to decline her offer and get out of there. "Thank you so very much for the offer, but I must be going. I need to get back home to prepare for another busy week."

Collecting my things, I slightly stumbled when getting up from the cushion I occupied. I quickly recovered and started towards the door.

"We were surprised to see you so soon after your hospital stay." The smile she wore was smug.

"Thank you so much for spending your afternoon with me. It's been enlightening." It was inconceivable that she or anyone else in Jefferson would have known about my recent visit to the hospital. I was on to something, but it was far more derelict than I initially thought. I remembered her being a psychometrist and didn't believe the tenth of a second that she slapped my hand would have given her that information. Something else was going on.

She opened the door and reached out to take my hand. I pulled my digits back. "Those hospital germs - just in case, wouldn't want to get you or your husband sick."

I moved as quickly as my weak legs would allow without appearing to run to my car. Passing by the windows, I peered inside as far as I could manage; I saw him looking back at me from his wheelchair. Her hand was on his shoulder as they each waved good-bye.

I pulled out of the drive and onto the main road, accelerating excessively to put as much distance as possible between the family home and me. Flying down the road and beyond Jefferson's City limits, my cell phone rang with an unhappy Andy on the other end.

"I can't take care of you if you don't do as I ask."

"You are absolutely correct. I am sorry."
"Where are you, and are you okay?"

"I think so. Yes, I am fine. I am headed home."

"Okay. Text me when you are home. Yes?"

"Are you still having weird feelings about me?"

"Broad question; No, I don't have any weird feelings about you. Yes, I am still concerned about your safety, but the intensity is lessening." The concern in his voice was nice to hear, although I never meant to cause him to worry.

"Glad to hear on both accounts! I will let you know when I am home. Although it will be a couple of hours. I am in East Texas."

"I am not sure I want to know."

"I will explain it soon." Hearing his name being paged in the background, I said, "Get back to work. When will I get to see you?"

"See you tomorrow evening." Blowing a kiss through the phone, he disconnected.

All the way home, the man in the wheelchair kept popping into my head. It was a face I had seen, but I could not place him.

Pulling into my garage and extracting myself from the car, my body told me I had been a bad boy and overexerted myself. I closed the garage door and entered the house, hoping I would find something yummy in the refrigerator for dinner. Walking through the laundry room from the garage, I heard the front doorbell sound. Opening the door, I found my neighbor standing there with a fresh plate of pasta, which literally had my name on it. "I won't stay. Saw you pull in the garage and thought you might want to eat."

"Juliette, you are so sweet!"

"My pleasure, and when you feel better, I want to hear about the handsome man I saw leaving."

"Absolutely, and I might even introduce the two of you." I took the plate, promising to return it clean. I closed the entrance door and moved toward my comfy spot on the couch.

I retrieved the list I had begun to compile earlier; the details gathered during my excursion were added. Below the list of people tied to each other somehow, another list was forming. I surmised that if I wrote it all out, perhaps the pieces would somehow fall into place. The man in the wheelchair kept popping into my head. I knew we had connected at some point in time. But when and why? It was not coming to me.

One key takeaway from the journal was that all the entries didn't belong to Viscount Dench. The information written in French was another man's penmanship. The styles were similar but not exact.

My remedial reading in French proved to be somewhat helpful as I managed just enough insight to know they were comparing notes on tests that were being conducted, theories tested by trialing their methods. In the 1800s, this approach would be very forward in its thinking. Generally, colleagues kept their information contained until they had a reliable result.

So why would these two men be comparing tests and outcomes? What would they gain from different methods being applied to one standard? Then the lightbulb illuminated.

The Five Practices; they were testing their theories based on their individual skill sets. The other man in the notebook was Henri De Lyon: Physician and Spiritist comparing notes on their goal. The journals must have traveled back and forth between the two men comparing notes. But when did the other men come in? Where were their journals?

Going over my time spent with my supposed cousin, I couldn't get it out of my head; the comment made about my recovery. I replayed how she swatted my hand away from the book; it was as if she wanted to control what I saw. Thinking I wasn't able to discern the foreign writing, she moved slower on those pages. She and the husband in the wheelchair were hiding something. I had no proof, but I didn't believe she was related to me in the way she suggested; if she was my relative, why had she claimed she couldn't speak French?

The mystery letter with no signature had supposedly been left at the hotel. She claimed she hadn't noticed the date, odd considering she knew every other detail. It was written to suggest it was from Lily and Edgar, the red-eyed couple. Did she know I had connected with the red-eyed couple on numerous occasions? I asked more questions than I had answers to, but I was obliged to chase this mobocracy of sorts to an end.

I put the paper and pen down out of frustration; I was getting nowhere, and the list was vexing me. Time to relax in front of the TV and wind down was my response to the irritation. A freshly opened bottle of Merlot was on the bar to aerate while I moved to the kitchen to clean up my dinner dishes.

Standing at the kitchen sink, washing my plate for its trip home to the neighbor's house, I found recognition in the picture I had not noticed before.

The man standing behind Viscount Dench was the man in the wheelchair. The man in Jefferson was Carlton, the butler.

Chapter 15

Unintentional Harm

I was asleep when Andy arrived at my place. I suspected he would show up sooner than he planned, so I texted him the front door lock code. My intention for him to access the house was not well thought out; I did not have the foresight to include the alarm code. Awoken by the short beeps from the house alarm, I called out, "1972."

"What's 1972?"

"The alarm code."

Shortly after the noise stopped, the handsome doctor entered my bedroom. "How did you know it was me?"

"An assumption; I didn't hear any glass breaking or doors being kicked in, so it stood to reason in my groggy state; it was you. I would have rethought my assumption if you had not responded when I called the alarm code. What are you doing here? You said it would be tomorrow night before I would see you."

"I got a colleague to cover for me. I needed to check on you. Don't know why I just can't shake this eery feeling I have."

"I can probably answer that question." Propping myself up on the pillows, I told him about the trip to Jefferson and my working through our families' entanglements over the last 200 years. At times he laughed and thought it outrageous; other times, he was speechless. Each time he would chuckle at something I brought up, I would remind him of our encounter on Marsalis St. and the bruises recently found on me. Holding on to the main point until the end, I asked, "How long was Carlton in service to your family?"

He quietly thought for a moment before responding. "I really don't know. He was with my dad since he was a child. He relocated to the States when my parents did. Why?"

I asked him to retrieve the photo from the other room along with the magnifying glass. Holding the picture up to the lamp to fully evaluate the man, he concurred the man behind Viscount Dench looked exactly like Carlton.

We argued the facts of how much we looked like our great-great-grandfathers and how Carlton must have been a descendant of the man in the photo. It was not uncommon for servants' families to continue on with lives of service, so that was plausible. The issue at hand was the realization that even though we highly resembled the men in the photos, the minute differences suggested a relationship existed but eliminated the notion of exact duplication.

The photo of the man hiding in the shadows didn't appear to be similar; he looked exactly the same as Carlton did the day I met him. We finally determined we were drawing conclusions based on memories. He hadn't seen Carlton since his father passed away, and I hadn't laid eyes upon him since the first year of college.

"As a physician, I will say it is improbable they are the same man. He would be close to 200 years old by now."

"Against my better judgment, I am going to say that we have to go and ask him."

"Let's check with Mom and see what she knows. It's too late to call her tonight; let's catch up with her tomorrow. She has a tennis lesson at the club in the morning; let's connect with her over lunch."

In agreement with the plan, Andy slipped off his clothes and crawled into bed next to me. College was the last time I had been in his arms, and even then, we were clothed. This new sensation of his bare flesh touching mine was exhilarating; furthermore, the fact that we had never engaged in sexual activities made this all the more exciting. I laid my right hand on his. Entwining my fingers with his, I pulled him close to me. Two middle-aged men going back in time to feel like teenagers.

"What kind of guy do you think I am?" he said as he began to kiss the back of my neck. Smiling to myself, I replied, "The kind that knows waiting a little longer will only enhance what we feel for each other."

"Yep," was all he responded with before falling asleep.

Andy woke and was out of bed before me. He kissed me before heading out for a morning run. I heard the front door close, which prompted me to find my way to the kitchen for that required morning cup of coffee. I didn't expect to see the French press filled, waiting for me to extract it. What a great cup of coffee it was!

Back from his run, he showered and threw his scrubs back on. "We need to stop by my place for me to change clothes. It's on the way."

We pulled into the building's drive in the center of downtown Fort Worth. No sooner than I could ask if I should wait, the valet opened my car door.

"Come on up; no reason for you to sit in the car. Besides, I have something I want you to see."

"You could have shown that to me last night."

He just smiled and gave me a little wink before giving directions to the valet to hold the car upfront; we would return shortly. The towers' front doors parted as we approached; the elevator closing behind us, up we went. Even though I was certainly not poor, I had forgotten how Andy was raised and all the luxuries he still enjoyed.

Ascending to his floor within a second, or so it seemed, the elevator gently stopped. Voila, we were in his apartment without pesky hallways or neighbors to engage with on the ride up or down. Just through the elevator doors, his home awaited him.

"This is way more space than I need; hell, I am hardly ever here. When the building was renovated from a bank tower to condos, Mom and Dad bought this as an investment. Mother said it had never appreciated enough to sell, and when Dad passed, she decided to sign it over to me."

I observed the three-hundred-sixty-degree view and thought to myself, "Fuck, he has the entire floor!" Andy disappeared, leaving me to roam the apartment, where I internally critiqued the decorating. I made my way around the single-floor mansion, taking in each and every nuance of the furnishings. The art collection was impressive; seeing the pieces reminded me of time spent at the Kimball Museum during our freshman year. "What was it you wanted to show me?" I called out through the vastness, assuming he could hear me. He replied via text.

"You'll know it when you see it."

Continuing through the rooms, I found what he was talking about. On the wall in front of me, perfectly placed between two exterior windows, was a Toulouse-Lautrec: Jane Avril on the Moulin Rouge. I had fallen in love with her on one of our art outings and made such a fuss he kissed me to stop me from talking.

"I hoped you'd remember. It isn't the original but is one of 342 serigraphs he signed." Andy pointed to the pencil signature in the bottom right corner.

"How could I not remember? You kissed me right there in the museum, standing in front of the painting. Then you said you wanted to make a moment that would be etched in my mind forever."

"And I was right. You still carry that memory."

"Your apartment is beautiful, very well appointed."

"Mom did it. She put her focus on this after Dad passed, and well, I am sure you recall she doesn't do anything halfway. And speaking of Mom, we had better go."

The valet closed my car door, and off to the country club we went. Lunch was ordered along with a pitcher of gin martinis. Andy declined the liquor and ordered an iced tea, acknowledging he was driving. I was happy to hear the accident had proven a lesson for him.

"Mom, do you know how many years Carlton was in service with the family?"

"What an odd question. I am not sure. He was with your father since birth, so I assume he worked for the family prior to that."

"Have you spoken to him since he retired?"

"I haven't. He and I didn't really gel. I didn't like having live-in servants, but somehow he managed to convince your dad to stay with us when we came over."

The young waiter returned to the table with a slender pitcher filled to the brim. The glass of iced tea was delivered as well. The server provided extra attention to Andy upon its delivery. I didn't blame him; Andy was a well-known doctor who was openly gay and single. That said, I was not above tripping the young man or pushing him down the stairs if he didn't exercise some restraint.

"Dear boy, my son is here with his boyfriend; please don't be so obvious in your flirtations." She winked at me as the embarrassed waiter toddled off.

"Mother, I hate it when you do that."

"You would think you would be used to me by now, my love." After raising her glass to signify a toast, she took a drink of her gin. "Now, back to Carlton, why the questions?"

Andy looked at me, indicating I should go into the history of events leading us to this point in time. "It appears that our families have known each other for a couple of centuries. In the photo of Viscount Dench and my great-great-grandfather together at Dench Chateau, dated 1853, there is a man in the background who strongly resembles Carlton. I wondered if his family had served the Dench's for an era or two."

Over her martini glass, she pivoted her eyes from Andy to me. "Is your family name De Lyon?"

"Yes, ma'am, it is."

Tipping her glass up to let the last drop pass her lips, she pensively called out, "Waiter, I am going to need another pitcher of these, please. So the stories your father told are true. And let me guess, the picture you have is of the seance that was conducted, where three of the men died."

"Mom, how do you know about this?"

"Your father, God rest his soul, and Carlton had endless discussions about that night and what the men were attempting to do. Carlton was quite well-versed on the topic and overly preoccupied with the ins and outs of it. When your father died, and Carlton decided to leave our service, he took some books that were written by Viscount Dench. He had not asked for them, and I confronted him about it when I discovered they were missing from your dad's study. He claimed he had no clue what I was referring to."

"Black bound books, fading parchment paper, and handwritten notes in English and French?" I interjected.

"How do you know that?" she queried.

I pointed to the pitcher of martinis and asked if I might have a refill before responding. She didn't wait for the waiter to return; she leaned forward to fill my glass with her eyes fixed on mine.

"His supposed wife showed them to me."

Sliding back into her chair, she pursed her lips. Slowly but with purpose, she exhaled while blowing a sigh across them. "May I ask where you were?"

"Absolutely, but may I first ask if you know where Carlton went when he retired?"

"He moved to a large home in Jefferson, Texas. I believe it's a B&B. I am guessing that is where you saw the books."

I confirmed with a nod and brought Mrs. Dench up to date on the house belonging to my ancestors and Carlton's wife, my supposed distant cousin. Lunch was served while we continued to dissect the implications.

"Andy, how do you remember Carlton?"

"Well, Mom, he was always kind to me. He made sure I had everything I needed. He behaved on the border of inappropriate for a servant but nothing egregious."

"When you were born, he took to you like you were a fine wine. He never treated anyone else as well as you, not even your father. I always thought it was odd, but your father disagreed. I was so thankful when he left that I didn't make a fuss about the books. I was just happy to have him gone from the house. He totally creeped me out."

Into our third round of martinis, Mrs. Dench was becoming very vocal. "And what was even odder, the man didn't seem to age until you were born. While at your father's funeral, I found some old pictures at Dench Manor, photos of Carlton with your father. Based on the date written on the back of them, your dad would have been 8 or 9. Carlton looked to be around thirty, which would have made him well into his eighties by the time your dad died."

The last of the martinis consumed, Andy escorted his mom to her car and sent her home. He was very specific with her driver that they were not to stop anywhere on the way, no matter what she requested.

Work at the hospital the following month was brutal on Andy. While he toiled away healing those he could, I spent my days figuring out who I wanted to be when I grew up. I refused to answer emails or join conference calls for work. In my mind, I was on medical leave with no paycheck coming in; I was clearly within my rights to ignore them.

I received the news via certified letter; my company had been sold. My shares were to be paid in full at their current valuation prior to the close of the sale. With a little due diligence on my part, it proved reasonable that I walk away. Deciding my focus would be on investments going forward, I deemed it a decent way to live.

In our free time together, Andy and I delved into getting to know each other. The most difficult challenge we faced was why the toilet seat was not put down after one of us peed. We had opposing views that were deeply embedded in our core values; somehow, we managed a path forward.

Expecting Andy to arrive around 7:00 PM one evening, I was busy preparing Coq Au Vin when the doorbell rang. Turning the cooktop to low, I ran through the dining room to open the door. The outline through the front door's bubbled glass resembled Juliette; I was hoping she hadn't smelled the amazing aroma from my kitchen. "Please don't be coming to bum a plate," I thought to myself.

Bounding up to the door, I pulled it open; it was not Juliette. A half-smile greeted me, along with a request to come in.

"I am in the middle of cooking dinner, and Andy isn't here, but please come on in."

"I apologize for my verbal parade at the club last time we saw each other. I hope I didn't say anything too offensive."

"Not at all; you were just very relaxed with the words that flowed across your lips."

"Oh, good, listen, I came to see you about the information you brought up regarding Carlton and the family. It caught me off-guard. I hoped the legends were put to bed and out of my life." She opened her

Gucci bag and retrieved a small parcel before handing it to me.

"This is one of the journals from Viscount Dench's library. No one knew this existed except my husband. I don't know why he hid it; my sense is it contains something he was afraid of people knowing. He did not even share its contents with Carlton. I have to believe Carlton didn't know about it, or it would have disappeared as well. I am not sure I want to know what is going on with these books, but my instinct tells me you need this. My husband predicted one day, you would come back into our lives and would be able to put a stop to the chaos; I have hope that he was right. When Andy called and said you were in the ICU, the same hospital where he worked, I knew what my husband had been telling me was true." As she continued to speak, I guided her across the threshold and into the foyer.

"Four books were compiled prior to the seance in 1854. Each participant brought his own notes relating to his practice, except for Dench and De Lyon. Carlton has the physician and spiritist journal, the book yours and Andy's great-great-grandfathers co-wrote. The other book he took was from a psychologist. This is the journal from Andre-Pamphyle-Hyppolite Rech, the psychiatrist. My late husband claimed to not know where the occultist's book was, but I think he did. I believe his mother had it. Andrew should not know this came from me. He will think I am hiding information from him. There was more to his father's leaving England than his dad wanted him to know, and I would like to leave it that way."

While she was delivering her request for silence, I heard the recognizable sound of Andy's car pulling into the driveway. Guiding her towards the kitchen, I said, "Andy is coming up the drive; thank you for the book and the information. Stay and have dinner; I will say I invited you."

Entering the kitchen, Andy peered around the room, searching for his mother. "Mom? What are you doing here?"

"Hello, Andrew."

Interrupting to avoid him asking any more questions, "Family dinner night. Would you be a dear and decant some wine while I finish setting the table."

Andy was very astute; I assumed he noticed only two place settings were on the counter when he arrived. I would explain it all to him later. I was not going to grow this relationship on lies and misleading information. I would deliver the book to him and tell him the truth after his mother left.

After food and drink were consumed, I requested Mrs. Dench play piano while I cleaned up. "I would adore hearing the piano; music in the house is so important. And as I recall, you play beautifully."

She agreed to a concertina before leaving. I assumed Andy would not begin asking a bunch of questions while his mother was still there. The short interlude gave me time to wrap my head around what she had said. I was deeply concerned about what Andy's dad was hiding from him; what was it he never told his son?

With the dishwasher loaded, I opened another bottle of wine and joined the Dench duo in the living room for a drink and conversation. It remained very light-hearted, which was a welcome relief from the past.

Saying goodbye to his mom and requesting a text when she arrived safely home, Andy and I retreated to the family room. I reached for the remote to activate the television; Andy intercepted it and said he would rather we have some quiet time together. Retrieving the wine decanter from the counter, I filled our glasses and gave him a kiss.

"Thank you for having Mom over; that was a nice surprise to have both of you without other interruptions."

"I am glad she joined us for dinner, but it's not really that clean-cut." Crossing to the mantle where I had laid the book earlier, I slowly handed the book his mother had delivered to Andy. I explained she dropped by to deliver it, not expecting to run into him.

"Apparently, there are some issues from your family's past that your mother would like to leave there. She doesn't want you to think she is hiding anything from you and feels nothing good will come of you knowing. Before you even ask, she didn't tell me a thing. Let's give her this and let her enjoy her years in happy times like we had tonight."

Lying in bed later that evening, we found comfort in each other's arms allowing Andy to release a huge sigh. "It is difficult for me to understand what my father would want to keep a secret from me. Before his death, we were finally getting along. I never doubted his love for me, and I knew he had some real shit go down at Dench Manor; what else could there have been to hide?"

"Mind you, I am just hypothesizing, but I think your dad was doing his best to protect you. He was trying to keep you safe and out of harm's way."

Laying quietly before he finally responded, "I think we need to go see Carlton. I think he knows what is happening and hopefully can help us resolve it."

“What if he is the cause?”

“At least we will finally know. Come what may?”

“Come what may,” I replied.

Chapter 16

Spirits Who Hide

Carlton sat in his wheelchair, staring at the small journal. He looked through the pages, clearly seeking something specific. Closing the book after inspection, he quietly assessed us before beginning to speak. "I didn't begin to age until the day you were born, Andrew. I was frozen in time at age 31."

"How old are you?" Andy inquired.

"One-hundred-eighty-four."

"That's not humanly possible."

"Andrew, human is the key to the mystery herein. The exterior body is human, the soul inside is torn between worlds."

Almost without notice, the exit door quietly slid its deadbolt into the frame. Then, without a sound, she appeared beside him, smiling, "You need not be afraid." Her figure morphed into transparency as she moved away from his side. She reappeared, comfortably sitting in her favorite chair.

"Your great-great-grandfathers are the reason I am stuck here in between dimensions, half in this body, half out. As the manservant to Viscount Dench during his trials with Monsieur De Lyon, I was keenly aware of their goal to communicate with the non-living. The five men at Dench Chateau managed to open a gateway between the realms, allowing each dimension to touch the other. They opened an entryway to the living that should have never been disturbed. Their practices were designed in hopes of opening communications with the dead; they never intended to actualize them."

Carlton shifted his aging body in his wheelchair. "Five spirits entered the room that night, each one brought forth by a man at that table. As with the living, souls on the other side can be good or evil. They can be mischievous, mean, or funny; their characteristics are as varied as any person you might meet in this world. Not understanding what they were attempting, they summoned spirits that were random imps. Viscount Dench and Monsieur De Lyon quickly realized the danger of what they had done. They witnessed their three friends rising upward, suspended in the air without rope or wire, their life source being forcibly drained from within them."

His wife once again appeared beside him without warning, adjusting his blanket while he spoke. "Monsieur De Lyon reacted using his gift of communicating with spirits; he began commanding them back through the portal. His commands were unsuccessful, just as yours were during your attempted cleansing; each spirit refused to go. Viscount Dench and Monsieur De Lyon, fearing for their own lives, fled from the home, unaware I had been observing them in the background. Neither man had any knowledge of my reading their journal. The book they shared moved back and forth between their homes. They did not concern themselves with me as it was assumed I was an inept, uneducated servant, unable to read, much less understand a foreign language. They believed their manuscript was safe from interpretation."

Looking directly at me, he continued, "Just like you lied about knowing another language Hank, I pretended to be incapable of understanding their correspondence. On my travels between their homes, I cultivated their notes over each journey. Crafting my plan while quietly waiting in the background. Another spirit was summoned that night, an entity for myself. I wasn't prepared for the price I would pay for inviting it."

Andy was unbelievably calm during this revelation. He sat ever so still on his perch with no emotion displayed as the old man spoke. "I have been searching for all the books in hopes I might recreate the seance and release my lost soul to its appropriate dimension. Be it heaven or hell, travel to the other side, allowing this mobile corpse to die and finally find my hereafter. With this book, we are one step closer."

Goose pimples rose on my arms; I began to feel that familiar chill in the air. The cold that had accompanied past events. "You said, 'our,' what do you mean by that?" I asked.

Andy followed with, "What does this have to do with Hank or me?"

"Hank is a spiritist, just like his ancestors. I need his ability to speak to the phantasms to open the gateway. It appears you are unaware of the power your great-great-grandfather bestowed upon you; Andrew, my boy, you are a light seeker. Your universal power of love and single consciousness is needed as the catalyst to reopen the portal."

I looked towards his wife, who had once more faded into oblivion, before asking, "Carlton, what were you trying to achieve by reaching out to the dead?"

"I was the bastard brother of Viscount Dench, sired by a servant who impregnated our mother. Had she not died during my birth, she and I would have been sent away from the manor with nothing to own but shame. Her passing left me abandoned, thus avoiding questions within the household; it was decided I would be raised in servanthood at Dench Manor."

"I carried my mother's royal blood just as your great-great-grandfather but was degraded into servitude. My mother never disclosed who she was engaging with sexually before I was born; I assume it was the man who raised me as we were very much in favor of one another's appearance."

The chill in the room continued; the sun shining through the windows did little to warm me. "Why are there four souls trying to take me to the other side?" I blurted out without pause.

Andy was once again silent, his warm hand reaching for mine ever so gently.

"You have the ability to unlock the passage and send them to their hell. The two of you hold the bloodlines that allowed the dimensions to be crossed; your alignment can resolve this for all. Should I not rid this body of its spiritual parasite before becoming a corpse, I will be stuck here forever to roam this place. I want to be free. I have witnessed enough tragedy; I want to live in the dimension my wife is in. A world where we can be together, not blocked by this withering body."

I felt Andy's hand release mine as he turned to Carlton. "Was my grandmother haunted by one of the spirits from the seance?"

"She was. Born into the Dench dynasty with a connection to evil, she was drawn to follow their guidance. Your great-grandfather knew she wasn't pure from the day she was born. As soon as it was realistic to do so, she was sent away. Your great aunt Lily refused to see her as evil; she did all she could to help Gert, even to the point of moving here to the States to try and save her. She hoped the child your grandmother produced would cure the evil; alas, it was not your father who would make the difference."

Carlton told Andrew how Lily arranged for the baby to travel to Dench Manor from the institution where Gert had given birth. He would be raised at the manor where Carlton would spend his life serving him. "The hope was by keeping your father away from his mother, he would stay safe. Historically the gifts of light and communication skipped a generation leaving your father without multi-dimensional cognition, leaving him helpless to deal with his mother's spectral attachment."

Andy learned his father ran away in 1957, traveling to Texas to visit his sisters. Finding a letter of Lily's involvement in his arriving at Dench Manor was the catalyst prompting his departure. Making the passage to Texas to see his sisters, he was unaware of their true relationship. "Your father hoped Lily would shed light on who his birth parents were. All Lily would tell him is that his mother had been raped by a man who worked at the facility where she lived. Your father noticed other oddities during his visit to Fort Worth; the interactions between Lily and Gert were unfriendly. They were not the loving sisters portrayed by his parents. Upon his visit to Gert, something transpired that began his search for the journals."

Andy sat quietly, absorbing the information shared.

"Your dad wouldn't discover Gert was his mother until several years later when he was at Oxford. He found detailed notes regarding her exorcism, which included a reference to a child born in 1942 in an institution."

While watching Andy absorb what Carlton was saying, I quietly interjected, "I assume he chose to confront his grandparents after the discovery of Gert being his mom?".

Carlton nodded, "Taking the journals from Dench Manor before exiting the UK, he felt he could expel the demon holding his mother captive. What he didn't understand is that he lacked the paranormal gift necessary to complete his quest, as well as the information required from within the final book. Alas, it would not matter; by the time he arrived, Gert was already dead." Carlton suddenly spun his chair, looking at me. "You know where they are, don't you?"

I did, I knew exactly what he wanted, and I knew exactly where it was. "Was it happenstance that my mother met Andy's grandmother, or was it a supernatural necessity?"

"You know the answer to that as well. You can talk to the invisible beings around us; ask them if you want confirmation."

Irritated by his response, I turned to Andy, who was now deep in a trance, staring off into the distance, disconnected from the room. I followed his gaze out the window to the man standing in the street. "Andy, is your dad speaking to you?"

"No, he is just there. He is trying to tell me something, but he can't."

Carlton laughed, "Hank, tell him what his dad is trying to communicate."

Not knowing if I was being pulled into a manipulation Carlton was instigating, I said, "He is letting you know he is nearby to protect you, and he believes in you and is proud of you."

Carlton turned his chair towards the window; Andy was released from his trance, the entity no longer visible. The spirit gone from the street, Carlton continued, "Two very odd things happened the year you were born; first was me finding the journals in your dad's possession, and the second was the release of the spell keeping me young."

He pointed to me while muttering, "I have read the journals from cover to cover, and nothing was revealed until you showed up. Meeting you in the pool house that day, I immediately recognized you as a descendant of Henri De Lyons. Believing fate sent you, I combed through the books once more. That was when I found what I had missed previously. I discovered it was the pairing of you two that could open the inter-dimensional gate."

"I believe it is time for Andy and me to go."

"I think you should stay with us for a little longer. There is much more to tell you." His smug voice floating across the air enraged me. I don't recall moving my feet, but there I was, looking directly into his eyes.

"You don't have any power over us, and as I see it, you need us to relieve you of this aging body. You said you didn't want to be stuck here; you need the other item and our assistance to leave your rotting body."

The staring contest betwixt us continued until the door behind us unlocked and slowly opened. There she was again, his wife and hotel proprietor, visible and holding the door open for us.

Walking towards the car, Andy requested that I drive back to Fort Worth. He needed time to take in what Carlton had said. The hours passed slowly for me while Andy sat very quietly in the passenger seat. As we neared the exit to my house, he requested we proceed on to his place instead. I remained on the freeway continuing towards his condo; he remained very quiet until we were safely ensconced in his home. "I needed to feel the safety of my dad; that's why I wanted to come here. His personal effects here give me the sense he is close by and protecting me. I find it very comforting to feel him near me. Do you think my dad is stuck here too?"

I slowly formed my response; I wanted to comfort him and speak honestly. "I believe he is watching over you and is not stuck in one place or the other. I think he is in the first heaven. He can connect with you when you need him, and when you no longer do, he will move to the next level of enlightenment. I think he is just watching out for his wonderful son."

"Thank you for that." He stretched out his arms and motioned for me to join him on the sofa. Knowing he was very emotional, I took him in my arms and let him be. His head on my abdomen, he said, "Carlton implied my grandmother wants to hurt you. Do you think that is true?"

"I don't know that I believe Carlton is right. I do, however, know where the other information is. It has the key needed to verbalize the portal opening. If she does want to stop us, it is because she fears leaving this realm. Perhaps she fears a level of hell she hasn't known and is doing her best to keep me away from the information."

After sitting in silence together and watching the sunset on the horizon, he asked, "Is she tied to the white clapboard house."

"She remains there, as does your great aunt and uncle, but completely by choice."

Andy pulled away from my holding him and looked at me, questioning what I meant.

"Your great aunt and uncle stay to protect me while Gert stays to protect herself."

"I am sorry, but I am not following you."

"Your grandmother is staying there to protect the last book; I am just not exactly sure why."

"If all the others have been recovered, why do you think this one hasn't been found yet?"

"Gert disassembled it while she was in the sanitarium. I need to go to Marsalis St. to retrieve them."

"Them? I'm confused."

"The information you found about my mom taking your grandmother out of the sanitarium before your aunt and uncle were murdered ties this all together somehow. It seems like it is a part of Gert's plan."

"She knew she didn't have to worry about leaving this realm after she died if no one could compile the books. To add an extra level of protection, she took the pages from the book and mailed them to my mother individually. She reasoned Norma wouldn't open them and would most likely destroy them, leaving the remaining details scattered to the wind. But my mom cared enough for Gert that she kept every one of them. She attempted to destroy them a few years ago by torching them; I stood by her and watched them burn, only to have them reappear in the little house. The letters are somehow protected, even from Gert."

"I am not following you," Andy said in desperation.

Over a bottle of Rosé, I brought him up to speed, revealing what had happened with Jaime. "Do you think Jaime was being controlled?"

"I think he had his own kind of lunacy, but I am willing to believe anything is possible now."

"So what do we do? It's not safe for you to go back to the white clapboard house."

I had recently discovered something else I did not share with him but knew he needed to know. Proposing some dinner and a little more wine, I managed additional time to determine how to tell him. We took the elevator down to the street and made our way to one of the wonderful restaurants in the city square. Settling at a table for two, I ordered another bottle of Rosé and summoned my courage. Before I could start, Andy told me about his work requirements.

"Remember, I am back on call starting tomorrow. And, I thought it would be nice if you brought your things over to my house while I am at work."

"Andrew! Are you asking me to move in with you?"

"Well, yes, sort of."

"Sort of?"

"It feels like the next correct step for us. We have had so many interruptions in our being together. I want to eliminate any obstacles to being with you. I mean, we have the day-to-day stuff, but I need you with me for however long we have on this earth. Or realm, as you would say."

This was an unexpected suggestion. I didn't know how to respond.

"And if you don't like the condo, we can redo it or sell it. Perhaps live in Westover Hills, a place near the hospital for me and one that brings you joy."

"I like how that sounds; let's figure out how to make it work."

I believed he and I had to face his grandmother and her fellow spirits if we were ever going to live a life free from turmoil. I understood all relationships have some type of snarl, but this relationship with the spirit world needed to end.

Laying my silverware on my plate, I smiled and said, "You're not going to like what I have to say, but here goes. I have to return to Marsalis St. with you to close this out. The letters aren't the only thing we need to resolve this. Another item is needed to ensure we do this right. The table our ancestors sat at in Bordeaux, the evening that has lived on for almost two hundred years, resides in the little house on Marsalis St. The table made of French pine, the table Gert placed Lily and Edgar on for their final rest. It is the conduit needed to summon the spirits. It has been here in Fort Worth, TX, right behind the white clapboard house all along."

"Are you sure?"

"I recognized it in the photo given to me when all hell broke loose the last time I was there. All the pieces point to the one place Gert has been protecting all these years. Carlton said you had the power to protect me and to help open the gateway. Trust your dad to guide you. Gert won't hurt either of you. I believe your father will be there to protect you through this."

Chapter 17

The Curandera Knows

Staying at Andy's place, most nights were sleepless for me. I didn't know if it was the new surroundings in the condo or perhaps the fear of it not working out with him. I had not lived with anyone since Jaime, and this was unnerving. When I did manage to get some sleep, my dreams were bizarre. Nonsensical wanderings to places I had never been, people I had never met, and worlds I didn't know existed.

On the other hand, Andy quickly adjusted to my being there; his quick adaptation provided me with some emotional comfort. It had been agreed we would stay at the condo while my house was in the process of being sold; after that, we would combine resources and buy a place we could both afford equally. Although I had to admit, I did like all the convenience of high-rise living. There is something to be said about the farmers market or butcher shop located a short walk from the front door. In addition, a hot latte topped with cinnamon was easily acquired just beyond the building's lobby. I quickly grew to love it, becoming very comfortable with this new lifestyle.

With my moving in with him and preparing my house to sell, the conversations surrounding the white clapboard house fell to the wayside. I was unsure where Carlton fit into it all and needed to give my brain a rest. It wasn't until much later fate decided to push the issue forward.

My house sold quickly, and determining whether we should stay in the high-rise or find a new home was a priority for me. My family recently started pushing me to resolve the sale of the white clapboard house; I explained to them my time was occupied with moving and such. I knew I couldn't put it off forever without some hassles from them, but I wasn't ready to deal with it. Three months passed before the house on Marsalis Street came back to the forefront of my mind.

Heading back to the condo from my morning routine one day, I encountered a woman leaning against a car on the street. I recognized her but couldn't immediately place where from. She was very well dressed, reclining against a Mercedes. I smiled at her and said, "Good morning."

She then replied, "I have been waiting for you."

"My apologies, ma'am; I don't know who you are. Have we met?" I slowly backed away from her, unsure who this woman was. Then it came to me; she was the Curandera from the Northside, the woman who listened to me and prayed over me.

"You have been showing up in my visions lately, more and more over the last month, each image more vivid than the one before. I believe the spirits who seek to harm you are growing stronger. I see a Congress forming, but they are missing a spirit to complete their grouping. They need another unholy spirit on this earth to fulfill their ritual. My cards tell me you are the key to stopping a level of hell from becoming a part of our world."

"Your cards? Your visions?" I recalled who she was but was uncertain about her abilities.

"My success being a Curandera is that I also am an occultist; I seek truth through rituals like tea leaves or the Tarot cards."

Not sure of her intent, my inability to discern her purpose for being there made me uneasy. I proposed we find somewhere to grab a beverage and talk in more detail about her visions. Acquiring a latte from the local coffee stand, we began to stroll around the square before she asked a very pertinent question. "Are you aware of your abilities?"

Thinking about how I should reply, I gave her a thirty-five thousand-foot overview of my life. Listing out the energies encountered from other dimensions, I was cautious about providing too much detail or insight into my past. I still wasn't sure I could trust her.

"My readings and visions are getting stronger; regardless of whether I use the cards, transcendental meditation, or tea leaves, all present the same message. 'Do not let the six become one.' I am not clear what this means, I am missing a piece of information to pull this together, but I sense you know what that means."

Slowing my walk, I reached for her hand; I hoped my senses would confirm if she was telling the truth. She took one hand and then the other; looking me straight in the eye, she said, "Your fears are making you foolish. You have the power to do this, whatever 'this' is."

I couldn't explain why, but I had a sense of calm from her touching me. She appeared sincere and genuinely wanted to help. We parked ourselves on a bench by a water feature; taking in the elements around us, I started asking questions of her. I attempted to trip her up and see if she said something that only certain people knew. She was consistent in her responses, and my sense of her never changed. Finally, I asked, "How did you find me?"

She paused before answering. "I looked your name up from the credit card slip when you bought the items in my store. Using your name, I looked up your address and found the house had recently been sold. I called my realtor cousin, who reached out to your agent. My cousin said your agent wasn't timid about telling where you and your husband lived."

If what she said was true, she had expended a lot of effort to find me; this must be important to her. Time passed quickly while I gave her in-depth details about the spirits and the turmoil they had caused over the years; the three attacks, the three saviors, and the prediction of the fourth attack. Sharing the recent events of the picture and its information coming out of nowhere flowed outward without pause. Still not entirely trusting her, I held back details regarding the letters and my theory about them.

I am not sure how long I had been talking to her when we were interrupted by my handsome boyfriend. "I thought I might find you here." Introducing himself to my companion, he said, "Hello, I'm Andy."

Clara stood and shook Andy's hand. After holding his hand for a moment, she turned to me and said, "He is one of the people who saved you. He is a light seeker; his aura is pure." Turning back to Andy, she said, "Mucho Gusto, I am Clara." Turning to me, she smiled, "Tu esposo es muy guapo!"

Andy placed his focus on me; "Esposo? Hank, what's going on?"

Clara quickly engaged with Andy. A bond rapidly formed; I sat back and watched their interactions while they conversed. She told Andy of her intense visions, how her need to find me had become so strong her Novio began to think she was having an affair. The morning migrated into the afternoon when it dawned on me that Andy should have been at the hospital. "Why aren't you at work?" I asked. "Tell you in a minute." This was code for we needed to speak in private. I thanked the Curandera for her time and asked if she would let me know if this continued.

"Andy and I do have a matter we need to address between the spirit worlds, but we are still reeling from the implications of it all. Now with the new information you bring, I just don't know." I pulled a calling card from my pocket and gave it to her. "Here's my number; feel free to call me anytime."

She took the card as Andy and I turned towards our building. Heading for the apartment, we took about thirty steps when I heard her speak, "Boo Boo."

Turning back towards her, I blurted out, "I beg your pardon?"

"It was your childhood name, your nickname."

I had not been called that name since my mother passed. I stood still, looking at her as I spoke. "It was what my family called me when I was young."

"Do you not see them flowing all around you?" She queried.

"I don't. Whom are you talking about?"

"There are several spirits around you, telling me you're safe. They are indicating they are here for you. An older man and his wife, one I think is your mama and maybe a brother."

I didn't understand why I couldn't see them; everything was off being near her. It was as if she was using my gift without me knowing it.

Suddenly she stumbled backward. "Wow! That was weird. I have never had that happen before. I have never seen or spoken across the dimensions, not even as a child."

I was giving her a blank stare when Andy spoke. "Hank? Henry? Are you ok?"

"It's as if all my senses are gone."

I suppose his intuition drove him to grab my hand and lead me to her. Holding onto mine, Andy took her hand before closing his eyes. He let go of each of us abruptly. Pointing to her, he said, "You have to go with us to stop the six becoming one. And you know why." He immediately began to walk towards the condo, indicating we should follow. We didn't know what had happened or why he was taking command, but we followed without question.

Andy asked that I remain in the lobby with Clara while he went to the apartment to retrieve the journals. Carlton had recently sent them to him with a note saying he was quickly fading and requesting we contact him when we are ready to meet with the spirits.

Returning with the books in hand, he passed the Occultist journal to Clara, requesting she read the text out loud. Clara gasped for air when she opened the book. "I have not seen these writings outside of Europe. Where did you get them?"

"Please interpret the drawings on page 66?"

I didn't recall seeing any drawings in the book, but as she turned to page sixty-six, the parchment paper revealed a series of graphics laid out in a particular form.

"This is the symbol of love, followed by a symbol of judgment. Death by sword followed by the symbol for world or realm." She worked furiously through the information, attempting to align the message to the events. She finally stopped and looked up at us, "This is a prediction of the future, not a story from the past."

I looked at the two of them, "Some of those symbols were in a letter Gert sent to my mom."

Seeing her olive skin go pale, it was obvious she was being overwhelmed by fear. The realities of her visions and the prediction pointed her toward a reality she had not anticipated. "We must face the demon together. It is awaiting us with the intent to take a soul, a soul with great power, a catalyst required to settle a union. The six to become one."

Clara finished her statement and moved her eyes from me to Andy. "It is you they seek."

All my assertions were proved wrong. It was Andy they wanted, he was the catalyst needed, and I was the link leading them to him. I told him my realization. Speaking of my concerns for his safety, I reiterated I would not lose him again, no matter what.

He gently smiled at me. Looking intently into my eyes, he softly said, "For whatever reason, this fight has been dumped on us; let's finish it together."

Taking a seat across from me, he collected the journal from Clara while revealing the reason he left work to find me. "A nurse at the hospital revealed to me she was a psychic. This came about after she had asked me how you were doing. She said she remembered you from the ER. I told her you were well, and she quickly responded that she wasn't so sure. I pushed her to explain to me what she meant. She admitted that she peered into your life when you came into the hospital. She had seen those types of bruises before and wanted to confirm her suspicions. She said you would meet an occultist who would complete the circle needed to stop the six."

It was clear what Clara had been stating was indeed valid. The three of us must go to the white clapboard house and face the impending task.

Crossing the bridge out of downtown towards Marsalis St., I began to see the night filled with spirits stirring around the white clapboard house. Passing over the Trinity River and getting near the street I grew up on, I saw the haze begin to appear as we drew near. I had not revisited Marsalis St. since my last trip to the hospital; I was clueless about what to expect.

Filled with trepidation, I advised we move towards the little house via the side gate. With the two of them behind me, we started our journey past the white clapboard house. Removing the lock from the gate, I moved forward with purpose. I did not sense any specters near me but soon heard them knocking on the wall near us from within the white clapboard house. With each step I took toward the little house, the noise level grew in intensity from within. Hearing the banging against the wooden siding frightened me. I wanted the comfort of Andy's skin touching mine. I stretched my hand backward towards his; the instant the hand grasped mine, I knew it wasn't Andy.

I slowly turned around; I was at least twenty feet beyond where they stood. I did not know whose hand I was holding. As I began to turn back, their grip intensified; my fingers turning blue from a lack of blood flow. Three loud knocks on the wall beside me rang out, and the hand released me.

The banging on the wall grew in intensity, drowning all other sounds out. The drumming was so intense I could see Andy calling to me, but nothing he spoke was audible. The deafening noise was so extreme I looked around to see if the neighbors' lights had turned on, but alas, none appeared in the darkness between the houses.

The cement path to the little house appeared longer than I remembered. For every step I took, the walkway appeared to extend two additional feet. The little house was distant but visible. One foot after another, I continued on the path, pushing forward with all my strength. Finally, I saw it.

A dim glow emanated from inside the little house, a low lux of light emitted through the single window on the left side of the little house. Shadows came and went; others were waiting for us in that room.

Seeing the movement, I stopped advancing toward the little house; the knocking on the walls abruptly ended. Silence, once again, the world I was accustomed to, returned. I turned back to find my comrades. Each of them forced their way through the time warp I had exited; Clara covered her ears due to the noise I could no longer hear. As she and Andy pushed through, an ethereal mass enveloped them. It appeared to hold the spirits back, allowing Andy and Clara to pass by the white clapboard house. They now moved without restriction, heading towards me.

Andy, reaching my side first, smiled at me. Each of us found solace in the other's touch while waiting for Clara to catch up. Once she was next to me, I pointed to the light coming from the doorway; it now burned brighter. Looking to each other for strength, we nodded our heads in agreement to proceed forward. Our surroundings were once again normal; each step taken was a step towards the now-open door.

Entering the little house first, I saw the white pine table with vacant chairs surrounding it. A wheelchair-bound old man was at the table, waiting for us to arrive. I pushed past the threshold towards the table; Andy followed. Soon, we heard a rustling sound behind us. We both turned to see Clara stuck in the doorway. She was aloft; her rapidly moving feet had no traction; she was not moving forward.

"Carlton, you must let her in; she has to be here to read the hidden symbols in the book," Andy explained.

His thin skin, barely covering his skeletal hand, rose and waved as if to signal her approval to pass. Once again, her feet touched the floor, and she entered the room.

"Have a seat, my friends. It's time to begin our journey."

Andy made a point of sitting between Clara and me, taking the chair directly across from Carlton.

"Andrew, is your father here?" Carlton asked.

"Why?"

"I want to make sure he bears witness to your suffering this evening. He should see the pain, the same angst I endured all those years being a slave to him. Who is this, and what is it you think she can read that I cannot?"

Andy reached for Clara's hand and smiled, "She is an occultist and can decipher the final book. She is the key."

Looking past depleted nose cartilage, his voice was low and airy. "Most interesting, you have studied the books then? Good boy. But they aren't enough to save you and your love."

Andy turned to me and blew me a kiss, "Don't worry, my love, I will always be with you."

"I am not worried." My response was spoken with complete calm in my voice. Carlton looked at me, his eyes questioning my confidence. "Henry, do you see anyone around us?"

I took a moment and closed my eyes. Letting my senses reach out, I began to feel each of the spirits in the room. Opening my eyes, I met his stare. "I do, Carlton, and I don't think they are who you expected. Each is light, and they are here to assist us."

Carlton looked at Andy. "That's because the others haven't arrived yet. I spent my life under your family's superior attitude, treating me as a mere servant, none of them knowing I carried the same royal bloodline of our ancestors. The self-righteous who denied me my right to live amongst the elite. Your father's love for you was greater than anything in this world; he knew you were special. The more he studied the journals, he began to understand your importance to this world. What he didn't know was I was waiting for you to develop your skills; then, I could reunite the spirits and take control over this realm. I am the one who revealed to your father who his mother was. I persuaded him to move here where Hank lived. I needed you together in order to complete the Congress, and now, here we are at the table where it all began. Andrew, you shall die a painful death. When I absorb your power, I will join the six into one!"

He lifted his bony arms and hands to the table, laying a cigar box in its center.

"Henry, you are a very clever boy to figure out that Gert dissected the book into what looked like love letters. She was not actually insane until your grandfathers tried to fix her; this worked perfectly into my plan. I convinced her Lily and Albert were the guilty parties who took your dad away. It was I who managed the papers for Norma to retrieve her from the institute. Her anger at Lily and Edgar made it easy to push her to kill them. I suspected Lily took the last journal from Dench Manor; I didn't know she hid with Gert when she was sent to the nut house."

His pale sallow fingertip lifted the lid before handing the box to Clara. Quietly she reached for the container, pulling it towards her. She began to untie the bundle with great caution; she moved as if she anticipated something would take hold of her.

Andy smiled at Clara and said, "It's all right; untie them and release them. It is necessary."

The untied lavender ribbon lay on the edges of the box. The letters remained within. The room was now completely still.

Carlton pulled his hands to his chest, crossing them on his bony ribcage; he began to chant. Quietly at first, then growing louder with each repeat flowing from his lips.

Ever so slightly, the table began to tremble. A slow rocking motion at first, then complete calm. Carlton repeated the chant, louder this time. Each time he spoke, the table moved more aggressively than before. Unexpectedly a letter flew up from the box. Carlton's fluid wife entered the room, taking the letter to the far edge of the light. Soon another spirit followed, taking another and opening it while moving beyond the table. Each of them floated carelessly midair, looming, awaiting their instructions.

Carlton continued his chant calling the spirits into the room. Each appeared and approached the table, taking a letter from the box in sequential order. A circle of dark souls began to form around us. The letters opened, each one facing Carlton.

The Congress was approaching completion; one more spirit was required to close the circle. Approaching the cigar box, the entity remained suspended at the edge of the table, peering into the box, its arms unable to reach inside the container. Carlton leaned forward from his wheelchair, his malformed hand reaching inside the box only to discover no more letters remained. The Congress had not closed; the circle was incomplete.

Something was wrong; the Congress could not develop; it remained broken. The gap in their circle allowed me to see beyond them. I saw the protectors nearby. Carlton needed the last letter. Without closing the circle, the light spirits made him vulnerable. He began to shout, "Where is it?"

Andy just looked at him.

Letting a shrill scream pass his thin blue lips, Carlton shouted at Andy, "What have you done with it?"

Carlton's anger grew, his rage infuriating him to the point he wanted to stand and strike us, but his feeble half-alive body was incapable. Andy reached for my hand, holding it tightly; he told me he loved me. "Come what may."

He turned his head to the occultist, and taking Clara's hand, he placed his sights on Carlton. "I was told never to trust you." Turning back to Clara, he simply said, "Now."

She began reciting the missing letter, the words required to open the portal. To N was how it started. The letter was spoken verbatim, voiced with such eloquence it became evident Clara was channeling Gert.

"I am here now and must remain until you leave. Go now and leave this place. Return to the home where you belong. The evil surrounding us is not strong enough to stop my love!"

The room began to swirl around us; the bodies of the damned were now confused. Taking aim at the three of us, the spirits started reaching out to us, their non-existent fingers grasping at anything they could touch. The same hands who tried to pull me into the ground were now tugging on all of us, reaching for our souls to take them to their hell.

Suddenly Andy shouted, "Hank, call out to the light; now is the time for them to help us."

I calmly closed my eyes and connected with each of the spirits who had always been around to save me. They pushed through the opening in the circle of the attempted Congress. Surrounding the three of us, they joined their energy, intensifying their light. The light encapsulated the three of us, forcing the damned spirits back and pushing them toward their crossing. My visions of them had never been so clear; the purity of soul from Andy enhanced my ability to see each of them there to save us.

Ma and Pa Day, Mom and my brother, Mr. Dench, Henri De Lyon, alongside many others whom I didn't recognize. Each one assisting in our rescue.

The room filled with energy; the protectors pushed the dark souls from the room up into the corners, away from the candlelight. A stream of light began to emit from Andy, crossing down his arms and into the Spiritist and the Occultist. The emanation continued growing brighter until each specter there to help us was connected. The light seeker united our souls into one force.

Clara continued reciting the love letter, a letter of hope and peace for the future. "Even when darkness is upon us, our protectors will guide us forward. Trust in the light. Trust in the love I have for you. Believe that when we join hands one final time, all will be resolved!" With each word, the light pushed beyond us, the darkness fading.

Time and space altered around us; we were no longer contained within the little house; the dimensions were no longer divided. Floating in a sea of calm, we watched the demons being carried away. I witnessed the supposed cousin, the wife of the butler, release the letter she held; she cried out in agony as she disappeared from sight. As each of the entities vanished from my view, the bright lights surrounding us began to fade. We were soon returned to the chairs at the table. The cigar box, now filled with the ashes of the parchment paper, sat directly in front of us. It was over. The crossover had been reversed.

The dim artificial light in the room still glowed, but it did not produce enough light to determine if Carlton was alive or dead. I left my chair to find the light switch by the door.

Flipping the white lever upward, it appeared Carlton had moved on to the spirit world. All that remained was dust within the tattered clothes he had arrived in. A sigh of relief was exhaled from the three of us remaining in the room. I followed the sigh with the proposal we leave the little house and move on with our lives. I felt different after what had just happened, but I didn't know why.

Grabbing onto Andy and making our way towards the exit, the light switch flipped off, and the door quickly closed on its own. Andy backed up to me and pulled my arms around him tightly. He was aware danger was still near. "Clara, can you see who it is?"

There was silence in the room. I reached around for Clara. Finally catching her hand in mine, she spoke, "It's him; he didn't cross over." Clara made her way to stand in front of Andy and me. She released my hand; taking a firm stance, she began to speak.

"In the name of all that is holy, all that is within Christ, you are commanded to leave this plane. With all that belongs to God and of this world, I command you to return to your realm."

The blow was quick and sudden; the thud of his hand against her face was deafening. She continued her chant even after he hit her again. The force was so intense she fell to one knee from the brutal impact.

She continued with the demand for him to leave this realm. "Carlton, with all that is holy and of Christ, I command you; go to your hell!"

As if watching slow-motion, Clara became air born. Lifted off the ground and tossed like a rag doll. Landing in the middle of the pine table with an undeniably loud thud, her bones cracking against the wooden surface. The parchment ashes from within the box remaining on the table floated upward, dispersing around the room.

The sound of a masculine female Brit in the distance permeated the room. "Save her! You know what to do."

Andy told me to hold tight as he placed his hand on the Curandera's body. The three of us united once more; he called out, "Grandmother, I need you."

Andy saw the apparition first; as it developed, it was obvious it was Gert. She entered the room where she had left her dead sister and brother-in-law. Dressed in the same suit worn in the picture with my mom, the photo Andy had retrieved long ago. The handsome woman acknowledged us prior to taking her stand against the former butler.

The ashes from the burnt parchment began to form; Carlton's ghastly spirit was now visible to the naked eye. The lambskin paper combined to generate a physical being to walk the earth. I closed my eyes and held tightly to Andrew Dench.

Gert began the battle with Carlton to save the life of her grandson and find peace for her family.

The wind swirled around us; the grunts and groans from the two battling spirits were horrific. The table Clara lay upon moved, pushed by an unseen force, pinning us against the wall. Against the knotty pine wallboard, my legs were being crushed by the power of the table forced into the wall. Andy maintained his grasp on Clara and me, keeping the bond secure.

Out of the corner of my eye, I saw my mother enter the room. She moved past me, stroking my hair before joining Gert. I heard Andy call out, "There's my dad!"

The ones who loved us no matter what had come to ensure we stayed where we belonged.

Gert and Andy's father joined hands with my mom. All those who came to protect us followed suit and joined together, creating a collective spiritual mass. Their march towards Carlton was swift and forceful.

A singular thud against the opposite wall brought it all to an end; the room was once again quiet. The light returned to the overhead bulb, and the door opened once again.

Pushing the table away from the wall, we quickly collected Clara, moving across the ash-covered floor, out of doors. The air was clear; everything appeared normal at the white clapboard house on Marsalis St.

The physician within Andy took over; he checked Clara for broken bones or contusions. Not one could be found. There was not one single mark on her.

We returned Clara to her car and made our way to our home. We didn't speak goodbyes; we parted with a hug between the three of us. It said all we needed to at that moment in time. Arriving at our floor, a place where I knew Andy felt safe, I asked, "How did you know Gert was going to be the one to save us?"

"When we were in Jefferson, it wasn't my dad who told me not to trust Carlton. It was Gert out in the lane I was staring at. Sorry, I lied when you asked if it was my dad."

"No worries, so you knew then something was up?"

"Yes, but I didn't know what."

I sat pondering where the last letter in the box ended up. I was standing there when Mom put it on the fire with the rest of them. "Andy, do you have any idea what happened to the love letter? It was with the rest of them."

Andy did not immediately respond. It appeared as if he wanted to tell me something but wasn't quite sure how. "Let's just say you weren't the only one to visit the white clapboard house alone."

What did he mean? I wasn't following his train of thought.

"In addition to my grandmother telling me to not trust Carlton that day in Jefferson, she told me to collect the letter without you. I went to Marsalis St. before coming home one day. The gate was unlocked, and the door to the little house was open. The letter was on the table waiting for me."

"Where is it now?" I didn't sense it nearby.

"It is with Clara in one of the journals. I separated them so no one can repeat what happened." Andy took my hands and smiled at me. "Now, what was that Clara was saying about me being your husband?"

A small tear ran down my cheek. "Would you like to be?"

Leaning in to kiss me gently, he whispered, "I've already bought the rings."

Moving to lie on his chest and release the years of madness from my soul, I asked, "Do you think it's over?"

"Yes, my sweet man, it's over."

"Andy, I feel different. I can't explain it."

"Clara released you from your burden of being A Sensitive. That's why she saw the people around you in the park and why you weren't aware. She absorbed your powers when she touched you. I don't think it was intentional; I think it was time for you to be released."

And he was right; for the first time in my life, I felt like just one of the collective world.

The End

About the Author

This is the second fiction novel by Thadeus Parkland. The supernatural events in the book actually occurred in the house on Marsalis St., where he grew up. While ghost hunting in East Texas one Christmas break, Thadeus revealed these events to friends who suggested he write them down.

An experience on that trip resulted in one friend describing him as A Sensitive.

Other works available at P1Press:

Deathbed Confession: My Son Was A Stolen Baby

The Girl Who Stole My Chair

8 Things You Should Know To Launch A Product Line

Ready To Own A Salon? 10 Things You Should Know

P1Press

ISBN 978-1-7329729-3-3